THE SHRINKING JUNGLE

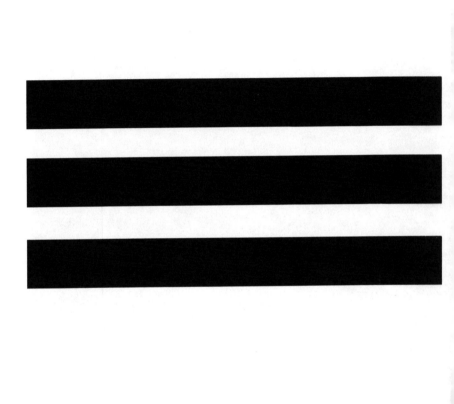

THE

SHRINKING

JUNGLE

Kevin T. Jones

A Novel

THE UNIVERSITY OF UTAH PRESS

Salt Lake City

The Defiance House Man colophon is a registered trademark
of the University of Utah Press. It is based on a four-foot-tall
Ancient Puebloan pictograph (late PIII) near Glen Canyon, Utah.

19 18 17 16 15   2 3 4 5 6

LIBRARY OF CONGRESS CATALOGING-IN-PUBLICATION DATA
Jones, Kevin T., 1951-
The shrinking jungle / Kevin T. Jones.
    p. cm.
Stories about the lives of some of the last tribal peoples in the deep forests
of Paraguay affected by the expansion of modern industrial society.
ISBN 978-1-60781-196-1 (pbk. : alk. paper)
1. Guayaki Indians—Fiction. 2. Indians of South America—Paraguay—Fiction.
3. Jungles—Fiction. 4. Life change events—Fiction. I. Title.
PS3610.O6266S57 2012
813'.6—dc22
                                            2012022702

≡ CONTENTS

☰ ACKNOWLEDGMENTS

The support and encouragement I have received from my best friend and wife, Barbara Evert, are the most important factors in getting this book published. Her confidence in me has kept this dream alive. Our son, Nick, has inspired me to write and has always had a great interest in the Aché and their lifeways. He has created some wonderful line drawings and other art depicting the Aché people.

I would never have met the Aché had it not been for Kim Hill, and I am ever grateful that I was able to experience these wonderful people who love Kim so. I am also grateful for the support and assistance of my colleagues: Ana Magdalena Hurtado, Kristen Hawkes, Hillard Kaplan, Heather Dove, James O'Connell, Duncan Metcalfe, Ken Juell, and Laura Fonoti. Not only did they assist me in the field and the laboratory, but they also supported me immeasurably following my injury in an automobile accident in Paraguay.

We received assistance and friendship from many people in Paraguay, for which I am grateful. Most of all, I thank my Aché friends and mentors who showed great kindness and patience, especially Pedro Bepurangi, Roque Chachugi, Julio Kuaregi, Dolores Kry'ygi, Bepegi, Martín Achipurangi, Enrique Tykwanangi, and Ruben Chachugi.

Thank you also to all my family and friends who encouraged me, and especially to those who read parts of the manuscript and helped make it better, including Kim Hill, an anonymous reviewer for the University of Utah Press, W. Michael Gear, Kathleen O'Neal Gear, Heidi Roberts, and Kate Toomey. I especially thank Reba Rauch, acquisitions editor at the University of Utah Press, for taking a chance on an unusual book written by someone who had never before attempted fiction.

Thank you all.

≡ INTRODUCTION

In the early 1980s, I had the great fortune to be part of a team of anthropologists from the University of Utah, led by Kim Hill and Kristen Hawkes, that studied the Aché Indians (pronounced ah-CHAY), who live in the thick forests of eastern Paraguay. Hill had lived among the Aché and learned their language while in Paraguay with the Peace Corps in the late 1970s, and his friendship with them, along with his mastery of the Aché language, provided a wonderful opportunity to learn from these amazing hunter-gatherers.

The Aché had been full-time hunter-gatherers until relatively recently when Paraguayan loggers and homesteaders intruded into the heavily forested region south of the Mbaracayu Mountains. Some bands did not make peaceful contact with Paraguayans until the 1970s, including one group that Hill met as they were brought from the forest in 1978. Hill cared for the members of that last band to leave the forest and saw that they were fed and treated for the inevitable colds and related illnesses for which they had limited immunity. His devoted attention endeared him to the Aché, and he continues to be a friend and advocate for them today.

A traditional Aché band consisted of some 20–40 people, generally composed of a half dozen or so nuclear or extended family groups. They moved camp nearly every day and ranged widely through the forest, with the men hunting and the women gathering (although not exclusively). As Paraguayans made deeper and deeper incursions into the forest, the Aché way of life changed. Violent confrontations became more common, and the ancient lifeways of the hunter-gatherers began to unravel. During my limited time with the Aché, I was astounded by some of the stories that our friends told. I found their experiences to be both interesting and revealing, relevant even to my life as a North American. I wrote down some of the stories, and Hill related many other experiences of the Aché to me.

This book is a compilation of some of the stories, interwoven in the fabric of fictional Aché characters. I have tried to be faithful to the Aché and their customs, but I realize that the richness and depth of any culture is too great to condense into a few pages. My goal in writing the book is to share in a small way the story of these people: people who are still alive today, coping with the most astounding culture shock imaginable—stepping directly from the Stone Age to the twentieth century. I hope I have described the people and their practices reasonably well, and I have tried to make the book readable and interesting.

There are some very good sources of information about the Aché. I highly recommend the following:

Batten, Mary, with photographs by A. Magdalena Hurtado and Kim Hill. 2001. *Anthropologist: Scientist of the People.* Boston: Houghton Mifflin Company.

Clastres, Pierre. 1998. *Chronicle of the Guayaki Indians.* New York: Zone Books. The original French edition, *Chronique des indiens Guayaki,* was published by Librairie Plon in Paris in 1972.

Hill, Kim, and A. Magdalena Hurtado. 1996. *Aché Life History: The Ecology and Demography of a Foraging People.* New York: Aldine de Gruyter.

≡ THE CHARACTERS IN TURTLE'S BAND

Note: All Aché people are named for animals by their mother at or around the time of their birth. The name reflects an animal the mother prepared and cooked while she was pregnant. The name consists of the name of the animal, plus the suffix *gi,* which indicates the reference to a person, not an animal. The word for the nine-banded armadillo, for instance, is *tatu,* so a person named for it would be Tatugi. I have used English common names for the animals throughout the book to avoid the possibly confusing Aché terms.

In addition to their true names, nearly all Aché have nicknames, which often describe the person ("Big Scars," "White Skinned," "Tall") or refer to something they have done ("Stabber," "Growls a Lot," "Weakling"). To lessen confusion, I have not used many nicknames in this book, except when Turtle refers to Anteater as "Sores" and other occasional references.

Grandmother Boa (Memboruchugi): The wife of Grandfather Jamo Paca and the mother of Armadillo and Deer from an earlier marriage. Grandmother and Grandfather wed when their children were adults. She is a wiry, but strong, woman in her late fifties or early sixties.

Grandfather Jamo Paca (Bywangi): The husband of Grandmother Boa and the father of Turtle and Blackbird. *Jamo* is the Aché word for "jaguar," but it also refers to older men or grandfathers as an honorary addition to their true names. He is relatively tall and gangly and is in his late fifties or early sixties.

Armadillo (Tatugi): The daughter of Grandmother Boa, the sister of Deer, the wife of Snake, and the mother of Catfish and Monkey. She is very attractive with flashing eyes and a quick smile. She is about thirty.

Snake (Membogi): The husband of Armadillo and the father of Catfish and Monkey. He is an orphan. He is very friendly but somewhat shy and is a very good hunter. He is in his midthirties.

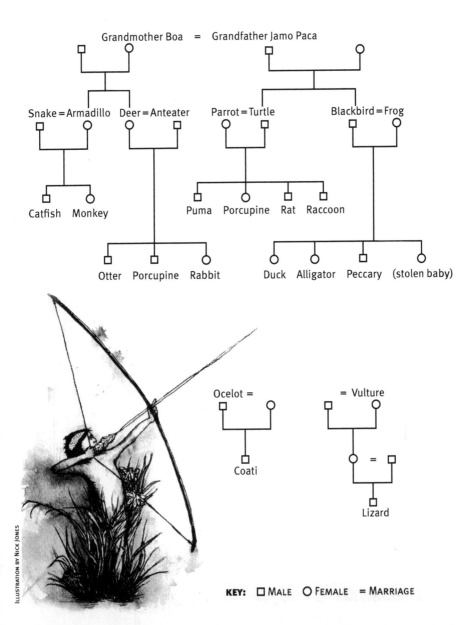

Grandmother Boa = Grandfather Jamo Paca

Snake = Armadillo   Deer = Anteater   Parrot = Turtle   Blackbird = Frog

Catfish   Monkey

Puma   Porcupine   Rat   Raccoon

Otter   Porcupine   Rabbit

Duck   Alligator   Peccary   (stolen baby)

Ocelot =

Coati

= Vulture

=

Lizard

KEY: ☐ MALE   ○ FEMALE   = MARRIAGE

ILLUSTRATION BY NICK JONES

Catfish (Bekrorogi): The son of Armadillo and Snake and the brother of Monkey. He is about nine years old.

Monkey (Pwa'agi): The daughter of Armadillo and Snake and the little sister of Catfish. She is about four years old.

Deer (Buachugi): The daughter of Grandmother Boa, the sister of Armadillo, the wife of Anteater, and the mother of Otter, Rabbit, and Porcupine. She is in her late twenties.

Anteater (Kuaregi): The husband of Deer and the father of Otter, Rabbit, and Porcupine. He is in his late twenties.

Otter (Cherygi): The son of Deer and Anteater and the brother of Rabbit and Porcupine. He is about nine years old.

Rabbit (Atagi): The daughter of Deer and Anteater and the sister of Otter and Porcupine. She is about six years old.

Porcupine (Gui'igi): The son of Deer and Anteater and the brother of Otter and Rabbit. He is about four years old.

Turtle (Krombegi): The son of Grandfather Jamo Paca, the brother of Blackbird, the husband of Parrot, and the father of Puma, Porcupine, Rat, and Raccoon. He is an intense man with a squarish head and strong brow. He is in his midthirties.

Parrot (Gerogi): The wife of Turtle and the mother of Puma, Porcupine, Rat, and Raccoon. She is in her midthirties.

Puma (Bwapirangi): The son of Turtle and Parrot and the brother of Porcupine, Rat, and Raccoon. He is about twelve years old.

Porcupine (Gui'igi): The daughter of Turtle and Parrot and the sister of Puma, Rat, and Raccoon. She is about ten years old.

Rat (Bujagi): The son of Turtle and Parrot and the brother of Puma, Porcupine, and Raccoon. He is about eight years old.

Raccoon (Bejyvagi): The son of Turtle and Parrot and the brother of Puma, Porcupine, and Rat. He is about six years old.

Blackbird (Kuyrachigi): The son of Grandfather Jamo Paca, the brother of Turtle, the husband of Frog, and the father of Duck, Alligator, Peccary, and the stolen baby. He is about thirty.

Frog (Jy'ygi): The wife of Blackbird and the mother of Duck, Alligator, Peccary, and the stolen baby. She is in her late twenties.

Duck (Chimbegi): The daughter of Blackbird and Frog and the sister of Alligator and Peccary. She is about eleven years old.

Alligator (Japegi): The daughter of Blackbird and Frog and the sister of Duck and Peccary. She is about ten years old.

Peccary (Chachugi): The son of Blackbird and Frog and the brother of Duck and Alligator. He is about six years old.

Ocelot (Kajagi): The father of Coati. He is not related to others in the band. He is in his midforties.

Coati (Tykwanangi): The son of Ocelot. He is approximately twenty.

Vulture (Brikugi): The grandmother of Lizard. She is not related to others in the band. She is in her late sixties or early seventies.

Lizard (Chejugi): The grandson of Vulture. He is approximately seventeen years old.

Some Aché terms

Apa: Literally means "father," but it was used before contact to refer to the Paraguayans. The original meaning was "fathers with explosions." I have used Apa to refer to the Paraguayans.

Bayja: Attracting, as in attracting animals to come to a person. The word refers to a condition that results from a killing or bloodletting or after a man's wife has given birth. Living creatures, including spirit animals, are drawn to a bayja person.

Chija: Strong, courageous.

Berendy: A spirit that sometimes appears as a furry creature in the forest, a flash of light, or a loud noise.

Membo: A large poisonous pit viper of the species *Bothrops neuwiedi*. This snake is commonly called the fer-de-lance, lancehead, or *jararaca*.

Kwanto: A spiny plant with long, spikelike leaves.

Timbo: A climbing vine common in Paraguay, sometimes called a milk creeper for the liquid it produces when cut. Aché use the juice for cleansing wounds and healing in general.

The Aché have lived in the forests between the Paraguay and Paraná rivers as long as anyone can remember. In the deepest forest, away from the large rivers and meadows, where the hardwood trees grow strong and tall, and vines and brush in unrelenting competition tangle the forest floor, choking out light and impeding travel, the Aché flourish. Slipping silently through the jungle pursuing game and gathering fruit and honey, they live where no one else can: a world that is hostile and alien to others, a world that is theirs and theirs alone.

The forest is their ally, their provider, their protector. This forest that rises like a wall and clings to the rolling hills with a grip too strong to break fully has always stopped intruders at its edges. The Guaraní with their complex society and growing population have for centuries pecked at the perimeter of the Aché sanctuary to no avail. The great forest that stretches from what is now Brazil through Paraguay and into Bolivia, in the heart of South America, has always been the home of the Aché and tribes like them—the Hêta, the Siriono, the Guarayos, the Kaingang. Within its limits, they have established a way of life that is as old as human history. The tribes that surrounded them—despite their technological superiority, statelike organization, and great numbers—have never penetrated the forest, have not defeated those who dwell there, have failed to swallow them as they have so many others whose environment is less forbidding.

The coming of the Spanish in the sixteenth century with their horses and metal did little to change the inviolability of the forest, and four centuries after European arrival, the Aché remained its citizens, masters of a lifeway that is in some ways simple, in many ways complex, in most ways harsh, and—until recently—viable.

In 1965 the United States had more than 180,000 troops in South Vietnam and was bombing North Vietnam. Thirty-five people died in race riots in Watts. Craig Breedlove drove his car, "Spirit of America," six hundred miles an hour on the Bonneville Salt Flats of Utah. Roberto Clemente of the Pittsburgh Pirates was the National

League batting champion. Sandy Koufax pitched a perfect game. Runner Michel Jazy of France set a world record in the mile of 3:53.6 and bragged that he smoked a pack of cigarettes a day. A missile silo in Searcy, Arkansas, exploded, killing fifty-three. Malcolm X was assassinated in New York City. The United States conducted twenty-nine known nuclear tests.

And in Paraguay, an expanding population and growing demand for timber led more and more woodcutters and farmers to enter the forest armed with axes and shotguns. Each day more trees fell, more of the jungle was cut and burned away, and the home of the Aché, which is everything to them, was threatened. Near Naranjito, a band of twenty-seven Northern Aché camped in the thick, open jungle they called the good forest, a place they knew well, a place where they were comfortable. They knew nothing of the World Series or Malcolm X or nuclear weapons. But then, neither did the men who stalked them.

≡

Tucked unobtrusively into a small camp pocketed in the verdant vegetation that was their home, the Aché slept. Cuddled together on palm-leaf mats within a ring of smoky fires that separated them from the forest, they slept, their bodies sprawled and intertwined, touching. Hard, scarred, brutally muscular men curled around tender babies. Lean, strong, ruggedly resilient women nestled with slender children. Wizened, wiry grandparents lay dreaming on the jungle floor that was the only bed they had ever known. The band shared sleep as they shared their food, their lives.

In the diffuse light that comes before dawn, a teenage boy named Lizard raised up on one elbow and peered into the forest, roused by a rustling noise in the brush that could have been made by a bird lighting on a branch. He listened for a moment and slowly rose to his feet. Moving silently, Lizard stepped between two of the smoldering fires and paused when he was just past the edge of camp. A stern-faced man, Turtle, sensed Lizard's movement and sat up on his mat, watching. The sharp snap of a twig in front of the boy brought the man to his feet, and in an instant, his bow and arrows were in his hand. Then came the shotgun blast.

The violation caused by gunfire is something that forests become accustomed to. In some forests, shots are as common as birdsongs and seem less of a trespass. Other forests—alive and mature, filled to over-flowing with life—seem ripe for the shotgun, yet they are the ones most shocked by its intrusion. Thunder echoes in a storm, and the living jungle is prepared. But an explosion of gunfire surprises the forest, consumes the gaps between the trees, shakes every molecule of every organism, and begins a loosening, a disruption that cannot be repaired.

The Paraguayan jungle is filled with life—from microorganisms to giant trees, from burrowing armadillos to soaring harpy eagles—and the air is alive with sound. Birds trill and screech, frogs blurt love songs, insects buzz and chirp sophisticated melodies. Leaves chatter against each other in the breeze, branches scrape and drop, trees creak and fall. The jungle, filled with sound, is an enveloping milieu, and it was shattered by the shock that raced in radiating waves from the muzzle of a farmer's gun.

1 ≡ THUNDER

Catfish ran from the terrifying sound. He ran as fast as his legs would carry him, ignoring the vines and thorns, frantically trying to keep up with his mother, Armadillo. Tears streamed down his face, and his uncontrollable sobbing made him oblivious to the frenzied flight of others around him. He could hardly see his mother in the predawn light as she strode quickly and quietly away from what had been their camp, carrying his younger sister close to her body. He caught only an occasional glimpse of her and ran toward the slight movement her passage created in the brush.

And then it came again. *Bawhoom*—the loudest and most horrifying sound Catfish could imagine, the thunder of the Apa.

The blast filled the forest, and when Catfish turned his head for a second to look toward it, he lost sight of his mother. In a panic, he scrambled madly toward the spot where he had last seen her and continued on, still running as fast as he could. He raced through a stand of thick, spiny *kwanto* toward a slight crease in the vegetation that he hoped his mother had made. As he dashed past a large, densely foliated laurel, a hand reached out and pulled him into the brush.

"Catfish, it is me. Be quiet."

It was his mother. Armadillo pulled him close and hugged her two children tightly against her breast. They trembled with fear, and the jerky, arrhythmic breathing of the children was all that betrayed their silent sobbing.

They cowered in their dark hiding spot, occasionally catching the sound of excited voices muffled by the forest, or the crashing of someone sprinting through the brush. They remained silent and motionless like fawns waiting quietly for their mother while the jaguar stalks nearby. They knew only that the band had scattered the way minnows flee a shadow, running from the most feared thing in the forest—the Apa—the white men.

The Apa were the fathers who make explosions, who possessed fantastic tools and wonderful plants and animals, the masters of brutal and terrifying attacks. The Aché had fought and fled the Apa since before their grandfathers were babies, but now the Apa were intruding deeper into the forest, violating the Aché refuge, savaging the only people who knew how to live in the jungle without destroying it.

The young mother, Armadillo, peered intently out from her sanctuary. Her children huddled between her splayed legs, shielded by her encircling arms from even the scattered beams of early morning sunlight that now penetrated the protective foliage. She listened, and as the minutes slowly crept by, the forest gradually absorbed the sounds of panic and confusion and replaced them with the pacifying hum of the jungle. Still she waited, knowing that any movement would alert the watchdogs of the forest—the crickets, the birds, the frogs, the cicadas—and the dampening of the symphony would alert others to the Aché presence.

There were others nearby—she had heard them—but she couldn't be certain they were Aché, her people, members of her band. They might be Apa, waiting to kill her and steal her children. She would remain hidden until she knew it was safe.

Mosquitoes, wakened by the growing warmth of the day, hovered about them and began to attack. Armadillo endured their stings, and with slow, deliberate movements, brushed them off her children. She nursed her young daughter and softly stroked Catfish's hair, helping both of them to remain quiet. The still, heavy air made the children drowsy, and the little girl, Monkey, closed her eyes.

The sharp cry of a toucan startled Catfish. He squirmed, and the baby started to cry. Armadillo quickly offered her breast to the child and tried with little success to quiet her. Then, above the soft complaints of the uncomfortable four-year-old, they heard someone call, "Hoo. Hoo. Aché, come here. Aché, come here."

The sounds were coming from nearby, perhaps only a hundred

yards away. Catfish started to get up to run toward the voice, but Armadillo stopped him.

"Wait, it might not be safe," she said, taking him by the wrist.

"But that was Jamo Paca calling. Grandfather Paca wants us to come," Catfish said. "The Apa are gone."

"Just wait, Catfish," said Armadillo. "The Apa may be hiding."

Then they heard louder cries, and this time they knew it must be safe.

"Hoo. Hoo. Aché, come here quickly. The Apa are gone. We must find everyone and leave this place. Come here quickly."

The man calling was Turtle, the most powerful man in their band. They pushed the branches aside, crawled out from their hiding spot, and started toward the voice. Catfish ran ahead, eager to see the others.

He heard some movement in the brush and looked over to see his cousin, Otter, a boy his own age, about nine.

"Otter," he called, "We got away from the Apa. We're real men now."

"I'm not afraid of the Apa," said Otter. "We are big strong men. They can't hurt us. Let's find the others."

The boys hurried through the thick brush toward the sound of voices and came to a small opening in the vegetation. There they saw several Aché standing in a circle, looking down at something and talking. Catfish ran up to them and peered between a man's legs so he, too, could see.

He froze as he looked, and so did Otter. They could see the seated man's back, covered with blood from five or six ragged holes. The blood was beginning to clot around the puffy wounds and ran in thick, shiny, bright red trickles down toward his buttocks. The boys couldn't see the man's face, and he wasn't speaking, but they knew from the pattern of scars on his muscular back—scars every adult Aché has—that he was Anteater, Otter's father. Catfish shuddered and felt cold, and suddenly the great fear that had overwhelmed him earlier returned with greater sharpness.

Otter pushed his way through the group and sat next to his father.

He put his arm around the sitting man's leg and laid his head on his father's knee.

"Are you going to die? Did the thunder pierce you?" the boy cried. Otter hugged his father's leg, and his tears ran down the man's shin.

"The Apa pierced me," Anteater said, running his hand over his son's smooth back. "But it doesn't hurt. I am strong."

"Where is mother?" Otter asked suddenly, looking around at those standing nearby.

"She is coming with Snake," someone said. "She will be here soon."

By this time, Armadillo had arrived. She lowered her daughter from her shoulders and knelt behind Anteater. "We need *timbo*," she said. "Catfish and Otter, go get some milk creeper so I can wash Anteater's back."

The boys hurried into the forest. Otter cried as he ran, and Catfish cried, too. They had never experienced anything so crushing.

It did not take them long to find the timbo vines that provided the milky juice the Aché use for cleansing wounds and purifying people who have been afflicted by spirits. The boys pulled the vines down by hanging on them and broke them off by twisting them. When they each had two six-foot pieces, they hurried back to the spot where the band was gathered. They gave the creeper to Armadillo, and Catfish went and stood behind his sister.

He helped Monkey to her feet and held her hands. They stood and watched as members of their band—their family and friends, all the people they really knew—tried to save a wounded man. Others, including Catfish's father, Snake, were out trying to find the remaining band members so they could bring them to this spot and learn what had happened to everyone.

Armadillo took a piece of vine, bent and twisted it, and crumpled it in her hands. She carefully wiped the blood and dirt away from the open wounds with the juice that ran from the crushed wad. Someone handed her a large leaf, folded and filled with water from the small stream that ran nearby. Armadillo dabbed her crumpled sponge in the water and continued cleaning Anteater's back. As she blotted the blood from one of the holes, a small pellet fell and landed on the ground between her knees. She picked it up and looked at it for a moment.

"What is this?" she asked, handing it to Turtle.

Turtle, the intense, powerful man who led the band, took the ball in his cupped palm, rolled it around with the tip of his finger, and then brought it close to his eye. "This is how the Apa kill," he said. "They throw these stones with their thunder. The thunder sends them flying through the air to kill. Anteater is lucky; he will not die. His back is strong. Lizard is not lucky; they destroyed his face."

"Lizard was pierced, too?" Anteater asked.

"Lizard was hit first," Turtle said. "His face is gone. He is dead."

Catfish winced. He hadn't heard that Lizard was dead. Lizard was not even a man yet; he was just a teenage boy. Catfish liked Lizard because he let the younger boys follow him through the forest. He had helped them make small bows and arrows and showed them how to shoot at birds and fish. And now he was dead. The Apa had shot him in the face with their thunder.

How wrong he and Otter had been earlier, he thought. They had boasted that they weren't afraid of the Apa, that they were strong, that they were men. They had felt good when they heard that the Apa were gone, and they were proud to be Aché because the Aché were strong, and their men were able to fight off the Apa. But the Aché hadn't won any battles. The Apa had attacked their camp, the men had fought to allow the women and children to escape, and the Apa had shot them. How many more were hurt or dead, he wondered? And who were left to fight the Apa the next time?

"Here comes Snake," someone announced, and Catfish turned to look as his father, stern and intent, pushed a branch aside with his bow and held it for the two women following him.

"Mother," Otter cried as he ran to embrace Deer. "Father's been hurt."

"I know; Snake told me," his mother replied as she hurried to her husband's side.

As she reached the group, the second woman, Frog, sank slowly to her knees. She sat on the heels of her feet and held her hands together between her legs. Her eyes were swollen, and her face was wet from tears. She stared at the ground in front of her.

"They took my baby," she said in a high, songlike voice. "The Apa stole my baby. My poor little baby. The Apa will eat her. They will cook her like a peccary and eat her."

She wailed, and the other women went to her, put their arms around her, and cried with her.

"I was holding her next to me as we slept, and when we heard the thunder, I tried to run away with everyone else, but I fell down and dropped her." She looked up and scanned the faces of those around her with grief-filled eyes. "Then an ugly Apa came and kicked me and grabbed my baby. He would have killed me, but then he saw Anteater, and I ran away. My poor baby. They are probably eating her now. She was such a good baby, so strong. Now she is in some Apa's stomach."

"We must leave this place, or the Apa will come back and eat us all," said Turtle. "Hoo, hoo, Aché, come here," he yelled. "Hurry. The Apa are gone. Come here. The Apa are gone."

"We can't wait much longer," he said, pacing. "We must leave this place. If the rest of the group aren't here soon, we will have to leave them. I killed one Apa today, and I want to go kill them all, but the women and children are not safe here. We must go deeper into the forest." He cupped his hands around his mouth. "Hoo, hoo, Aché," he called. "Come here. Hurry. Come here."

People straggled in—singly and in groups of two or three—and when someone was heard in the brush, everyone in the small clearing looked closely to be sure it was an Aché. When Turtle's oldest son arrived, looking lost, his mother ran and hurried him to the place where her other children were sitting. The Aché were anxious and excited, and everyone wanted to find out what had happened, who had been killed or taken or hurt.

"We should have camped farther in the forest," said Snake. "Our camp was too close to the garden we raided."

"The Apa are coming deeper into the forest," agreed Turtle. "The last time we were here, there wasn't a single Apa trail within two days' walk. Now there is an Apa house only a half day's walk away."

"We made a mistake to go to the Apa garden yesterday," Snake said quickly. "We should have waited. But when we saw the corn, we couldn't resist taking it, and the axe was just sitting there. I didn't think there were any Apa there. There was no smoke. I thought they were gone. They probably followed our trail back to the camp."

"They didn't follow the men's trail," said Grandfather Jamo Paca. "They found the trail the women and I made yesterday and followed it. I saw their trail, and it came right up the one we made yesterday."

"They must have found us last night and waited until morning to attack," said Blackbird, the father of the stolen baby. "That must be what caused the noise we heard last night."

The other men drew their breath in agreement.

"Lizard was the first to hear them this morning," said Turtle. "I saw him sit up and listen, and I listened, too. We both heard a branch move, and he jumped up, and I got my bow and arrows. Lizard started from the camp and had only gone a few steps when a twig snapped. We saw an Apa stand and point his thunder at Lizard. They just looked at each other. I don't think Lizard had ever seen an Apa before, and he just stared at him. Lizard didn't look scared, but the Apa did. He looked like the monkey caught in the jaguar's paw, waiting for the big cat to finish licking his lips and kill him. But the Apa had the thunder, and with his big scared monkey eyes, he pointed the thunder at Lizard's face, and fire came from it and tore Lizard's head apart. That stupid Apa.

"He didn't even see me. He stared at Lizard's head and then watched his body jump and move. I think he was so proud of what he had done that he couldn't look away. While he was still watching Lizard, I pierced him in the chest." Turtle touched his finger to his rib cage, indicating where the arrow had entered. "I was lucky the arrow didn't hit a rib. He didn't even flinch. He just looked at the arrow and looked at me and fell forward so the arrow came out his back and stuck straight up."

"I saw Turtle shoot," said Snake. "The Apa was soft. The arrow pierced him the way it goes through water." The old man, Jamo Paca, laughed, and Snake continued. "I got my bow and arrows and ran to the bushes on the other side of the camp. We all ran. Everyone would have escaped, except Frog ran the wrong way. She ran toward the Apa, and one grabbed her baby. Anteater went to help her, and that's why he got shot. But first he shot an Apa in the mouth with an arrow. It went right in his mouth and out his cheek." Snake poked his finger into his mouth and showed the way the arrow had gone. "Anteater started running, and another Apa came up and pointed his thunder, and fire came from it, but the fire didn't reach him. I didn't think he was pierced. Then we all ran away from the camp into the woods. They didn't follow us."

"We waited until we heard them leave," Turtle said. "Snake and I followed them to be sure they were gone, and then we came back to the camp. The Apa took our axes and machetes. Now all we have is one old stone axe that Blackbird took. They took or burned everything else—the water baskets, the bowls, the carrying baskets and mats. Now we have nothing." Turtle paused, and everyone looked as two more Aché entered the clearing.

"We buried Lizard and built a tiny house for him on his grave and a small fire," Turtle continued. "The vultures won't eat his eyes out now. He will be happy and won't want to hurt us. We will cry for Lizard and the baby when we camp.

"But now we must leave quickly; now everyone is here. We'll head straight for the Big River. Snake got fire from the camp, but we must make only small fires so the Apa can't find us. We can go now. Anteater will be all right. He can walk."

Catfish listened closely to what had happened, and it made him feel cold. He started shaking and shivering. He was frightened by how much damage the Apa had done in only a few minutes. Friends and relatives had been killed and wounded, their possessions had been stolen and destroyed, and they were leaving this place that only yesterday had seemed so peaceful. The cold fear he felt now was stronger than even the terror that had gripped him when he was fleeing the Apa. That had left him when he had found his mother. This, he knew, would stay with him forever.

"Catfish, Catfish, I can take Monkey now," Armadillo said, tousling his hair. "We are leaving and will walk fast. I want you to stay close to me. Don't wander off—we have to stay together. We have to be careful because Turtle and Anteater are *bayja*. They drew blood, and the animals will come to them. The jaguars will be attracted to them, and Lizard's spirit will come after us. We must be careful and watch and listen." She bent down, hoisted Catfish's young sister up, and swung the child onto her back. "Are you ready? Let's go."

Anteater's wife helped her injured husband to his feet. After an unsteady moment, he was able to walk, using his unstrung bow as a staff. Turtle headed into the forest leading the way, and the others fell in behind. They had just gotten under way when Vulture, an old, shriveled woman, long widowed and the grandmother of Lizard, began wailing.

"I cannot leave; I have lost my pets," she cried. "You must help me find them. I have lost my coati and my monkey. They will die in the forest. I am going back to look for them. You can leave me if you want, but I am going to find my pets."

She turned and started back toward their morning's camp. The pets were the only family she had left.

Snake ran and took her arm. "Come with us, Vulture. Your pets will be all right. They will find plenty of food to eat in this good forest. The Apa won't bother them. I will get you new pets. I will get you monkeys and coatis and peccaries—all the pets you want. Come with us now and stop worrying about your pets."

The confused old woman relented and turned to join the rest of the band, now reduced to twenty-five people. They traveled in single file with Turtle leading the way. Two men trailed behind to guard the rear, and two others walked parallel to the band at some distance on either side. They hurried straight north at a very fast pace.

Turtle moved through the forest the way a hunter does when pursuing game. He did not skirt around thickets or bogs but went straight through them. Walking was difficult for the injured Anteater and the women with small children.

Ordinarily the women walked together while the men hunted.

They frequently stopped to forage, to feed and care for their children, and to rest, for they normally carried heavy loads in their large baskets. One of the men usually led them through the forest and marked the trail by bending twigs or saplings to direct them away from wasp nests or around thick brush. But they could not afford to be slow today, and no one complained.

Catfish settled in behind his mother as they traveled silently through the jungle. He moved mechanically and efficiently as he ducked under vines and climbed over fallen trees. They passed through a stand of palm trees where they had camped two nights earlier. When he remembered the palm fiber they had eaten there, he realized he was hungry. He thought also of Lizard, his dead friend who had found the palms, and how he had helped the women chop them. Lizard had often stayed with the women and children, leading them through the forest and helping them gather fruit, chop palms, and take honey.

Now Lizard was dead; he was no longer Catfish's friend. His spirit would be lonely and try to take living Aché with him. The thought of spirits who took the form of jungle animals and hunted the living haunted the Aché; they tried to leave the dead behind, to bury them quickly and leave the area so the spirits couldn't find them. The band was especially vulnerable today because two of the men, Turtle and Anteater, were bayja. They had spilled blood, and anytime a man killed or injured another, or when his wife had a baby, he became bayja. Such a man was charmed—a gatherer, a magnet for the animals of the forest. His condition attracted animals, and a bayja man could kill many of them while hunting.

At the same time, he was in great danger because not only were deer and monkeys attracted to him, but so were the jaguars and snakes. Most dangerous of all were the spirit animals, which most often took the form of jaguars. A bayja man could exorcise his spell by killing many animals and being cleansed with timbo water, but until then, he was constantly in danger, and so were those with him.

Catfish had heard many stories about bayja. His father, Snake, had been orphaned before he was Catfish's age because his own father was bayja. Snake's mother had just given birth, and the band was walking to a new camp when the animals started coming to Snake's father. They ran out of the forest and straight to him. He killed a deer and a collared peccary and a paca while walking in line with the women. He wasn't even hunting. Everyone in the band had been laughing and talking about what a good hunter Snake's father was and that he was breaking the spell by killing so many animals when the jaguar attacked. It jumped Snake's father from behind and bit his neck. He died instantly.

The other people in the band climbed trees. Snake's mother pushed him up a tree and started climbing up behind him when the jaguar came for her. She was almost out of reach when the jaguar jumped and grabbed her foot. It snarled and growled, held her foot in its mouth, and raked at her leg with its claws. She tried to cling to the tree, but the jaguar was too strong and pulled her to the ground. The jaguar ripped open her belly and left her for a moment while it took her baby and tossed it high in the air, playing with it the way a cat tortures a mouse.

Snake watched from the tree as the jaguar ate his mother's face and ran off with the baby in its mouth when the other men in the band chased it. From that day, Snake had been on his own, haunted by the vision of seeing his parents killed so quickly and savagely. Snake was strong—as anyone without family must be—but when he told the story, tears came to his eyes, and he was always very careful when he was bayja.

Catfish's fear of the Apa, his worry about bayja, and his sorrow at the loss of Lizard combined to give him a feeling he had never had before. He hated the Apa for attacking them: killing and kidnapping, stealing and destroying, causing the bayja, making them fear Lizard's spirit. Over and over he fantasized killing the Apa—every one of them—so the Aché could go on living as they always had. He had seen the hatred in his father's eyes this morning, and especially in Turtle's. And now the small, naked, nine-year-old boy followed his mother through the forest, unaware of what he was doing, while in his mind, he killed Apa and saved his family and friends.

2 ≡ THE RAGE

Several hours at a fast pace took its toll on the injured Anteater. Although he walked with determination and was very stoic about his pain, he began to slow down. He stumbled and fell to the ground with increasing frequency and each time rose to his feet with greater difficulty. Everyone was tired and hungry, but only the smallest children complained. The Aché knew they were running for their lives.

A small grove of trees, laden with plump, ripe kuri fruit, afforded them an opportunity to take a late-afternoon rest and eat something for the first time that day. Anteater eased himself to the ground and lay on his side, supported by his elbow. Catfish and several other children climbed trees and shook the branches, releasing the fruit so the others could collect it. The women and children scoured the ground, eating the juicy orange fruit as they went. Even Catfish's little sister foraged on her own, crouching and crawling through the brush, voraciously consuming the walnut-sized morsels. Catfish and the other children in the trees did not go hungry; they ate the fruit that did not succumb to their shaking. Occasionally they gathered a handful and tossed them directly to someone on the ground.

Anteater managed to gather the fruit that fell within reach of where he lay and also ate some that his wife brought. The men who remained in the forest away from the group ate little, only an occasional piece of fruit they found under the scattered trees.

Turtle waited alone a short distance from the women and children. He adjusted his bowstring and smoothed the flights of his arrows, paced, and tightened his bowstring again. Light skinned and blocky, and heavily muscled as all Aché men are, he was not extraordinarily imposing at five and a half feet tall, but he lived with great intensity. Whether he was laughing, fighting, hunting, or telling a story,

Turtle's close-set eyes were sharp and observant. Every move he made exuded confidence. Turtle refused to accept failure; he did not know compromise. To attempt a task was to concentrate on its successful completion. Turtle was rarely beaten and never defeated.

Turtle listened as the band foraged, but he did not eat; his angry stomach would not allow it. He would rather have kept moving, but he knew how fatigued everyone was, especially the children, and he was worried about Anteater. Anteater was a strong man, but he had lost blood and was very weak. The time spent resting would not be wasted, Turtle decided. A short rest and a little food should enable even Anteater to continue walking. Turtle wanted to put as much distance between the band and the Apa as he could; he would not be able to relax until he was sure they were safe.

Turtle felt the burden of responsibility for the band's safety, although he was not their leader in any formal sense. His voice carried more weight than any other individual's, partly because he was strong, confident, and a good hunter whom the members of the band respected. He had no authority or power other than his personal ability to convince, coerce, or intimidate the others. He could be frightening and had the advantage of strong kin connections—his father, Jamo Paca, and brother, Blackbird, were in the band, and they gave him a great deal of support. Nevertheless, he was no more than a consensus leader of a band of individuals who were not obligated to listen to him. Indeed, if he overstepped his bounds, anyone who disapproved could leave the band and join another.

When no more fruit could be shaken from the trees, Catfish and the other children came down from their perches. A few people continued to forage on the ground, but the supply there was nearly exhausted as well. Anteater grasped a hanging vine and hoisted himself to his feet. His legs trembled when they felt his full weight, but he wasn't going to allow himself to keep the group waiting; he had slowed them down enough already.

"Are you ready?" he called to Turtle. "Let's go."

Turtle set a slightly slower, but still punishing, pace. The band moved silently, resolutely, through the darkening jungle. One of the men who had been guarding the rear now walked with Anteater and helped the weakened man keep up. With fatigue and the waning light, a fog of depression descended on the Aché: they were hunters—strong and bold—who confronted danger and overcame it. They were the masters of the forest who made way only for the jaguar, a hunter like themselves: strong and fierce, and sometimes one of them, a spirit, a dead Aché looking for friends to take with him.

But now they were running like startled deer bolting through the jungle: hunted, not hunting. They were running from one of their favorite parts of the forest. It had few thorns and less slashing bamboo and tangled brush than most other places in their territory and was a place where hunting was easier and the palms were thicker.

Turtle feared he and his band would never see the good forest again. They were being chased from a place they loved, a place they had gone to as long as anyone could remember. They were losing not only a hunting spot but part of their lives.

As night fell, the men cut dry seed-pod spathes from palm trees and used them as torches. The band walked in a tight group, and although they moved slowly and stopped often for short rests, they continued to distance themselves from the Apa. Dark and threatening even at midday, the jungle comes smotheringly close at night, concealing dangers and creating them in the mind when none exist. Aché rarely ventured from camp in the dark of night, but tonight they fought their fears because they had no choice. They feared the approach of spirit animals, especially the jaguar, the brutal big cousin of the African leopard that in the closed forest home of the Aché knew no fear and that tonight might be the lonely spirit of Lizard seeking companionship.

Finally, the band stopped for a time beneath the sagging, vine-cloaked branches of a great cedar tree and rested. Those who could, slept, cuddled together against the night chill while the men took turns listening and watching with lit torches and ready weapons.

They resumed walking before the first light and remained alert to the approach of spirit animals, but none were drawn to the fleeing band. When morning came, they pushed on through the warmth of a sunny day, more slowly but always steadily.

The roar of the Apa thunder, the acrid smell of its smoke, and the searing pain of the flying stones hung in their memories like an indelible chilling void. Through the harlequin greens of the towering and tangled forest that was their home, they ran from the destruction caused by the Apa. They ran from jungle razed with steel, from the roaring inferno it became when consumed by fire to make way for garden crops. They knew that the destruction of their home by the Apa—the exploding trees and screaming winds sucked from the surrounding forest by the flames—would continue, would take them with it.

Armadillo carried her daughter, Monkey, on her shoulders as the band strung out through the forest. The women and children walked in the middle, led and followed by the men. Armadillo followed her mother, Grandmother Boa, and was followed by her sister, Deer, and her wounded husband, Anteater. The three strong women formed the distaff nucleus of the band and were not afraid to speak out on any matter. They had joined Turtle's group when Grandmother Boa married his father, Jamo Paca. Grandmother Boa's first husband, the father of Armadillo and Deer, had been killed when a tree wrenched from the ground by violent winds fell across his chest as he lay in camp tending a roasting capybara haunch. The daughters were young then and well known among the Aché for their beauty.

Armadillo, with her flashing eyes and confident manner, caught the attention of nearly everyone who met her, especially the men. She looked people in the eye, and smiled, and seemed happy to know them; she always listened when they spoke as if she was truly interested. People regarded her as a friend from the moment they met her, and even when she said something pointed, they weren't offended. Women wanted Armadillo as a friend, and men desired her as a lover or spouse. Younger men and boys her own age hung back, intimidated by the stares of the older men, even married ones, if they paid attention to her.

When Boa and her daughters joined the band, Turtle was still a young man, just a few years older than Armadillo. He was married to Parrot, and they had one child, and the band, which had long been led by his father, Paca, became known as Turtle's band because of the strong, bold, young hunter who had been in charge since his teens. Turtle was immediately attracted to Armadillo.

Armadillo enjoyed the favor of the already-famous man, and Parrot endured her husband's wandering eye with the sober resignation that came from tolerating the frequent aberrations of such a volatile man. Turtle pursued Armadillo without serious competition within the small band, and when—after several months of open flirting and not-so-secret liaisons in the forest—he proposed marriage, Armadillo was not surprised. She discussed the proposal with her mother, and Boa told her that if she loved Turtle, there was no reason not to marry him since powerful men sometimes took more than one wife. She also warned Armadillo that Turtle might not be satisfied with her, might desire other women as he wanted her now, and that she would have to share her husband with Parrot. Armadillo coyly avoided giving Turtle a direct answer while she made up her mind, and when he pressed her, she told him she wanted to wait until after the scarring ceremony that marked her entrance into full adulthood.

Four bands gathered in midsummer for cooperative fishing and the important scarring ceremony. They congregated in a great open camp near the Big River. Armadillo was proud to be a member of Turtle's band, for it was highly regarded. When Turtle and his father studied the fishing lagoon and decided where the cut brush should be placed, it was put there. When Boa wanted to gather oranges, most of the women went to the grove with her. When Jamo Paca told the story of the Red Flood, people gathered to listen, and when Turtle boasted about the new Apa garden he and his brother, Blackbird, had raided near the big-bamboo meadow, more people came and crowded the camp.

Armadillo heard the men whispering that she was Turtle's woman, and she smiled to herself. She felt important being associated with such an esteemed man, and she decided that she would marry him after the scarring. She was pleased that she could look ahead with confidence to marriage and children, and she was surprised by the suddenness with which she then changed her mind.

She had first noticed someone at the fringes of the camp, in the shadows, listening. He was a man others often overlooked, an orphan from a disintegrating band, a man whose future was as uncertain as Turtle's was assured. People said it was too bad he was an orphan because he had come from a good family. Though he was young, he already had a reputation as a good hunter. Like his deceased father, he moved carefully through the forest when he hunted, never rushing, and thus he often found game others might miss. Armadillo noticed how much meat he brought to the big camp and the way he averted his eyes when he spoke and did not join the loud young men when they bragged and sought attention.

He impressed her at the lagoon when others were rolling the brush through the water, fighting for fish that got caught in the branches, yelling and screaming and diving when a flash of scales showed in the frothy water. He was not in the center of the excitement, holding fish high above his head to advertise his skill. Instead, he worked quietly ahead of the advancing group, toiling alone to move fallen limbs and dead tree snags that hindered the progress of the fishing group.

Armadillo watched him work and admired this quiet, dark man. When she went to help him pull a waterlogged trunk up the steep lagoon bank, she saw behind his kind eyes an unassuming confidence that she alone seemed to recognize. His name was Snake, and from the time they first spoke at the edge of the lagoon and Armadillo gave Snake one of the fish she had caught, she knew she wanted him. When Turtle stared at Snake that evening and said loudly to Blackbird that orphans should catch their own fish and not depend on the generosity of girls, Snake stood quietly, not reacting to the taunts, content to know what his contribution had been without needing to impress it upon others. He seemed to grow taller in Armadillo's eyes, and she knew she loved him and would feel that way the rest of her life.

They announced their marriage before the communal gathering ended and had to weather the sometimes-cruel comments of others and the overt animosity of Turtle. Armadillo and Snake went as husband and wife as Turtle's band returned to the forest, both wearing the fresh scars of adulthood, and—despite the early opposition—their strength earned them respect in a vital Aché band.

≡

As the afternoon progressed, the fleeing band skirted standing water along a meandering stream, and when they crossed the flooded channel, the men and women came together. Snake relieved Armadillo and hoisted their dozing daughter, Monkey, to his shoulders. They pushed on through a vine-burdened forest of buttressed arboreal giants, where the understory was scant from the perpetual shade, and up a rise into ugly, spiny forest; then they slowed and followed the slight creases, rather than forcing their way in a direct line. Fatigue had become a member of the band and discouraged them from even speaking.

In those few short moments when dusk was preparing to collapse finally into dark, they stopped. Turtle and Snake pulled and broke the brush to ground level in a small, ten-foot-diameter area while most of the others scrambled to find firewood. With the brand they had retrieved from camp on the morning of the attack—and carefully carried and replenished as they traveled—they started a fire, then another, and another. The three fires were on the perimeter of the cleared area and were kept small, fueled by dry logs fed in a little at a time. The band wouldn't need large fires tonight because there was nothing to cook; they only wanted enough warmth to cut the night chill and protect them from predators.

Catfish sat on the ground near one of the fires. Beside him his mother was helping her sister, Deer, clean the wounds on Anteater's back. "We must pick the scabs off these wounds," she said, "or the pus won't have anywhere to go, and he will never heal."

As Armadillo and Deer worked, the other women began their ritual crying for the two children. They wailed in shrill voices, led by Frog, who was extremely shaken by the loss of her baby. The crying was much like a song without words. It had structure—the voices rising and falling in a kind of staggered unison—but it was always changing and harmonious. When his aunt and mother joined in, the camp and the area around it resounded with the mournful chorus, and Catfish felt warm and secure for the first time since the attack. The crying seemed to form a protective bubble of sound around the camp: something familiar, something reassuring, even though it expressed sorrow and death.

The crying did not seem as loud this time, probably because they were still concerned about the Apa. Catfish also noticed that Vulture was hardly making any sound—she was crying, but she wasn't showing much emotion, wasn't grieving like the other women. She should be one of the most upset, he thought. Her grandson, Lizard, had been killed in the Apa attack, shot in the face by their thunder.

Vulture just doesn't know what is going on, he decided. He remembered that she had been more worried about her pets than anything else. She has been getting confused lately, he thought: calling people by the wrong names, getting lost, and doing strange things like saving those monkey feet in her basket until they began to stink so badly that someone had to take them and throw them away.

Although the other men were now sitting with their families, Catfish's father, Snake, remained on the edge of the small camp. He stood with one foot on the ground and the other on one of the logs that fed the fire by Catfish. The end of his long bow was planted firmly on the ground in front of him, and he held it with both hands about three-quarters of the way up and leaned on it with his hands resting against his right shoulder. As he stared quietly into the coals, the light of the fire flickered on his naked body, accentuating the clean definition of his lean, powerful muscles.

He was a tall man by Aché standards and quite robust. His skin was the color of aged, vegetable-tanned calfskin in the soft light and appeared smooth; a close look revealed it was marked by an almost-uninterrupted array of scars, randomly crisscrossing each other: scars upon scars with hardly a spot unmarked, all given to him by the thorns, spines, bark, and slashing leaves of the forest and the teeth, claws, jaws, stingers, and beaks of the animals and insects. All Aché were marked this way; even the skin of Catfish, only nine years old, was toughened by uncountable cicatrices.

Cuts and scratches, gouges, punctures, and bites were an inevitable consequence of living in the jungle, and the Aché accepted them and paid them little attention. They were constantly acquiring new wounds, most of them small and irritating; some of them deep, anatomically revealing, and serious; some even critical and life threatening. Most of the adult men had at one time or another been shot by an arrow, often their own. Arrows fired upward seeking monkeys or birds sometimes flew astray when deflected by vegetation or—on their return from the treetops—glanced off a lower branch or limb and surprised a hunter with a quick change of direction.

Snake had a small circular scar on the top of his left shoulder that he had gotten when a plummeting arrow came straight down into the fleshy part of his shoulder and upper back. Turtle had removed the barbed arrow that was embedded in six inches of muscle by twirling it between his hands the way he might have spun a fire-starting stick. When the flesh was sufficiently shredded to permit the barbs to be extracted, he pulled the hardwood point straight up and out. The small scar that remained was scant record of a painful and serious injury, which had elicited not as much as a grimace from Snake.

The second toe on Snake's right foot was missing the nail and bent severely to the right due to an accident when his axe glanced off a lapacho tree trunk he was chopping to open a beehive and extract honey. An irregular toe and a button of scar tissue on his shoulder were visual testimonials to the difficulties of the jungle hunting and gathering life, but they were much less noticeable than the decorative insignia that had been carved into his skin when he reached manhood.

All Aché—men and women alike—wore decorative scars on their bodies the way others wear clothes. These markings identified a person as Aché forever and were a constant reminder that the bearer had battled flesh-rending pain and conquered it. Every scarred adult was no stranger to pain and knew that it could be overcome, that it was no longer something to fear. They knew pain would visit them frequently, sometimes linger, and even settle in as an unwelcome guest. But they also knew it could be put aside, controlled, ignored. They shared a bond of pain, a bond of strength over pain, and wore their incised reminders proudly and comfortably.

Each person's pattern of scars was unique, but all were composed of a number of straight lines cut into the face, chest, back, arms, and legs with a strip of razor-sharp cane or shard of glass picked up in an abandoned Apa camp. Rubbing charcoal powder into the wounds produced bluish lines in the scars of lighter-skinned Aché that were considered especially decorative. On darker-skinned individuals such as Snake, the tattoo-like lines were hardly noticeable.

Despite being cut into dark skin that minimized their contrast, Snake's scars were considered very attractive. The lines were clean, smooth, and symmetrical, the result of steady-handed execution and an unmoving initiate. He had one horizontal scar across his forehead and one on each cheek under his eyes. Three vertical cuts also adorned his cheeks, and another bisected his chin. On his back, four vertical scars ran from near his shoulder blades to his buttocks, and on his chest, a pair of especially prominent horizontal lines crossed each pectoral, one above and one below each nipple. Four wide and slightly puckered vertical scars marked his stomach—two on each side of his navel—and a series of vertical scars ran from his shoulder to elbow on each arm, and from hip to just above the knee on each thigh.

From just under Snake's lower lip protruded his labret, a pointed, three-inch-long, slender piece of monkey leg bone, carved and flattened on the end that rested against his gums. The hole to insert the labret had been pierced when he was in his late teens, not too long before he had received the scars that welcomed him to adulthood. Unlike the scars, however, only men wore the lip ornaments, and Paraguayans said it looked as if Aché men had stuck large toothpicks into their lower lips.

Snake's hair was cut in the traditional way, shaved almost completely off with a cane knife, except for a line of inch-long hair along the crest of his scalp running from his forehead to the nape of his neck, and a smaller band of long stubble encircling his head. Aside from the labret, and a necklace bearing the four canine teeth of an ocelot, Snake wore nothing. Even without clothing, however, he was exquisitely adorned.

Snake shifted his weight, and the log he had been resting one foot on rolled toward him and out of the fire, causing it to smoke. He laid his bow next to his arrows against a large tree and pushed the log back into the fire, adjusting the angle to produce better air circulation around the glowing coals. He glanced up, noticed Catfish looking at him, and lifted his head slightly and pursed his lips in a silent greeting to his son, which made Catfish smile.

Catfish greatly admired his father and often watched him, noting how he did things, how he carried himself, and his expressions and mannerisms, so he could imitate them. He learned some things and patterned his behavior on them without being consciously aware of them or understanding why, such as walking in the characteristic Aché way: lifting each foot rather high, shifting the weight smoothly, carefully placing the foot on the ground, shifting the weight smoothly once more, and beginning again.

Catfish did not know that this graceful, balanced way of walking was unique to the Aché, nor could he understand why they moved like that, for he had never left the forest, had never lived in a place where there were no branches and vines to step over, and had never seen anyone other than an Aché walk. He had never had a chance to notice that others were not so careful and graceful in their movements and could not know that they had no reason to be.

He could understand the reasons for some things he saw his father do, such as the way Snake was always careful to lean his arrows against a tree or bush at night so they would not be stepped or slept on; that way their tips would not be broken or their feathers frayed. When Catfish watched his father adjust his bowstring, he noted the way he wound the cord and checked for proper tension, and Catfish knew why it was important. When Snake straightened his arrows each morning, Catfish watched and learned how to sight along the shaft, thump the nock with his thumb to check for unevenness, hold the crooked part near the fire to heat it, and bend the offending section slightly past straight and hold it until it cooled so the straightening would hold.

Catfish understood the purpose of these things and knew that by paying attention, he would learn useful and important skills; more than that, he watched because he wanted to be like his father: a good hunter, a man who made few mistakes, a man who was kind and fair, a man whom the others in the group admired.

Catfish also watched Turtle, not because he wanted to imitate the influential man—even though Turtle was, like Snake, a good hunter who excelled at most tasks—but because Catfish was uncertain about what he might do. Turtle could be warm and charming. He was generous and told stories and jokes that made people laugh. He was very clever and could often find solutions to problems that confused others. He was in many ways an admirable man who was well suited to be a leader. However, he was unpredictable, and Catfish did not trust him. He had seen Turtle lose his temper on many occasions and lash out unmercifully at anyone nearby.

Catfish and the other children also feared him because they knew they were especially vulnerable. Less than a year before, Turtle had terrorized the camp when he had gone into the rage—the rage of vengeance, the rage any Aché man can experience when someone close to him dies or is killed, and the spirit cries for company.

Turtle's infant son had died from fever, and Turtle had gone into the rage. All the children were terrified because they knew what the rage meant and what might happen to them.

"I am so angry; I need to kill to quiet the spirits," Turtle yelled as he paced around the camp, swinging his bow like a seven-foot-long club. He grunted like a wild animal and made thrusting, stabbing motions with his sharpened bow stave. "My son is dead from the fever, and his spirit is alone. I must send him a companion." He spoke rhythmically, almost chanting, and his voice gradually rose as he intensified his frenzy. "I am angry enough to kill. I will kill so I no longer hear my dead son calling."

Catfish lay on the ground as if paralyzed. He wanted to become invisible. He felt as if the blood had drained from his body and he could not move. His eyes were only slightly open, and he looked at the dirt in front of his face without seeing it. He knew Turtle could kill him with a blow from his bow at any second. He tried to stop breathing, thinking that even the movement of his chest might attract Turtle's attention.

Everyone sat silent and motionless as Turtle's rage shattered the peace of their camp. Mothers held their babies and tried to quiet them, and fathers sat looking at the ground, knowing that to do anything would only make things worse. Then Otter's little sister, a weak child who often cried, twisted her head and pulled away from her mother, Deer, who had been covering the child's mouth with her hand, and bleated out a shrill, scared-baby cry. Deer again covered her mouth, but the baby struggled to free herself and attracted Turtle's attention the way a wounded rabbit draws the hawk.

"Turtle, don't take my baby," Deer screamed and stood up, locking both arms around the baby's tiny body. "I won't let you take her," she cried and turned to flee into the forest.

Turtle grabbed the baby's feet with his left hand and violently stripped the mother's protective arms away with his right. Anteater, the child's father, had not yet returned from hunting, and the men who watched made no effort to intervene. The baby's cry stopped abruptly as Turtle turned his hips, and his chest, arms, and hands followed, swinging the innocent child like an axe. Catfish watched as her head struck the buttressed trunk of a fig tree, making a sound like a breaking melon; at that moment, she ceased to be Otter's little sister. Silence flooded the camp, and the rage was over for the moment.

From that day on, Catfish was never comfortable around Turtle, and even though he knew that the rage could come to any man, he had seen Turtle come close to having it several times for no real reason, and that made Catfish afraid. When Turtle returned from hunting each day, the children ceased being children—stopped shouting and running and laughing—and sat down and tried to become invisible. They waited to read his mood, to see if he was angry, to see if they risked offending him and having to face the consequences. Usually nothing happened, and they resumed acting like children after a short while.

Every man was treated with similar respect and apprehension when he returned from the hunt, but Turtle was especially troubling for the children, even his own. Catfish was most uneasy when Turtle was in camp and his father was still out hunting. Snake understood that and always attempted to return to camp each day before Turtle arrived.

Catfish had been worried all day because Lizard had been killed, and although Lizard was not a relative of Turtle's, one never knew, and the baby that had been stolen was Turtle's niece, the daughter of his brother, Blackbird. Turtle was angry today, very angry, but he was angry at the Apa. Several times Catfish had heard him say that he wanted to kill Apa, that he would kill the Apa to avenge the attack and teach them not to kill Aché. This had comforted Catfish because he felt the same way and was glad Turtle was not looking in his own band for an object for venting his anger.

When the women stopped crying, the camp was silent for a few moments, and then Jamo Paca began singing in a low voice. He sang a song about his youth, punctuated as most Aché songs are by a wordless, modulated refrain:

> Ey, ey ey ey eeey; ey, ey ey ey eeey.
> When I was a young man,
> We hunted tapir and peccaries.
> We always ate meat;
> We always ate fat.
> We never hunted monkeys
> As they are never fat.
> Ey, ey ey ey eeey; ey, ey ey ey eeey.
> We hunted in good forest
> And never had to run.
> We were great hunters
> And never went hungry.
> We always ate meat;

We always ate fat.

Ey, ey ey ey eeey; ey, ey ey ey eeey.

Catfish relaxed at the sound of singing, a sound that usually put him to sleep. He was tired and slept soundly; he didn't even wake when the men heard a sound in the forest, sat up listening, and grabbed their weapons before deciding that it was nothing more than a dead branch falling from a tree. The Aché slept piled on top of each other in the unusually small camp, and most of them alternated between the deep sleep of exhaustion and the inability to relax that often accompanies it.

3 ☰ ARROWS

The camp was stirring well before dawn. Men stoked and added wood to the fires and blew them into flame. Mothers nursed their babies, and the older children warmed themselves by the fires. Usually at this time, leftover food from the previous evening's meal was warmed and eaten, but today there was none. There was not even any water, for the Apa had stolen or destroyed all the containers.

Anteater was stiff and had a difficult time moving. He sat up and faced away from the fire to warm his tight and painful back. His wife, Deer, pulled the cracked, dried scabs from his wounds. Fluid drained from them, and she wiped it away with a handful of leaves. She gently squeezed the mushy tissue around the holes to flush out the pus, and as she did, a pellet came out.

"Look, Anteater, another one of the Apa's stones came out of your back," Deer said, showing her husband the lead ball.

"Good," said Anteater. "Squeeze them all out. I don't want them in me."

Deer felt around the four holes that still held shotgun pellets, and she could feel two of them.

"I can feel two stones," she said. "They aren't very deep. I think I can get them out."

She pinched the skin and muscle between her thumbs and fingers and worked the two shallowly embedded balls to the surface. The two remaining wounds were deeper than the others—in the thick muscle of Anteater's lower back—and she could not feel the pellets nor work them out, even after she probed tentatively with the wooden tip broken from one of Anteater's arrows.

"Squeeze harder," Anteater said. "I don't want those stones in my back. Dig them out if you have to."

27

"I felt with the arrow point, but I didn't touch anything but flesh. Maybe they came out already—I don't know—and if they didn't, maybe the pus will push them out. I can't feel anything in there; they are too deep and too close to the bone."

Anteater slowly nodded his head, pensively rubbed his index finger with his thumb, and turned to his son.

"Otter, bring my arrows so I can sharpen them."

Otter retrieved his father's arrows. Anteater took a large snail shell he had found as they walked and pecked it on the hard tip of his bow until he knocked a small hole in its side. He then used the edges of the hole to plane and sharpen the hardwood tips of his arrows. This was one activity that this morning had in common with all others. Each morning the men carefully inspected their arrows, straightening, sharpening, and repairing them, often working for nearly an hour, preparing their tools for a day of hunting.

Anteater sat on the ground, placed his arrows next to him, and lined them up with the tips pointing toward him. He worked on one arrow at a time, and as he finished each one, he placed it next to the others with the feathers toward him, so he could keep track of how many were done and how many remained. He had seven arrows, about the same number as all the men. One arrow had a blunt tip for shooting birds and small game, one had a big, daggerlike tip for shooting very large game such as tapir, and five arrows had a row of barbs running down one side and were used for other kinds of animals. The arrows were as long as a man is tall and had shafts made of cane and hardwood points. The points were long in relation to the size of the arrow, often comprising more than two-thirds of the length.

Anteater worked on his arrows, as did the other men, although he would not be able to use them; his torn back could not take the strain of pulling his powerful bow. He readied his arrows more to resume working than prepare for the hunt. He would not hunt with the other men until he recovered from his injury, which might take weeks, but he was determined to push himself to do everything he could. His arrows—of no use to Anteater right now—would be sharp and ready in case another hunter needed them.

The tip on one of Anteater's arrows was cracked and splintered from colliding with a tree limb high above the ground three days before. His shot had narrowly missed a screaming capuchin monkey, and the brittle hardwood point served its purpose well, breaking the slender tip, rather than impaling a lofty branch and becoming stuck. Anteater put the broken point in his mouth and clenched it between his teeth to break off the damaged part so he could resharpen what remained.

"Look at Anteater!" Armadillo exclaimed. "He is trying to be like the Apa. The one he shot in the mouth!"

Anteater leaned back and held the arrow with both hands. He squealed and pretended to be trying to pull the arrow from his mouth. Everyone laughed, and when Anteater removed the arrow and used his arm to push himself back to a seated position, he winced slightly from the pain.

He coughed loudly and spit into the fire. "Arrows don't taste very good. I think I'd rather have thunder stones in my back than have to eat an arrow." He chuckled at his own joke as he reached for the arrow and broke the tip off cleanly between his teeth.

The men planed their arrow tips and resharpened them; they also checked the straightness of the shafts, for the dampness of the climate made the cane susceptible to warping. Small cracks or splinters in the shaft could be mended with beeswax and wrapped with thin strips of liana bark. The vulture feather flights were also checked, and straightened and rewrapped if needed. The men paid careful attention to the condition of their arrows because a missed shot due to a faulty one was a poor excuse for failing as a hunter.

When the last arrow had been straightened and set aside, the men sat and played with the children for a few minutes. There was no discussion of strategy for the day, and the feeling that this was an unusual day like the previous two began to fade. As if by some prearranged signal, the men got up, and Snake and Coati, a young man with no family, started out alone. The others lingered while the women and children readied themselves. Otter carried his father's arrows as he had the day before, and he bore them proudly, and Vulture carried a brand from one of the fires. As the diffuse, colorless morning light grew, the band started walking north again through the dew-drenched jungle, heading for the Big River.

The band moved purposefully, although at a slightly more relaxed pace than on the two previous days. They made short stops to drink and eat fruit but allowed themselves no additional interruptions. Despite their hunger, they passed several honey trees and fresh armadillo holes, resources that they would usually exploit for a considerable amount of food. An hour or two of time, at this point, was more valuable than fifteen pounds of meat or a gallon or two of honey. They were still running.

Catfish understood. Hunger was an enemy he had learned to fear long before he had even heard of the Apa. He was accustomed to the hand-to-mouth existence of the Aché. With no means of preserving or storing food, the foremost question in everyone's mind each day was "what food will we eat today, and where will we get it?" The men hunted and the women gathered with some overlap. When food was available, everyone ate, and when it was not, they thought about eating.

Catfish had never known extreme hunger, but like all Aché, he was continuously anxious about it. He could remember clearly the few times he had gone an entire day without eating meat and had, until now, never gone without it for two days. When he saw the fresh armadillo holes, he thought about the juicy, white meat and salivated. The others did, too, but still they marched on.

When they came to a small grassy meadow and crossed the narrow, deeply cut stream that traversed it, Catfish knew they were not far from the Big River. The cool, sluggish water was chest deep on the adults, and they carried the children across on their shoulders. Catfish knew the spot. He and Otter had shot five little fish with their little bows and arrows just a month earlier and—like grown hunters—had proudly returned their prey to camp for the band to share.

Meadows speckled the landscape like patches of lichen on the bark of a tree and were the only places in Aché territory where sunlight could touch more than two persons at a time, but the band generally avoided them. Chiripá Indians, farmers of the once-great Guaraní chiefdoms, lived and traveled in the meadows, and so did the Apa. The Chiripá, like the Apa, regarded the Aché as fearsome, savage animals that should be killed on sight. In the open meadows, the Aché were vulnerable. They were visible and could be run down on horseback like stray cattle and killed or captured, but in the jungle— where horses could not go and the Apa and Chiripá were clumsy and slow—the Aché held an advantage. When the Aché had trouble with their enemies, it was usually in or near meadows, especially large ones that could be hundreds of yards wide and miles long. In these places, they moved quickly and looked about often, like a dog-fearing cat venturing across an open yard.

But this was a small meadow deep in the forest and isolated from any others, and they crossed it without fear. The tropical sun was growing larger, and its usually intense, yellow-white rays were acquiring the rosy cast that indicated its approach to the horizon. As the foot-weary band trailed into the trees, leaving the grassy opening in their forest home behind, and the doors of the familiar jungle closed behind them and shielded them from the discomfortingly direct sunlight, their breath came slightly easier. They walked through forest Catfish knew well and came to the overgrown camp where they had eaten the fish he and Otter had shot. A few yards beyond the old camp, they spotted Snake and Coati sitting on the ground, their backs against tree trunks, waiting for them.

Catfish ran to his father and sat between his legs, his arm around Snake's knee. He was glad to be close to his father again after the long day without him. The others spread out and began removing the brush and branches from around them, making camp.

"We're hungry," Catfish said. "We've only eaten fruit today."

He turned, looked at his father, and thought he looked tired. Snake gently squeezed Catfish's shoulder with his big, thick-fingered hand and smiled at his young son. His eyes twinkled under strain-thickened lids, and he turned and pointed over his right shoulder, indicating the direction with a slight extension of his lips. Catfish's face lit up, and he stood up, looking where Snake had pointed. Spotting a furry shape in the leaves a dozen feet away, he ran to it and turned, beaming, toward the camp.

"Otter, come here; I need help," he called and bent over and picked up a yard-long lizard, thick in the middle and covered with iridescent scales. "We have teju lizard to eat and capybara!"

Several children hurried to Catfish and the game, and he handed the lizard to Blackbird's oldest daughter, Duck. Catfish and Otter tugged at the lianas Snake had used to bind the feet of the capybara for carrying, but they could hardly budge the huge rodent, which at a hundred pounds outweighed both of the boys combined. Turtle's son, Puma, helped them, and together the three boys half dragged, half carried the animal to the camp.

Turtle began preparing the capybara for cooking, and Frog, Blackbird's wife, butchered and cooked the lizard. Both men and women cooked and butchered game, although men usually handled the larger animals. All meat was shared equally within the band, regardless of who killed it, and they ate together as a large family. Since Snake had killed the capybara, he could not eat any of its meat, nor could Coati eat the lizard, for he had killed that. The hunters would not go hungry, however, because they could freely partake of each other's kill.

Since there was meat to cook, and the threat of an Apa attack had considerably diminished, the band set up a more normal camp. An area about fifteen to twenty feet in diameter was cleared, and each family made a fire on the perimeter. There were six fires in all: the families of Turtle, Snake, Blackbird, and Anteater each had one; Grandfather Jamo Paca and his wife, Grandmother Boa, had a fire; and the widower, Ocelot, shared one with his son, Coati, and the old widow, Vulture. The fire was the focus of activity for each family, and they spent most of their time in camp near it: cooking, eating, working, and sleeping. There were no real boundaries or divisions in the camp, though. People moved freely from fire to fire if they wished, and conversations often included everyone in the band; privacy was one thing the Aché knew little about and seldom desired.

Turtle made a large pile of wood and lit it with a smoldering brand. He blew on the coals and adjusted the wood until he had a roaring fire. When it had burned back and was hot and glowing, he spread the wood out just a little and untied the vines that bound the feet of the capybara. Grasping the hind feet, he flopped the carcass on the fire, and it crackled and sent up a billowing cloud of smoke as the hair burned off. A few seconds in any one position was enough, and he moved it forward and back, turning it over, spreading the legs, laying it on its back, and scraping it vigorously with a flat piece of wood until the capybara was black and naked. He then lifted it from the fire and set it aside for butchering.

The lizard needed very little preparation. Frog had taken the heavy animal from Duck; removed the tail, which she placed in the coals; and split the carcass down the middle for roasting. She turned the tail several times, and the thin skin blackened and blistered, revealing the moist, white meat. In just a few minutes, she removed it from the fire, gingerly pulled and snapped the tapering end that was already cooked from the thick base, set it aside, and returned the rest to the coals to continue cooking. Blackbird, who had been squatting beside the fire, reached for the cooling portion and put it in his mouth.

"Give some of that to Snake," Frog reminded him quietly. "He can't eat any capybara because he killed it, and this is not a large teju."

Blackbird grunted, broke the piece in half, and tossed a portion to Armadillo. She smiled, and Blackbird smiled back around the sides of the lizard meat he was already chewing.

Turtle was hot and dirty from singeing the capybara, and when beads of sweat rolled down his steamy brow, they washed away the soot and left clean streaks in their wake. He pulled the wad of ferns from the small slit in the belly where Snake had earlier removed the intestines and, using a sharp piece of cane, enlarged the hole. He pulled out the liver, heart, and lungs and handed them to his wife to cook in the hot coals of the fire. Then—with the touch of a surgeon—he began removing the skin. He was not simply skinning the animal, for the Aché never tanned hides and rarely used leather; instead, he was removing a thick layer of meat that kept the subcutaneous fat attached to the skin. The Aché rarely skinned animals; like nearly every other part of the game they killed, they ate the skin.

When he had finished removing the skin, Turtle had a large, three-foot-square blanket of flesh some three inches thick. He hoisted it up, carried it to the fire, and laid it over the green-wood rack his wife had built. Suspended over the fire, it would cook slowly and not lose its fat and juices. When it was done, Turtle would cut it into hand-sized pieces and pass them out to everyone in camp.

He paused for a moment to peel another strip from a finger-thick piece of bamboo and replace the already-dull, blood-covered knife he had been using. Returning to the capybara carcass, he quickly dismembered it, wielding the delicate cane knife with the deft precision that comes from years of practice. He cut the animal into segments that would easily fit on the small wooden cooking racks, using his detailed knowledge of anatomy to minimize the number of strokes needed from his scalpel-like blade. He made cuts at the precise spots necessary to release muscles from around a joint so he could bend it back and expose the critical tendons, which he severed with clean, sure strokes. Once he had removed the legs and passed them to others to cook, he took the axe and chopped along both sides of the vertebrae to remove the ribs and cut through the spinal column in four places to remove the head and segment the backbone.

When he had finished, he sat by the fire with his wife, who was already passing out the cooked capybara organs, and ate some of the liver. The rest of the lizard would be ready in just a few minutes, and some of the capybara—the feet, for instance—would be cooked shortly thereafter. The band would be cooking and eating for several hours: sharing the meat, the work, and the company of their families and friends; reinforcing their togetherness and reliance on each other; strengthening the bonds that held them together as a unit, an Aché band.

For two days, they had been strained as tightly as a damp bowstring shrinking in the morning sun. Now the tension was easing. The rewarding work of preparing a camp and food was a welcome replacement for the tiring and confusing act of running. They were on familiar ground here and could relax. The children caught large fireflies that were beginning to appear; they had such bright lights on their heads that they were sometimes used to illuminate small things that needed to be seen at night, like a splinter or a tick that had to be removed.

Catfish caught three of the light beetles, and he picked off their legs and wings and threw them high in the air, watching with glee as they caromed off branches and leaves. His deep-jungle, aerial light show was popular with the other children, and soon a dozen or more of the insects were sailing about, doomed by their bright sexual displays.

Armadillo tended the capybara haunches roasting over her fire and licked the juices from her fingers, wishing she had a palm-wood brush to catch the tasty drippings as she normally did. *I will make one as soon as I have a chance,* she thought. She looked around and saw that while the children played, the adults seemed absorbed by the cooking. Her eyes began to gleam, and she fought to hide the grin that tried to spread across her face.

"I wasn't at all afraid when I first heard the Apa's thunder the other morning," she said, looking down and picking at a small tidbit of meat that was separating from the cooking capybara thigh. "I wasn't even going to run."

"You're crazy then," said her mother, Grandmother Boa, from across the camp. "Did you think you were already dead?"

"It was a clear night, and there were no clouds," added Turtle's wife, Parrot. "I knew it wasn't real thunder, and I knew right away it must be something terrible. I was terrified. You were afraid just like the rest of us. You looked scared to me. I saw you run; you almost lost Catfish, you ran so fast."

"I ran, but it was only because everyone else was running. I didn't think it was the Apa's thunder." Armadillo used a stick to turn the meat.

"You must have been dreaming when you heard it," said Parrot. "We all knew what it was, and we have never heard the thunder that close before. Even if I hadn't known what it was, I would have run. I have never heard anything that loud."

"Parrot is right," said Grandmother Boa. "What else could it have been but the Apa's thunder? Nothing else makes a noise like that on a clear morning. What did you think it was?"

"I know you are both right, but I really didn't think it was the Apa's thunder," Armadillo said innocently. "And I wasn't dreaming; I was wide awake. When I heard it, I thought, 'There goes that Blackbird with his farts again!'"

The camp exploded with laughter, and Turtle laughed so hard he rolled backward and almost burned himself in the fire. Blackbird giggled like a child at the joke. He was used to teasing about his farts, for which he was notorious. "Why did you run then?" Blackbird asked. "The loud farts don't smell. What were you afraid of?"

"When I saw the others running, and even you running, Blackbird, I thought it must be the worst fart ever. I wasn't going to stay there and take the chance of ruining my nose."

Snake was still chuckling at his wife's joke minutes later when the rest of the lizard was ready and Blackbird handed him a large piece of the plump tail. Catfish stopped playing with his fireflies and sat between his parents to eat. He ate the meat from one of the lizard's legs, chewed the bone, and thought about his dead friend, Lizard.

All Aché babies were named for an animal whose meat the pregnant mother had prepared and cooked, and while she might cook dozens of animals, one always seemed to stand out. *If a woman is pregnant now,* Catfish thought, *she might choose capybara or lizard for her baby's name since this seems like a special meal. Maybe that's why the lizard let Coati kill him, so a new baby could be named lizard to replace my friend.*

But nobody is pregnant. Maybe it came to remind us of lizard and show us he is not angry and won't come to bother us. I hope so.

4 ≡ BIG RIVER

Morning came quickly, and Grandmother Boa was, as usual, the first to wake. She quietly fed her fire and rebuilt the roasting rack, which had burned and partially collapsed during the night. She arranged some of the leftover meat on the rack to warm and waited while others enjoyed the restful sleep that comes just before waking. The ground was carpeted with bodies, punctuated by the flaky ash and wispy smoke of the forgotten fires. The camp had been active well into the night, fed by the periodic arrival of juicy, freshly roasted meat from the grills and the spirited conversation, jokes, and laughter of the band members enjoying a release from their recent anxiety and confusion.

As the forest began to fill with the sounds of morning, and the numerous species of birds initiated their dawn-to-dusk chatter, the band eased into the new day. The adults woke first and, without rising, pulled the burned-back fire logs together and puffed them into flame. Pieces of roasted meat were reheated and handed to the waking children. Babies were the last to stir and signaled their arrival with squeals of hunger. Men checked their arrows but had little work to do; only Snake had used his weapons the day before, and he had killed the capybara with a single shot. Deer examined and cleaned her husband, Anteater's, back, which was beginning to heal, although there was increased swelling in the lumbar region where she had failed to extract the two deeply buried shotgun pellets. Armadillo sent Catfish to get leaves to wrap the leftover meat for carrying, and in a short while, the band was ready to move.

They walked north again as a group, and in less than an hour reached the Big River. They then turned upstream and went east, following the course of the stream but staying several hundred feet from the banks to avoid the tangled bamboo and branches that flanked the watercourse. Trees along the river bowed toward it in various stages of very-slow-motion descent, toppled by water-softened earth and the never-ending lateral, riverine meander. Turtle and Blackbird went ahead to search for a spot where the band could cross.

The creamy-brown water was less than a hundred feet from bank to sandy bank, but beneath the deceptively flat surface, the flow was swift and strong and, in most places, too deep for people who could not swim to ford safely. A pair of ducks startled by the band's approach noisily churned their way into water-skimming flight and disappeared around an upstream bend while mergansers in a back eddy near the opposite shore continued diving for minnows without apparent concern.

Blackbird and Turtle saw caiman tracks along the banks and noted the outlet to an oxbow lagoon in the trees across the river, where the crocodiles likely were, but put off pursuing the reptiles for now. When the two men came to a large tree that had fallen across the river with the tops of its branches just tickling the far bank, they gave a high-pitched cry to inform the others and walked out on the trunk to see if it was strong enough to be a bridge. They snapped off branches that obstructed passage and carried them to the far end. There they wedged them in places to add additional support or act as handholds in the final few yards where their bridge was more spindly and springy than substantial.

When the band arrived, they crossed in single file, being careful not to follow too closely behind each other and interfere when walking on the slender branches at the far end. Catfish trailed about ten feet behind his mother, who carried Monkey piggyback and held a bundle of leaf-wrapped roast meat in her left hand. They started on the three-foot-diameter main trunk some ten feet above the surface of the water at the near bank and walked on a downward slant along the fallen tree. Halfway across and five feet above the water, the tree branched out, and they traveled along a one-foot-diameter branch that disappeared into the river about fifteen feet from the shore, the part with the swiftest current.

From there they walked on smaller branches—some only an inch in diameter—at or near the level of the water. The branches moved rhythmically back and forth as they were first caught by the current and then snapped back again and again. For much of the last dozen feet, people were walking on limbs knee deep in the water, finding their footing by feel, moving with the waving branches, and grabbing as best they could for limbs above the water for balance.

Despite the difficult footing, no one slipped or fell, and even old Vulture, who was nearly seventy, did not miss a step. Usually each of the women, including Vulture, would have been carrying a heavy basket, which added to the difficulty of such crossings, but they always managed. When the day came that someone could no longer travel where the band needed to go—whether across a river or through a swamp, over a fallen tree or through a tangle of vines—that person's last day as an Aché was near.

When they reached the narrow beach on the north bank of the river, they stopped to drink and rest. Catfish and his friends sprinted in the shallows and pelted each other with handfuls of sand, filling the air with excited howls and squeals. Snake took the axe and cut several sections from the three-inch-thick bamboo that grew nearby to carry water in and fashioned wooden plugs to keep the containers from spilling. Turtle and Blackbird walked downstream to look at the oxbow lagoon they had seen earlier and, when they returned, reported that they had seen caiman and capybara tracks, and they would come back later and hunt there. Anteater sat on the sandy bank while Deer washed his wounds with *timbo* water, which felt good on the inflamed, swollen tissue.

When the water containers were finished, Snake gave them to the boys to fill and carry, and he went to Armadillo, who was waving a small leafy branch like a fan in front of Monkey, occasionally using it to slap herself on her back or arms. Tiny black biting gnats were swarming about—their numbers seeming to double every few minutes—and the youngest children, who were nearly defense-less against the savage, painful attacks, loudly voiced their discomfort. Snake noticed the puffiness in the corners of Monkey's clear, dark eyes and the pinprick bite marks atop rising welts on her chest and arms.

The little children always suffer the most from biting insects, he thought. *When they are older like Catfish, they can run and play, or slap themselves, or fan themselves with leaves, but the little ones can do nothing but cry. Their skin is tender, and the gnats can bite them anywhere.* He looked at his own feet, so toughened that a hundred gnats crawled and flew about them, unable to find a single spot where their bites could penetrate the skin and extract the desired drop of blood.

"Come on, Monkey," he said, lifting her high above his head. "Let's get away from these gnats. We'll go into the forest and leave them behind."

The tormented child exchanged her grimace for a big grin, her swollen eyes nearly closing in a happy squint.

"I'll carry Monkey," Snake said to Armadillo. "We won't be walking very far, and the other men and I won't leave to go hunting until we find a place to camp."

He hoisted his daughter to his shoulders, walked a few yards and stooped to pick up his bow and arrows, then headed into the trees. Turtle and his family had already started walking, and the others quickly followed. The air was cooler in the forest, and there were slightly fewer biting insects. It helped to keep moving, and when the band stopped, the smoke from the fires would keep the pests in check.

They walked for half an hour through the jungle and chose to camp on the south-facing hummock of a gently sloping hillside. Here scattered palm trees were interspersed in the hardwood forest. The men helped clear the area of larger brush and debris and then quietly slipped into the forest to hunt. Blackbird and Turtle headed toward the lagoon to hunt capybara and caiman, and Snake, Coati, and Jamo went north to look for peccaries. There would be plenty of time for hunting because the day was still young. Ocelot would stay with the women and help them chop palms.

The women gathered dry logs and branches and made fires that would burn until after they abandoned this temporary home for another. They worked quickly because there was much to do: their entire stock of possessions, each item necessary for survival, had to be replenished. In the coming days, they would be busy making carrying baskets, sleeping mats, fans, slings for transporting babies, water containers, and cooking vessels. Replacing and repairing these items was a never-ending task even under normal circumstances, but such a full-scale effort involving everyone in the band was unprecedented.

When she had finished building a fire and had pulled up all the small stumps in the cleared sleeping area, Armadillo rose and indicated that she was ready to begin foraging in the palms. Ocelot prepared to leave with her. Armadillo took the axe and started walking along the side of the hill away from the camp. After a dozen feet, she turned and looked back at Monkey, who had been watching with apprehension.

"Come on, Monkey, let's go cut some palms," she said.

Monkey rocked forward, put her hands on the ground in front of her, and lifted herself to her feet with an exaggeratedly childlike wobble. She extended her arms as if inviting an embrace and took a hesitant step in Armadillo's direction.

"Carry me, mother," she called in a worried voice.

"You're a big girl now; you can walk by yourself," Armadillo said. "Don't you remember? You have been walking in the forest for a month. I've only been carrying you the last few days because we had to hurry. If you want to come with me, you have to walk because I won't carry you. Come on, let's go."

Armadillo again started walking into the trees. Monkey watched for a second and then turned her head quickly to look toward the camp. Catfish was already off in the forest playing with his friends, and those who were left purposefully looked away, avoiding the child's inquisitive gaze, providing her with no alternative to obeying her mother.

Monkey turned toward Armadillo, who was getting farther away each second, and burst loudly into tears.

"Carry me, mother," she cried, taking a few tiny steps and falling to her knees. "I don't know how to walk. I'm afraid."

Armadillo ignored the child, despite the screaming protests that drowned out all of the usual jungle sounds. Monkey started to follow her, and then she cried and fell unnecessarily to convince her mother that she should be carried. It was a difficult period in Monkey's life, a traumatic time every Aché child must go through when he or she ceases being a highly protected infant and has to become an independent child. Armadillo nearly changed her mind and returned to assist her daughter but decided against it. She continued on, stopping at a foot-thick palm tree only two hundred feet from the camp, and began chopping.

Monkey screamed at the top of her lungs, and her cheeks glistened from streaming tears. She staggered and fell often, partly acting, partly due to her tantrum. When she finally reached her mother, Armadillo put down her axe and squatted and hugged her child. With her hand, she wiped away the leaves and dirt that clung to Monkey's teary face.

Armadillo smiled at her daughter, and Monkey stopped crying. She was glad to be by her mother again and be rid of the terrifying feeling when they were apart.

"You sit here, Monkey, and be good while I chop this tree down," Armadillo said, taking the axe and returning to the palm. "I will give you palm heart to eat in just a few minutes." She planned to cut the first tree, and Ocelot would take over after that. She first cut two vines and a gangly sapling that were in the way and resumed swinging the axe, delivering practiced, powerful blows that would shortly topple the palm. She swung the axe with precision, each blow deepening the waist-high notch that would weaken the trunk and cause it to fall in the desired spot. Much deviation in the direction the tree fell might cause it to lean against another in the close-packed forest or fall toward Monkey, but Armadillo had cut a thousand trees and knew how to direct them.

She grasped the hand-hewn handle with her hands a foot apart and swung the axe as if it were an extension of her body. Her feet were firmly planted on the leafy ground about shoulder width apart, and she pivoted at the hips, throwing her arms and shoulders into each stroke. Her eyes concentrated on the spot she intended to hit, and her powerful arms, back, legs, and shoulders all cooperated in delivering the blow.

A strong, muscular woman, Armadillo had broad shoulders, thick forearms, and large hands. Her legs were powerful from years of carrying heavy loads over varied terrain, climbing trees, running through the forest, and gathering food. Beneath her tight buttocks, the large muscles of her thighs bulged with each expert stroke of the axe. She was thick in the midsection like most Aché, not fat, but muscular, like a weight lifter whose thick torso multiplies the power that he can exert with his arms and shoulders. Child bearing had added slightly to her girth and lengthened her breasts, which had been giving milk for eight of the past nine years.

Still, she had not lost the beauty that had distinguished her as a young woman, and her quick smile continued to win friends. Her jet-black hair was cropped short, and it roached up along the top and back of her head, accentuating her high forehead. The scars on her face and body were slender, light, and clean, and her expressive, almond-shaped eyes shone brightly above high cheekbones and full, pouting lips. Around her long, graceful neck hung a string necklace bristling with dozens of monkey canine teeth. Both men and women appreciated her sharp wit, and even more importantly, she was a capable and reliable mother, a hard worker, and a valuable member of the band.

The axe was worn almost to the point that it was hardly a tool anymore. It was dull and so worn that it was impossible to sharpen it. The blows bruised or crushed the burnt orange wood of the pindó palm tree, rather than cut it the way a metal axe would. A stone axe, even a new one, never cuts as well as even a dull metal one, and this one was old and worn out. But it was the only axe they had, and until it could be replaced—either with stone or new metal ones stolen from the Apa—it would be used constantly.

When the notch was two-thirds of the way through the smooth-barked trunk, the tree moved slightly toward the cut, and Armadillo knew it was about to fall. She put the axe down and walked to Monkey, who was well out of the way, and waited. The stressed wood let out a deep, groaning creak, and the green-leafed crown shuddered high above them as it began its arcing descent. The fall was broken by the ever-present vines, which held the tree midway down for a long second before releasing it to crash to the jungle floor.

When the last of the vines and branches that accompanied the tree had fallen, Armadillo picked up her axe and went to work. She walked to the top of the fallen palm and cut two armloads of fronds for making baskets and mats and set them aside. Then she chopped into the center of the crown and removed the terminal bud, the heart of the palm. It was covered with stringy fiber, and Armadillo pulled the coarse brown strips away from the white heart as she walked toward Monkey. She broke a fist-sized piece from the cylinder of palm heart that was as big as her forearm and handed it to her daughter.

"Here is some palm heart for you to eat, big girl," she said, taking a smaller piece for herself.

Monkey reached eagerly for the sweet, tender morsel, and while she and Armadillo were eating, Deer and Parrot walked up.

"We heard the tree come down," Parrot said. "We came to get some fronds so we can start making baskets."

"I cut some fronds and left them by the tree," Armadillo said. "Here have some palm heart first. I'm going to pound palm fiber from this tree; then Ocelot can use the axe and cut more trees."

"Frog and I have been getting bark to make carrying slings and tumplines," Deer said. "If we take turns with the axe, we should have plenty of fronds to work with and palm fiber and hearts to eat."

Parrot and Deer walked with Armadillo to the fallen tree and gathered up the fronds she had cut. She had selected only straight, undamaged plumes, ones that were still growing and not withered or discolored from disease or desiccation. In camp each frond would be inspected, and many would be discarded because of small flaws that affected the quality of the basket or mat made from them. Parrot and Deer also took what remained of the palm heart and headed back toward camp, their heavy loads balanced on one shoulder and nearly enveloping them.

Armadillo returned to the tree and cut two notches across the trunk about a foot apart, then connected them at the ends and pried up in one piece the section of bark between them. She pounded the exposed, soft, stringy wood with a dozen blows from her axe, and when it was shredded and spilling out of the opening in the trunk, she took a handful, gave it a shake to release it from the rest of the tangled mass, and brought it to her face, inhaling the moist, sweet smell. She put some in her mouth and chewed and sucked on the wad of fiber for a minute and then spit it out. She then scooped up all that she had pounded and carried the loaf-sized wad to Monkey.

"I have some palm fiber for you to eat; it is sweet and very good," she said to Monkey, who dropped the stick she had been using to poke at the rotting wood of a fallen tree beside her and reached for the moist fiber. "I am going to pound a little more, and then we'll go back to the camp."

Monkey noisily sucked mouthful after mouthful of the sweet, cool palm fiber, working each quid until the sugars and starches were gone and then spitting out the wooden wad that was left. Armadillo returned to the log, pried the bark from a six-foot section of the trunk, and resumed pounding. With her axe, she crushed, tore, and broke the wood of the palm and softened it to extract the edible parts from the indigestible cellulose. In half an hour, she was finished and gathered the fiber into a huge ball that she carried against her chest. She called to Monkey, who this time followed her without complaining, and they returned to the camp.

The small camp was crawling with activity. Parrot and Grandmother Boa were readying palm fronds to make baskets: spreading the slender leaves where they attached to the stiff central spine, drawing them quickly through glowing coals over and over again to dry and soften them, and hanging them on pole racks strung between nearby trees and bushes to dry further.

Deer, Frog, and Frog's eleven-year-old daughter, Duck, were making twine from shredded bark to use to construct slings for transporting babies and the tumplines for women's carrying baskets. With nearly continuous motion and nimble dexterity, they stripped two-foot lengths of the bark from piles in front of them, rubbed each one between their fingers and thumbs, separated it into two pieces, and rolled the strands with their palms along their thighs, twisting the fibers into a smooth, tightly wound, two-ply string. Hundreds of yards of the twine were needed for immediate construction, and it was an important item to have for stringing teeth for necklaces, constructing the men's bowstrings, and making all kinds of repairs. All of the women were skilled in making string and plaiting baskets, and they did it wonderfully, as if by second nature.

Anteater, who had stayed in camp with the women and children, was also busy. He had saved the large, sharp incisors and four of the leg bones from the capybara and was making carving chisels. He trimmed an end off each of the leg bones and socketed one of the incisors into the marrow cavity of each bone. The bone served as the handle, and the tools were used for wood working, such as cutting barbs in new arrow points, or carving the socket for a stone axe head in a wooden handle. Similar chisels made from the teeth of smaller rodents were used to make holes in teeth to string them into necklaces. Anteater carefully matched the teeth and bones to guarantee the best fit for each tool, and the tooth was held tightly in the handle.

"Here is palm fiber to eat," said Armadillo as she emerged from the green wall of vegetation that rose up wild and chaotic at the edge of their camp. "Ocelot is cutting more trees. We can get a lot of good fiber from them." She dropped the heavy ball of fiber near the middle of the camp, took a couple handfuls for herself, and went to her fire.

"I will go pound palm fiber," said Frog as she stood up and headed into the forest. "Vulture is out getting more bark for twine. I wish we had more axes, even stone ones. It's not so bad today, but it will be difficult when we are on the move and only one person can work at a time. I hope the men can make some new stone axes soon."

Armadillo poked at the largest log in her smoldering fire with a stick to expose some hot coals, added a few smaller pieces of wood, and revived the flames with long, slowly blown puffs of air. She reached for some palm fronds and joined the task of preparing them. Monkey picked up a broken piece of frond and dragged it through the hearth, mimicking her mother.

"Look at Monkey," said Parrot. "She is going to make a basket. She is just learning how to walk in the forest, and she is already working on a basket. Next thing you know, she'll be trying to find a husband."

"She's not ready for a husband just yet," said Grandmother Boa. "She doesn't know how to make a man do what she wants the way we all do. When she can say to a man, 'I sure would like some honey,' and he jumps up and grabs an axe and runs into the forest looking for bees, then she'll be a woman and will be ready for a husband. When the time comes, she'll find out how easy it is to get what she wants from men. It's much easier than making baskets."

Anteater loudly expelled a breath of air through his teeth and shook his head without looking up from his work.

"Anteater knows I'm telling the truth," Grandmother Boa continued. "These big strong men just hate to admit that it's the women who run things. We know how to make these men follow us around the way a baby peccary trails its mother. We know what they want, and if they don't treat us the way we want them to, we don't give it to them."

The women all laughed again, and Anteater hunched over even more, pretending to be so engrossed in making his carving tools that he couldn't hear.

"Monkey won't be a woman for a while yet, but Duck over there is learning," said Parrot. "Look at how well she makes twine. She will get a good husband someday. Have you noticed how much attention Coati pays to her? He makes certain that she gets plenty of meat to eat, and he pokes her and tickles her whenever he can, and she doesn't seem to mind."

"She already knows what she is doing," added Deer. "I've seen her give Coati that coy smile and look at him with flirting eyes. She knows more about being a woman than just how to make string."

Young Duck was blushing but grinning, too, because it was true, and she liked being called a woman. Anteater continued to pretend that he was deaf.

"Deer is not the only one to notice Duck's flirting," said Armadillo. "Turtle and Blackbird and Ocelot have noticed, too. That's why they make sure that Coati sleeps in the middle of the camp, where they can keep an eye on him."

"That's true," said Grandmother Boa, "but I don't think the men are only worried about Duck. They've seen how the rest of the women look at Coati. His skin is so light and pretty, and he is a good hunter. The men make him hunt the farthest away from the women, where they can watch him. They're not so worried about him flirting with the little girls; they're concerned about him having a little fun with their wives."

The women exchanged glances and giggled, and Anteater looked up and smiled at Grandmother Boa.

"That's not true, Grandmother," he said. "We're not worried about our wives and Coati. What do we have to worry about? What woman wants a boy when she already has a man? We're concerned about Coati having his way with you, Grandmother Boa. We've seen you look down there when he walks by. We're afraid you may go into the forest with Coati and die from the excitement."

The camp rocked with laughter, and the conversation that accompanied the work carried them quickly through the day.

A light rain was beginning to fall when Snake, Grandfather Jamo Paca, and Coati arrived. They dropped their game outside camp and walked in quietly, and without speaking went to their fires and sat down. Monkey walked up behind her father, put her arms around his neck, and leaned on his shoulders. In a few minutes, Catfish, too, went to Snake and began searching his back and neck for ticks. The rain was slowly but steadily increasing in intensity, and shortly Snake rose and picked up the axe, which was lying in the middle of the camp.

"We had better build a house," he said, heading into the jungle.

Coati stood and went with him, and Jamo Paca and Anteater followed. The rain was falling harder, and the women hurried to shield their fires with palm fronds and help their children move under the protective canopies of nearby trees.

Snake and Coati quickly began cutting and breaking slender saplings and segmenting them into various lengths. Anteater and Jamo Paca carried the first half-dozen poles to the camp, and when a few more had been cut, Coati took them and followed the others. Jamo Paca and Anteater returned to the forest, and Coati began setting up the poles to support the roof. He took a forked pole, raised it high above his head, and thrust it into the soft, sandy soil, embedding the end. Coati then pulled the pole from the hole it had made, raised it, and thrust it in again. He repeated this motion until the forked branch was well seated in the ground. He tamped the soil at the base of the upright forked pole with his foot, wiggled it a bit to be sure it was firmly set, and went to get another. He measured the proper distance and position and set three more forked poles in the earth. When the four uprights were in place in a rectangular layout, Coati laid longer poles across the forks of the uprights to connect them. He then laid shorter pole rafters across the short axis of the rectangle and lashed two that would not lie properly in place with vines.

The rain was coming down hard and steadily in wind-blown waves as Snake returned to the camp with more poles, and he began setting the corners of another house, immediately adjacent to the first. Jamo Paca cut huge quantities of fronds from palm trees felled earlier, and he, Anteater, and the women carried them to camp and put them in a great pile near the edge of their cleared spot. When the cross-pieces were in place on the structure Coati had made, he and the others began piling fronds on top of them.

Soon the platform was covered with a two-foot-thick layer of palm fronds, and they all hurried to help Snake complete the second structure. When the two unwalled, flat-roofed houses had been completed, the people got under them and tended their fires. In a short while, they had roofed over most of their camp, placing the structures so the fires were just inside the drip line near the outside edges of the houses.

As soon as the structures were up and the chilling discomfort of the rain had considerably diminished, the Aché began processing an armadillo and two capuchin monkeys killed by the hunting party. Jamo Paca singed and butchered the monkeys, and Deer prepared the armadillo. Both first cut off the tails and put them on the fire to cook; they would be done and ready to eat, along with the organs, before the rest of the meat had even begun to roast.

The smell of the roasting meat was just beginning to permeate the still air pocketed under the palm-roofed shelters, and the rain was slowing a bit as it often does prior to unleashing a deluge—the way a running jaguar gathers himself before springing—when Turtle, Black-bird, and Ocelot arrived in camp. Dusk was not yet fully upon them, but the darkness initiated by the storm made the hour seem much later. The hunters slipped quietly under the shelters, and no one acknowledged their coming with more than a glance.

They, too, had been successful today but not with the capybara or caiman they had intended to hunt. They brought a large female paca—a rodent smaller than a capybara but still substantial at more than twenty pounds. The usual silence that accompanied the hunters' return was broken when Snake took the axe, went to the uphill side of the shelters, and dug several small ditches to divert the water that was running in growing rivulets through their camp away from the fires and shelters. When he finished, he sat next to Armadillo and ate some monkey tail.

"It's too bad we haven't been able to make any pots yet," mused Armadillo. "We have so much palm fiber that we could squeeze some in water and cook the meat in it. I love meat cooked in palm broth."

"We could put palm hearts in it, too," added Deer. "But we don't have those things, so why talk about them. We won't be able to make pots for days. We need baskets and slings and mats more than we need pots."

"We can make pots anytime," said Frog, "and they're not that important. We have done without them many times when our pots were all broken and we could not get clay. What we really need is axes."

"We will not have axes until we can go to the mountains and get stone," said Grandmother Boa. "Deer is right; first we have to make baskets and slings. Then we can worry about getting axes."

"We will get axes before you women are even ready to make pots," Turtle said, breaking his silence. "We will get axes and machetes and kill the Apa who attacked us. We won't have to run to the mountains and work for days pecking on rocks so we can make dull stone axes. We will go kill the Apa and show them that we are not afraid. We will kill them and take their metal axes." He rose up on his knees and became animated. "Then we will have axes and machetes and can go hunt in the good forest and not have to be afraid of the Apa."

The Aché sat quietly. A light breeze shook the trees above them, and the dense drops that fell from the leaves spattered more heavily than the rain. Then the rain intensified. "We have run too far in the forest to attack the Apa," said Snake, speaking as if to himself. "They are too far away."

"We ran this far to protect our families," Turtle said, facing away from the camp as if he were speaking to the forest. "Women and children can't fight the Apa, and men can't fight if they have women and children with them. The Apa didn't bring women and children with them when they attacked our camp, did they? We won't, either. I will go and take Blackbird, Coati, Ocelot, and Snake with me, and we will show them that Aché men are not afraid. We will show them what happens when they attack Aché camps and steal babies. We will make them fear us because we are strong, we are brave, we are Aché."

The hard-pounding tropical rainstorm beat a steady rhythm on the leaf-roofed shelters and draped curtains of cascading raindrops around them, walling off the rest of the world. Droplets of water splashed up from the ground outside, and occasional random drips that trickled through the frond thatching wet the Aché, but the fires, the closeness of huddled bodies, and the mild spring temperatures kept them comfortable. Catfish nestled with Monkey between Snake and Armadillo and felt protected and warm. He became large with pride when Turtle spoke of killing the Apa and making them fear the brave, strong Aché.

Catfish had spent his day with the other boys in the forest, stalking and killing imaginary Apa. They had made bows from spindly branches strung with slender lianas and shot twig arrows at rotten-log Apa. They surrounded an Apa camp, crept slowly and silently through the understory, and attacked unmercifully, filling the sleeping Apa logs with tiny arrows and shouting "*tu, tu,*" as they let fly their twig projectiles. They plundered stick machetes and axes from the defeated enemy and later told stories of their bravery when they sat in camp eating palm fiber their mothers had pounded. Catfish was proud to be Aché and dreamed contentedly of revenge and the possibility of freedom from fearing the Apa.

"The Apa found us in the good forest, and they know that we got away and ran," said Snake, raising his voice above the drumroll backdrop of the pummeling rain, speaking—as Turtle had—to the forest. The men avoided directly confronting each other because they both knew the conversation could easily escalate. "They have probably been looking for us. Maybe they are looking now; maybe they followed our trail. If we go back to attack them, they will be ready for us. It is too soon."

"Some may think it is too soon," said Turtle. "Some may think never is too soon, but they are wrong. Now is the time. We must go now to the same place and attack the Apa where they attacked us. If we don't, the Apa will know that we are afraid. They will cut down the trees in the good forest and build houses. We must show them that we will fight, that they cannot drive us away so easily. Without the women and children, we can get there in one day, spend the night in the forest, and attack them early in the morning before the sun comes up. Then we can be back here by the next night. The Apa can never catch us in the forest; they are too slow, and they will be afraid to come into the forest because they know that we are not afraid to kill them."

"The Apa may be looking for us right now," said Snake. "They may be looking near the Big River. What if they found our camp while the men were gone, and only Anteater and Jamo were here to protect the band? I want to attack the Apa and kill them, but I don't think it is wise to try it now in the good forest, where they are ready for us. I think we should all go to the mountains and get stone and make axes. I would rather work hard to chop trees than risk losing our families. We will have many more chances to attack the Apa. We can kill them then and take their axes and machetes."

"I agree with Snake," said Anteater, sitting up and joining the conversation with the jungle. "We will have our chance again to kill Apa. They aren't going to go away. But now they are ready for us. They are ready to fight. We can't think they will all lie around sleeping and let us run up and kill them, can we? They will have guards, and their dogs will warn them when we come out of the forest. It is foolish to attack when your enemy is ready for you. You don't attack a jaguar when he is ready for you, or you will be killed. You attack the jaguar when he is trailing a peccary. You attack him when he is thinking about something else, when he doesn't know you're there."

"Some in this band are afraid," Turtle said sharply. "They are afraid because the Apa shot them, and others are afraid, too. They are fearful and want to keep running and let the Apa cut and burn down the forest until we have to hide in the dirty, ugly forest, where we can't hunt and can't chop palms. Then we won't be Aché anymore. The only thing we will be is alive.

"I do not want to be frightened like a deer. I am an Aché, and Aché do not run and hide. Aché stand and fight. If we attack the Apa now, they will know we are not deer; they will know we are men, Aché men. We attack them now while they are thinking how strong they were to kill Aché and steal Aché babies and chase the rest away. We must show them that we are not afraid. We must attack them and make them afraid of Aché, make them fearful to come into the forest.

"The Apa may be ready for us, but we will be the attackers, we will be the hunters. When the jaguar attacks you, you fight back. You can't wait until he forgets about you to fight him, or he will kill you. You fight then, or you are dead. If we don't fight now, we are dead. Those who are afraid to fight the Apa are not Aché, and they may as well be dead because all they will do is run until they die. I am not going to run. Turtle is not afraid. Turtle would rather fight than run and hide. Turtle would rather die than run and hide."

A moment of silence shrouded the camp, and the rain continued unabated while everyone thought about what Turtle had said. Turtle was known for his bravery and his hatred of the Apa, and the Aché admired him for those traits. He was angry now and had spoken cruelly of Snake and Anteater, nearly accusing them of cowardice. Catfish's warm feeling of pride became a flush of burning embarrassment for his father, and he thought that Turtle was right. The Aché should attack the Apa and kill them, not run and hide.

"The Apa is a more dangerous foe than even the jaguar," Snake said in a soft, but confident, voice. "The Apa are like us, but they have axes and machetes and thunder, and they can make animals do what they want, like the ones with strange horns that pull their carts, and the dogs that hunt for them and guard them. They have loud carts that they ride in that need no animals to pull them. If we go fight them the way we would fight other Aché or even the Chiripá, we will lose.

"We must stay away from them—ambush them when we can, fight them when we must—but we must not be foolish. I don't know what we should do about the Apa, but I know that we can't kill them all. We must stay away from them and try to protect our families. We all know what happened to Big Armadillo's band. All but two people were killed or captured. Do we want that to happen to our band? Do we want everyone to die so we can get vengeance?

"Snake is not afraid to fight Apa. Turtle and I have fought side by side and killed Apa. I am not afraid to die—no Aché is—but a dead Aché or one captured by the Apa and kept like one of their animals is no longer an Aché. We must not be foolish in fighting the Apa, or we will not have a chance. I think it would be foolish to go back to the good forest and attack them now. We should wait and attack them when they are not ready for us. I don't mind working hard and using stone axes. We can go to the mountains, get stone, and give Anteater time to heal, so he can be strong again. I would rather use stone axes and have my children live than try foolishly to steal metal axes and have them die."

"If you are men, you will go kill the Apa," croaked Vulture, her nearly toothless mouth a gaping crater in her pale, wizened face. "You must kill everyone in their band, cut their bodies into little pieces, and leave them for the animals to eat. They killed my grandson, Lizard, and made me lose my pets. Stop talking about them and go do what men should. Kill them all so the Aché can live in the forest the way they always have. Shoot them full of arrows. They've bothered us enough. Turtle is right. Go kill them."

"Even Vulture knows what we should do," said Turtle, rising up on one knee and facing Snake.

Everyone watched as Turtle's anger increased. By facing Snake, he was violating decorum, risking the kind of direct confrontation that could be divisive, perhaps fatal, to a band. "The old woman is not afraid," he said angrily, gesturing toward Vulture. "She knows we must kill the Apa. Snake and Anteater are not even as brave as old Vulture."

"Kill the Apa," Vulture said emphatically. "Cover the ground with their blood. Break their heads open, and let's be done with the Apa."

The entire band followed the debate, and the meat cooking on the racks all around them was forgotten. Catfish felt confused and numb. He had always thought of his father as brave and strong, but now people were saying he was afraid. Was Turtle right? Was Snake afraid to fight the Apa? Was he more frightened than a shriveled old woman?

Catfish curled himself into a tight ball and felt as if he were sinking into the ground. He could not believe what he was hearing because, for the first time, his image of his father was tarnished by the worst blemish he could imagine: the accusation of cowardice. Catfish found himself siding with Turtle, a man he feared. He felt detached and surrounded by a cold, dark blanket that was smothering him.

And then Jamo Paca spoke.

"Snake and Anteater are not cowards, and Vulture is not brave," he said sternly. "Vulture thinks we can kill all the Apa and never have to worry about them again. Even my son, Turtle, seems to think he can kill them and drive them away. We can't kill all of the Apa, and killing a few of them doesn't drive them away; it makes more come in their place. My father fought Apa, and so did my grandfather; they were great fighters, but still, every year there are more Apa and less forest for the Aché. Someday there will be no forest for the Aché, and maybe there will even be no Aché, but that day is not here yet. Snake and Anteater are right. If we go fight the Apa when they are ready for us, we will lose."

The old man paused for a moment, glanced at his wife, and continued. "When I was young, I knew a man named Sunfish who had lived with the Apa. He had been captured by them when he was a boy, and he lived at an Apa's house for a long time until he could escape. He said that the man took him to a place where there were as many Apa as trees in the forest, and they lived in houses made of stone that went on and on as far as he could see. The Apa man had many axes and machetes just for himself, and he killed animals with his thunder every day. That man told Sunfish that the Apa would chop down the entire forest someday, grow corn and manioc, and raise their strange-horn animals.

"The Apa have cut down most of the forest I lived in as a boy, and I know I will never go there again. Now they are cutting the good forest, and we cannot stop them. Big Armadillo tried to stop the Apa, and it was foolish: his band is gone. Do we want to do what Big Armadillo did? We still have plenty of forest to live in here between the rivers. We must share it with other bands, and maybe we will have to fight other Aché to live here, but fighting Aché is not like fighting the Apa.

"I don't think we should go to the good forest and fight the Apa. I think we should go to the mountains and make stone axes. Don't let Vulture decide what we should do; Vulture doesn't know about the Apa. She was going to walk up to the Apa and ask them if they had seen her pets. She was more worried about her pets than about Lizard.

"Let's not talk foolishly and fight among ourselves. We have a good band, a strong band, and the Apa could not destroy it. We must remember to be Aché, and Aché do not get angry with each other. We know how angry you are, Turtle; we are all angry, but we must not do things hastily that endanger the entire band. I am hungry now. Let's eat some of this good meat."

6 ≡ BOWS AND HONEY

Jamo's speech effectively terminated any further discussion of returning to the good forest and attacking the Apa. Most of the band members were in agreement, although they had been reluctant to oppose Turtle until Jamo spoke. They ate in silence, and everyone noticed with some uneasiness the intense glare Turtle leveled at Snake, as if he blamed Snake for turning his father against him. The rain continued steady and monotonous until just past midnight, when the clouds broke and the first-quarter moon bathed the cooling jungle in a clear, pale light. The Aché slept nestled like spoons among their smoky, damp-wood fires, and the crisp wet morning was a welcome arrival.

The camp was littered with hundreds of spent palm-fiber quids, spit out and ignored, and the lumpy orange carpet contrasted sharply with the deep greens and browns of the forest. Bones and bark and fragments of fronds dotted the floor of the camp as well, dropped in place and discarded without concern; trash buildup was not generally a problem for the Aché because camps were usually abandoned after one night or sometimes two. If a group remained in one spot for a longer period of time, such as when two or more bands got together for visiting, ceremonies, or cooperative fishing, the camp area was occasionally tidied up; usually, however, that was unnecessary.

Camp was particularly quiet this morning. As the first rays of sunlight brightened the treetops above them without yet touching the sodden jungle floor, and the smoke from the fires drifted aimlessly, unable to rise and not quite certain where else to go, families spoke in muffled tones or not at all and prepared for the day. Snake and Catfish shared a piece of the thick, white meat from the paca's pelvis and chewed slowly and thoughtfully while Armadillo pried the occipital bone from the base of a monkey skull so little Monkey could eat the brains, a delicacy reserved for the very young and very old.

A flutter in the leaves of a sour-orange tree high above them caught Snake's eye, and Catfish followed his gaze and saw a toucan alight on a slender branch. Snake turned slightly toward Catfish and—without taking his eyes off the large-beaked bird—motioned with his head and a slight extension of his lips toward his bow and arrows. Catfish rose and—moving smoothly and steadily—went to his father's weapons and carried the bow and a blunt-tipped bird arrow to Snake.

Snake took the bow and slowly restrung it. He lodged one end against a tree trunk, lay back on the ground, sprung the bow in the middle with an upraised foot, and slipped the loop of the string over the near end. He reached to take the arrow from Catfish, and while maintaining eye contact with the preening toucan, he maneuvered for a clear shot, carefully nocking the arrow and positioning the bow by feel. When he was almost directly below the bird, and only a dozen feet from the shelter, he raised the thick palm-wood bow above his head and slowly drew back the arrow, pulling the one-hundred-pound draw of the powerful bow without a hitch, stopping only when his right hand was past his ear. There he paused, holding the bow drawn; he was taking final aim without quivering when a loud pop sounded without warning, and Snake's bow broke in two, right where he was gripping it between the base of his thumb and palm.

The sound startled his intended prey, which flew off with a rasping cry. Snake flinched as the bow stave of the failed weapon caromed off his head and fell to the ground at his feet. All eyes were on him as he contemplated the arrow and limp string in his right hand for a second. He then turned toward the band and, with an impish smile, expelled the breath he had been holding in a disgusted "teeh."

Jamo chuckled quietly and was joined by Anteater, and then Snake, who laughed loudly as he returned to his fire, dragging his ruined weapon by its string. The entire camp, including Turtle, laughed with him, and the tension of the morning broke nearly as quickly as the pull on the string had snapped Snake's bow.

Snake sat down with his family. He removed the string from his broken bow, wound it around his hand, and tied it in a ball.

"I will have to make a new bow today," he said, looking at the fire.

"You can use my bow," said Anteater. "It's almost new, and I won't need it for a while."

"It is good of you to offer, Anteater, but you need your bow," replied Snake. "You have been using it to lean on when you walk, and you are getting stronger already. You worked hard last night when we made the houses. I think you will be hunting with us again in a few days."

"I don't know," said Anteater. "My back is getting better; it doesn't hurt very much anymore, but I am weak. I was very tired last night after just a little work."

"I think I should make a bow now, before we start moving again," said Snake. "I'll have time to work on it in camp while the women make baskets. I saw some spiny palms yesterday that would be very good for making bows, and they are not too far from here. That bow was getting old anyway."

As the band resumed its normal morning routine of eating, caring for children, and repairing arrows, conversation was minimal, and the silence was easy, not troubled and stifling as it had been earlier. Catfish was not certain he understood what had happened the night before, but his respect for his father, rather than being diminished, had been heightened. He realized now for the first time that the Aché men, strong and cunning as they were, were not invincible. It was a disappointing discovery for the young boy—as most increments of maturing are—but it gave him a greater appreciation for the complex decisions facing the band and the need to plan and consider alternatives.

The image of Apa as numerous as trees in the forest remained in his mind and made his stomach quiver, and the idea of attacking the Apa and killing them all, which had seemed so desirable only the night before, was today a discarded dream. He wondered how Turtle could have even considered it and began to think of him the same way he thought of Vulture—someone who isn't fully aware of what is going on around him.

"If you are going to go chop one of the spiny palms we saw yesterday to make your bow, I will go with you, and when you are finished, I can chop honey from the tree we saw near there," Jamo Paca said to Snake.

Snake drew his breath in agreement and eased himself out from under the shelter. He picked up the axe, spun it in his hands, and hefted it, noticing how worn and dull it was and thinking about how important it was for them to obtain more axes.

"Are you ready?" he asked Jamo. "Let's go."

Snake started from the camp heading north, and Jamo rose to his feet, took a burning brand from the fire, and began walking. Catfish and Otter scampered after Snake up the gentle hillside.

The two men and two boys meandered through the heavy, wet forest the way good hunters usually do: looking and listening, collecting information on the plants and animals, getting to know the crowded jungle in an intimate way. They traversed the forest between their camp and the spiny palms the way a hunting dog crosses a field—stopping here to investigate a burrow, moving one way to follow a scent or a sound, turning to continue in the right direction, stopping again and looking around and back, and searching some more.

The scarred and graceful men made their way unhurriedly through the boldly three-dimensional forest, where there was as much to see above them as any other direction; they were citizens of the jungle. The slight and tender boys who followed learned from them and with them, a learning that never stops, for the fantastic living diversity that is the jungle looms lush and bewildering and dangerous to one who does not know it. Life is everywhere: life upon life, within life, rushing, racing, random and layered and fingered and twined; everywhere an exploding palimpsest of the competition that is life.

The Aché had not the shell of the armadillo, nor the claws of the jaguar, nor the spines of the *kwanto*, nor the poison of the fer-de-lance to protect them. They had not the specialized jaws of the leafcutter ant, nor the tusks of the peccary, nor the talons of the harpy, nor the roots of the palm to help feed them. Natural selection had not shaped them for life in the jungle, for their bodies differed only slightly from those of their ancestors, who had braved the tundra of Siberia and Alaska during the last ice age and come to America.

Their life in the jungle was something they created, a niche opened not by a special design but by diverse knowledge and the ability to devise innovative solutions to the never-ending and always-changing problems of survival and reproduction. They knew the jungle not through inheritance or instinct and only minimally through instruction. The way they knew it was through experience, gained by spending every day among its thousands of species and having a purpose each day, one that rewards knowledge and punishes ignorance. They were not visitors in this forest, for information to visitors is inconsequential. They were residents, members of the community whose survival depended each day on their ability to obtain food and shelter, defend themselves, and avoid making foolish and costly mistakes.

Many Aché did not survive, and there was so little margin of error between life and death that when a member of the band became an impediment to the survival of others, he or she was abandoned, or even killed. An old man, who one day was capable and independent, might the next day be weakened by illness, and the group would leave him behind. A child born with imperfections likely to burden its parents and the band was killed.

It was not easy for the Aché to do these things, and they were not without compassion, but they had little choice. To increase the workload or impede the movement of a band weakened it, and the members of a weak band were vulnerable. A band that did not cleanse itself put its members in jeopardy, and in the thick green forest that was their home, the Aché knew this. They lived in the jungle, and their way of life was suited to it, the result of many trials and errors, a system of solutions to the problems of life there. The way of life that was the Aché was the jungle.

When they reached the place where they had seen the spiny palms the day before, Snake combed the area, searching out the widely scattered trees and carefully inspecting each one. In a short while, he found a suitable palm—slender and straight with no scars or irregularities that would affect the grain of the dense, hard wood.

While Catfish and Otter played nearby, and Jamo remained in the forest, Snake stepped on the springy branches of a young maté tree, bending them out of his way, and attacked the palm with his axe. Clean and powerful strokes, patient and measured, cut into the wood. Snake pivoted at the waist as he whipped the axe head, his body jerking with the abrupt stop at the end of each swing. He cut a wider notch than he would have needed had he been using a sharper axe or a metal one, but still, in less than ten minutes, the tree came down.

Almost before the falling tree had stopped moving, Snake began chopping again about ten feet higher than the notch that had felled it. When he had cut through the gray-barked trunk, he rolled the ten-foot section from the bushes where it lay onto a small patch of clear ground. He then cut a sapling and made two long-handled wedges, which he used to pry apart the two halves of the palm tree as he split it down the center with the axe. After examining the two halves, he selected one, split it in two, and chose the better of those two pieces. With the axe, he trimmed it to about eight feet, shaved away the softer inner wood and the spiny gray bark, and planed off splinters and rough places. He would carry it to camp, where he would smooth and shape it and rub it with beeswax, and by tomorrow, he would have a new bow.

Snake looked over at Catfish and Otter who were a short distance away, quietly stalking a small lizard they had spotted on the trunk of a thick cedar tree. He watched them for a moment and thought about how much they enjoyed hunting, and how good they were at it for boys their age. He then returned to the split palm pieces and took the one that was the same size as the piece for his bow, split it in two, and trimmed the pieces to about six feet. When he was finished, he turned once again to the boys; they were looking up at the lizard, which had dashed up the tree and out of their reach.

"Come here, boys," Snake called to them. "I am finished. Let's go get Jamo Paca and chop honey."

Catfish and Otter abandoned their tiny quarry and went quickly to Snake, who was lifting the split sections of palm to his shoulder.

"Let me carry them," said Catfish.

"No, let me," cried Otter. "I will carry them."

"Here, Catfish," said Snake. "You carry the big piece, and Otter can carry the two smaller ones."

"What are the smaller ones for?" asked Catfish.

"There are two hunters in the band besides me who need bows," replied Snake. "I thought I would cut the wood for them while I was making a bow for myself."

"But the other men have bows, and these are so small that . . ." said Catfish, and then he understood. He and Otter broke into wide-eyed, excited smiles, and for the rest of the day, the proud, happy boys walked with exaggeratedly bold strides, held their heads high, and grinned each time they looked at each other.

Snake handed the rough lengths of palm wood to the boys, picked up the axe, and started walking in the direction of the honey tree. Catfish and Otter followed him, dreaming of hunting with their new bows, shooting birds and squirrels and bringing them to camp, and receiving everyone's respect. They dreamed also of shooting deer and peccaries—game much too large and difficult for small boys to hunt. But daydreams are daydreams, and the boys were happily full of them.

Jamo Paca arrived at the honey tree a few minutes before the others because he had gone there when he heard the axe work stop. He cleared some brush and vines away from the entrance to the hive, which was in the hollow core of a red tree, only a few feet above the ground. With the smoldering brand he had carried from the camp, he lit a small fire. He would use smoking sticks from the fire to calm the bees while he destroyed their home and took the honey. He sat down next to the fire and leaned against the tree, enjoying for a few moments the relief from mosquitoes and gnats created by the smoke. The insects were not extremely bothersome on this cool morning after a rain, but as always in the jungle, they were an incessant irritation to anyone who was not moving.

Jamo Paca rose when Snake and the boys arrived, and he noticed the two smaller staves that would become bows for Catfish and Otter.

"I see that you have cut wood for three bows," Jamo Paca said to

Snake. Turning to the boys, he said, "The young penises are going to be great hunters. I hope you don't kill all the game so an old man like me will still have a chance."

The boys grinned, and the two men chuckled. Young boys without pubic hair were called penises, and they were often teased about their hunting prowess or their exploits with women, which they didn't mind. They relished any interaction with the grown men, and to be teased about their participation in adult activities reinforced their status as men-to-be.

Jamo took a burning stick from the fire and held it near the entrance to the hive. He blew with puffed cheeks on the stick and directed the smoke into the hole as the confused bees came and went. After a scant minute, he tossed the sticks toward the fire and reached for the axe.

"Now we won't have to risk the safety of the whole band when we want to steal axes from the Apa," Jamo Paca said to Snake. "We can send the mighty penises for them. The rest of us can wait here in the forest and eat honey until they return."

The boys exchanged sheepish smiles, and as Jamo began cutting a foot-square opening in the tree around the doorway to the bees' chamber, Snake peeled a platter-sized section of bark from a nearby dead tree to carry the honey, and Catfish and Otter went to get leaves to place between the honey and the bark.

The bees swarmed noisily about, angry but sufficiently drugged by the wispy smoke from the tiny blaze that they evidenced no hostility. Hundreds of worker bees cloaked Jamo's body, yet only a few stung him. He blew more smoke through the enlarged opening and then reached in; locating the finely constructed sections of comb with his hand, he tore them loose and dropped them on a layer of ferns Catfish and Otter had placed on the ground.

Some of the sections were heavy with honey, others were light and empty, and some contained only the cream-colored bee larvae. Snake compressed the dry, empty comb sections between his hands, flattening the hollow cells and forming the wax into a ball that he could take to camp and use to finish and waterproof the bows and seal the water-carrying baskets the women would make. Catfish and Otter squatted at Jamo's feet, picked up the pieces of comb as he dropped them, and placed the honey-laden ones on the bark tray. The boys busily took big bites from the larvae-bearing comb and chewed and sucked until the pale, bland larvae were consumed, when they spit out a masticated wad of beeswax. They all ate larvae, and they also ate some honey, but Snake warned that eating too much honey would produce a stomachache, so they saved most of the honey-filled combs to carry back to camp.

When no more honey could be reached in the hive, Jamo Paca joined the others and ate some larvae and honey. They licked clean the leaves he had dropped the comb sections on. They then broke pieces from a nearby dry rotten log, crushed them, and rubbed the powdered wood on their hands, chests, and faces to remove the stickiness. The dry powder clung to the honey, balled up, and rubbed off, leaving their skin clean and dry. When they were clean, they picked up their things and headed toward camp, for their jobs were finished, and they knew the axe was needed there.

On their way back, Snake and the boys looked for snail shells, which they needed to plane and smooth the palm wood for their bows. The delicately spiraled white and pink shells that were sometimes streaked with deep crimson were larger than Catfish's fist and were found almost anywhere in the jungle. Their occupants had died or been eaten by one of the numerous birds or predators of the forest. There were plenty to choose from in the brown leafy litter, although shells that were faded and weakened by weathering were not strong enough to take the stress of heavy use. Despite selecting carefully, Snake, Otter, and Catfish each had two shells by the time they reached home.

The sounds of camp floated out into the broadleaf evergreen forest, indicating its presence long before it could be seen. The cries of attention-seeking babies, the laughter of children at play, and the women's garrulous conversations were the familiar and welcome human sounds of home. Aché camps were rarely quiet, and the men often used the noise to guide them, especially if the camp was a new one, or they were returning at dusk, and the trails were difficult to follow.

Monkey was the first to notice the returning party and ran to greet her father. Snake reached down, took her tiny hand in his, and with one motion hoisted her to his shoulders. Monkey squealed with delight as she rode high above the others across the camp and around the palm-roofed shelters to her mother's fire. Armadillo looked up from the almost-completed carrying basket she was working on and smiled to greet her husband.

"It is good that you are back," she said. "We are nearly out of fronds for making baskets. We have been using some that are on the roofs of the houses, but they are bent and broken and not that good."

"Here is the axe," Snake said, dropping it next to the fire. He stooped and lifted Monkey over his head to the ground. "We got a lot of honey, and it is very sweet."

"Good," said Frog, who was sitting nearby. "I am hungry for honey. Duck, go fill the water containers so we can make honey water to drink."

Frog's daughter, Duck, put aside the fan she was twilling from a single palm frond and quickly collected the bamboo-section water containers. Her cousin, Porcupine, joined her, and the two girls hurried off toward the stream. They were as anxious as anyone to drink the cool, sweetened water that was a favorite of all Aché. They knew that eating honey in large amounts could make them ill, but when it was mixed with water, they could consume large quantities—sometimes the band drank several gallons of honey mixed in twice that amount of water in a single afternoon. Honey water was a kind of elixir for the Aché, and when they drank it, they felt light and happy and giddy.

Catfish and Otter leaned the palm-wood staves against the thick green roof of the shelter and sat down between their parents' fires. They were anxious to start working on their bows, and they began preparing the snail shells for planing by tapping them against the stone head of the axe to make a small hole in the side of each shell that would be the cutting edge, angled to smooth the soft, but resilient, wood.

"The penises can't wait to finish their bows," joked Snake. "If they work hard, maybe they can finish them today and go out and bring home some peccaries for us to eat."

The image of the slender little boys hunting peccaries prompted loud laughter in the camp, and the boys looked at each other and smiled.

"I don't think we'll hunt peccaries today," said Catfish in a loud, but boyishly high-pitched, voice. "We will hunt tapir today and peccaries tomorrow."

If the idea of Catfish and Otter hunting peccaries was funny, the thought of them hunting the four-hundred-pound tapir was hilarious, and the camp roared. Even little Monkey, who could hardly understand the jokes, laughed uncontrollably.

"I will go cut palm fronds so we can finish making baskets to carry all the meat our little penises are going to bring us," said Deer, standing and tossing aside the mashed milk-creeper stems she had been using to massage Anteater's wounds. She picked up the axe from between Catfish and Otter and left camp; in a few minutes, the measured sounds from the forest indicated that she had found a tree.

Snake prepared a snail shell and started trimming and shaping the largest piece of the spiny palm wood. His sure, smooth strokes produced a rapidly growing pile of shavings, and his bow began to take shape. He worked the wood into a two-inch-diameter, oval cross section and trimmed it to about seven and one-half feet with sharply tapered points at each end. He worked on the bow for the rest of the day, and when it was smooth and well shaped, he heated the beeswax, mixed it with charcoal, and rubbed it into the wood. Then he heated the bow to absorb the wax and give it the proper amount of curve.

Anteater helped the boys with their bows, the women made baskets and twine, and everyone drank honey water, and there was still plenty left when the hunters arrived with a deer and two coatis. The hunters had also captured three baby coatis for pets, and the widow Vulture was glad to have one of the inquisitive, raccoonlike animals to replace the ones she had lost in the Apa attack. She tied a string around its neck, tethered it to a sapling near her fire, and gave it small pieces of palm heart to eat.

7 ☰ A PROPOSITION

The band stayed in the same camp for two more nights and moved when the gnats that always multiplied in small camps in the forest became too numerous. In the following days, they changed camp as they usually did, moving every day or two, but they did not go far because they wanted to remain near the Big River. The hunting was good there, and the men went out daily and brought back capybara, monkey, armadillo, paca, deer, coati, and caiman to eat. They also gathered large quantities of honey—sweet honey, sour honey, and wasp honey. The women worked hard making baskets and mats and fans and slings for carrying babies, and the axe got little rest. The Apa were mostly forgotten.

Anteater's back was healing, and he resumed hunting, although the two wounds in his lower back did not close and continued to ooze clear fluid. He made arrows for Catfish and Otter, and the boys spent many hours each day hunting in the nearby forest. They were proud to bring small fish and birds they had killed to camp. One day they killed a large poisonous bothrops snake—the one Catfish's father was named for—and everyone in camp commented that the snake was fat and the meat was good.

Each day brought the band closer to a resumption of its normal routines, habits that the attack had disrupted. Replenishing their equipment was the most pressing task, and it progressed rapidly. Every woman now had a carrying basket—her most important tool—and the women also made palm-leaf mats to place around the fires and eat and sleep on. They also finished one-piece woven twine slings for carrying infants; these were like wide belts worn across the back and over one shoulder so the baby was cradled hammock-like at the mother's breast. When these items were completed, the women worked on baskets for carrying water, woven of cane strips and water-proofed on the outside with a layer of heated and charcoal-hardened beeswax. The last major implement was cooking pots, and the clay for them came from the banks of the Big River.

Armadillo was the first to be ready for pottery making, and she and Monkey left camp on a humid and overcast, but nonthreatening, afternoon to get clay from the riverbank. Armadillo lifted her new, still-green basket to her back and adjusted the tumpline across her forehead. Monkey stood and waited to follow her mother into the forest, and Armadillo smiled at her. With Monkey right behind her, she ducked under the large folded leaves of a philodendron that draped over a low branch on the edge of camp and disappeared into the jungle. Armadillo walked more slowly than usual to allow the youngster to keep up, and Monkey followed boldly and without tears. Even though the obstacles were large and difficult for the tiny four-year-old, she was not daunted.

"You are doing well, Monkey," Armadillo complimented her. "You walk in the forest like a grown woman."

Monkey quickened her pace and walked as though attacking the forest, pushing aside branches that would have, until recently, intimidated her and made her cry. She slipped through gaps in the vegetation and crawled under branches and fallen trees. She ignored the scrapes and scratches that always resulted, and she felt good. She was learning to be Aché.

When they reached the river, Armadillo began searching for good-quality clay. The gray alluvial sediments that lined the river course differed from the red sandy soil found nearly everywhere else in the region, and only certain places offered the fine smooth clay needed for pottery. Armadillo tested the clay in cut banks along the river and places where side streams entered the main channel. At each spot, she scooped out some of the moist, sticky mud with her hands and rubbed a small amount between her fingers. If the grain was too coarse, or if there were lumps or pieces of gravel in the clay, she rejected it and moved on. Monkey followed her mother, and Armadillo told her what they were looking for and showed her how to test the clay. They worked their way upstream along the river, and after an hour, Armadillo found a clay source that satisfied her.

She gathered leaves along the bank and lined her basket, then returned to the spot where she had found the clay. She first removed the sandy sediments that overlaid the clay to avoid contaminating it as she scooped it out. Then she dug into the clay layer and took a big double handful at a time. She patted the heavy gray gumbo with her hands to compact it, then placed the balls in her basket. She had to stop once and dig farther into the sandy bank to expose more of the clay before resuming. The sun was shining through a thin place in the afternoon clouds, and when she had enough, she pressed the balls of clay in her basket together to consolidate them and covered them with leaves.

When she was finished, Armadillo rose from her knees. Clay clung to her arms and legs and breasts; she even had some on her face and in her hair. Monkey, who had been playing in the mud, was covered. As the clay dried, it turned from dark to light gray and began to crack.

"Look at you, Monkey," Armadillo said. "You look like an Apa girl with your white skin. I am covered, too. Let's wash this clay off, and then we'll go back to camp."

They walked to the edge of the river, squatted in the knee-deep water of a small back eddy, splashed themselves and each other, and rubbed their bodies to remove the mud. Monkey giggled, took handfuls of sand from the river bottom, and rubbed it on her chest and in her hair. Armadillo splashed water on Monkey's head, and they both laughed.

"We had better go now," Armadillo said. "We have a long walk back to camp."

She stood up and ran her hands over her short-cropped hair, wringing the water out of it and down her back. Then she turned and started walking toward the bank.

"Let's go, Monkey," she called back to her daughter, who was still splashing in the shallow water.

Armadillo walked toward her basket and bent over and made sure the clay was secure and covered with leaves; next she took the carrying strap in her right hand and prepared to hoist it to her back. Then she saw Turtle.

He was standing on the upper bank, just at the edge of the rising vegetation. He was watching them, and when Armadillo saw him, he smiled and started walking toward her. Armadillo looked up and down the riverbank to see if anyone was with him, but there was no one. He walked down the bank, leaned his bow and arrows against it, and came across the narrow sandy strip of beach.

"I see you have been getting clay for pots," Turtle said. "We need pots. I am hungry for palm heart cooked in meat broth. We haven't had any since before the Apa attacked us."

"We have plenty of clay," Armadillo said. "It is good clay and should make strong pots."

Turtle walked to the water and bent over and drank from his hands. He splashed water on his face and chest and took another drink.

"I was digging an armadillo in the forest, and when I was finished, I heard voices, so I came here and found you. I am glad it is you, Armadillo. I like you. You are sweet. You have a sweet body."

Turtle walked over to Armadillo, stood very close to her, and looked in her eyes. She returned his gaze, then averted her eyes and looked at his shoulder.

"We could have fun together," he said. He touched her shoulder and ran his fingers along her upper arm, onto her back, and down her side.

"Let's go lie down," Turtle said, smiling. "Let's go lie down in the forest while your daughter plays."

Armadillo looked over her shoulder at Monkey, who was still playing in the water, and turned to look again at Turtle. His fingers were still touching her side, and he moved them down, brushing lightly along her hip and then back along her buttock, and he smiled again.

Armadillo looked into his eyes for a long second and began to smile. Then she turned and called to Monkey.

"Come here, Monkey; let's go. Turtle will walk with us back to camp."

Armadillo walked over to Monkey, picked her up, and carried

her out of the river. She went to the carrying basket, lifted it, and swung it onto her back. She called again to Monkey and began walking, and by the time they were in the cool shade of the forest, Turtle had disappeared.

Monkey followed her mother without complaining on the long walk back to camp. There were no trails and few landmarks, but life in the jungle had fine-tuned Armadillo's sense of direction. Despite taking a circuitous route necessitated by the terrain and vegetation, she had no difficulty locating their temporary home. They stopped once to eat fruit and rest and arrived in camp just as the orange glow in the west signaled sunset. Snake was already there, sitting by the fire talking with Anteater.

When he saw his mother, Catfish quickly picked up a bird that was lying dead at his feet.

"Look what I killed today—an *urraca* bird," he said, stretching the black and white bird out by its wing tips. "I hit it with a blunt arrow, and Otter got a green lizard."

"You boys are bringing game nearly every day," said Armadillo as she slipped the strap from her head and lowered her basket to the ground. "We'll not starve with you hunting for us."

Monkey went to Snake, crawled between his legs, and nestled against his chest.

"Monkey walked all day without crying," Armadillo said. "She is no longer a baby."

Meat was already roasting, and the camp was quiet except for some discussion of whether or not to build shelters. Rain did not seem likely because the clouds had broken, and the matter was settled quickly, although Parrot reminded everyone—as she always did when the topic came up—of the time the entire band had spent the night huddled under a coati-leg tree during a pouring rain because no one had thought they needed a shelter. They all remembered that night, but the reminder did little to convince anyone that rain was likely tonight, and the topic was dropped.

Turtle entered camp shortly after Armadillo and Monkey and seemed particularly stern. The children, who had been less boisterous than usual on this muggy evening, went to their parents' fires and sat quietly. Armadillo nursed Monkey for a few minutes, and the exhausted child fell asleep in her mother's lap.

As the evening darkness fell between the setting of the sun and the rising of the moon, the Aché ate, and the men talked about hunting. Late in the afternoon, Coati and Blackbird had seen the tracks of a large herd of white-lipped peccaries. The men were excited because peccaries were their favorite game. The meat was fat and juicy, and when the hunters found a herd, they could often kill three or four of the eighty-pound animals. Had it not been late in the day when they found the trail, Coati and Blackbird would have called the other men, and they would have run after the herd. Peccary herds move slowly through the jungle, and Aché hunters can outdistance them, although it may take hours of running to catch a herd. Peccaries make noise in the forest rooting and eating, and the men move stealthily when they near the herd and try to surround it. When the shooting begins, the peccary herd erupts chaotically, and each hunter may get several shots before the pigs disappear into the jungle.

The men talked enthusiastically into the night about the upcoming hunt, and Catfish lay on his back looking up at the sky through a break in the trees, thinking about hunting peccaries. He dreamed of running with the men and the excitement when the herd was surrounded and the pigs screamed and charged madly through the brush.

Catfish was looking up and listening and dreaming when he saw a bright light overhead—much brighter than a star but not as bright as the moon—and it was moving.

"Look, what is that in the sky?" he exclaimed, sitting up and pointing.

Conversation ceased, everyone in the band looked up, and some of them gasped.

"It is Berendy," said Snake. "Berendy is here, and he is going home."

Catfish had heard of Berendy but had never seen him, and his stomach and back tingled. The light moved across the sky—bright and slow—and it was hidden for a moment by leaves; then they could see it again for a few seconds, and it was gone.

"Listen," said Snake. "Listen. Now Berendy is going to crack, like a green stick cracks in the fire, like thunder. Berendy is going to crack."

Everyone was silent, very silent, and it seemed to Catfish that the entire jungle was still. And then he heard the crack: it was like thunder but not as loud. His heart raced, and he moved closer to his father. The camp was quiet for a few minutes, and no one moved.

"I saw Berendy once," Jamo Paca said, "and it wasn't far from here. I was hunting capybara along the Big River, and I was walking through thick cane when I heard something. I thought it was a capybara, and I went toward the sound. I was at the edge of the water, and the sound was in front of me, and I walked toward it, but I didn't see anything. Then I heard a sound behind me, and I turned and looked, and it was Berendy. He was like a man but bigger and covered with dark hair. He stood up and was very big, and he made a noise like a scream.

"I turned and ran. I ran fast away from the river through the big bamboo, and I got cuts on my arms and face and legs from the thorns. I ran through the canes and brush, and I came to the river again because there was a bend, and I stopped. I didn't hear anything, and I waited. I listened, and I thought Berendy was gone, and then I heard him scream. He was right in front of me near the river, and he was big and covered with hair.

"I pulled up an arrow and shot him in the chest, and he ran backward toward the river, and I heard a splash. When I went to look, I saw nothing in the river, and I never found the arrow, but I didn't kill him because he still comes. He still comes, and we all saw him and heard him tonight."

Catfish edged closer to his father and leaned against Snake's legs. He looked at the sky, and as the conversation died down and the Aché curled up by their fires to sleep, he thought about Berendy. He wondered how Berendy could be a light in the sky and big and covered with hair and chase people in the forest at the same time. The forest seemed dark and strange and unknown, and in his dreams, peccaries became Berendy, and Catfish the hunter was once again just a little boy.

When morning came, the men went quickly to work sharpening and straightening their arrows. They talked about hunting peccaries and were anxious to get going. They speculated that the herd would not be far because the trail was fresh when Coati and Blackbird had found it, and pigs do not usually move at night. That was good because the women could not trail behind the hunters today as they usually did. The women had clay and needed to make pots. If the men could find the peccaries early, they would not have to carry the animals a long way back to camp. Anteater sharpened his arrows, but he would not hunt today with the other men. He was not strong enough for a peccary hunt, so he would go out alone, hunting smaller game.

Deer sectioned the leftover armadillo meat with a cane knife and tossed one piece to each fire. The old widow, Vulture, took the piece of meat Deer threw her—a large portion of the back with the singed, brown armadillo plates still attached. The back was the best meat on the armadillo, and Coati and his father, Ocelot, looked across the fire at the meat in Vulture's hands and waited for her to share it with them. Instead of offering the meat, Vulture turned away from the men toward her pet coati, which was tethered by a short string to a slender tree, and placed the entire piece in front of the animal.

"Here is meat for you," she said. "I have the best piece of meat for you. It is good and fat. Eat all you want, and I will get you more."

Ocelot quickly leaned across the fire, reached in front of Vulture and her pet, and took the piece of meat.

"I am hungry, and my son is hungry," he said. "You must be hungry, too. The meat is for us to eat. Give your pet some berries or palm heart, but don't give it meat. We hunt to feed people, not pets."

Vulture wailed and reached toward the meat Ocelot was holding. "*Aiiieee*," she cried, letting most of the whining sound come out of her nose. She cried like a child whose parent had just taken something from her. Ocelot held the meat for a moment and looked at Vulture. Then he took it in his teeth and, using both hands, tore a large ragged piece from it and handed it to Vulture.

"Take this, old woman, and don't cry. You will always get meat when we have it. We won't let you starve. Here eat this meat, and you can find something else to give your pet."

Vulture snatched the meat from Ocelot and held it with both hands against her chest. She was leaning forward with her head down, and when she looked at him, he could hardly see her eyes peeking out from under her eyebrows. She looked around at the other fires, moving her head quickly and shaking it, and then she turned back toward her pet.

"Here is your meat, my little Lizard. Eat it, my grandson, and grow strong. Eat this good meat so you can be strong when you hunt peccaries today. Be strong, grandson, and bring meat for old Grandma Vulture to eat so she doesn't have to beg for meat from these stingy people."

She spoke loudly, and everyone listened. She was talking to her pet as if it were her grandson, Lizard, who had been killed by the Apa. She got water for the coati and let it drink from her cupped hand, and she talked to it about hunting peccaries; she seemed unaware of anyone else.

"Look, Lizard," she said. "There is a cloud. It is just a little cloud, but if rain comes, I don't want you to get wet. I will build you a shelter. You were born under a shelter, and I will build one for you now." She began reaching for twigs and branches and tearing leaves from bushes. "My daughter was a strong, generous woman, not like these weak, stingy women, and when she had you it was raining, and it was dark, and we were under a shelter. I was there, and you were a beautiful baby; we knew your name was Lizard, and we hoped you would be a boy. We were so happy under that shelter, and now we will be happy under this shelter. I am building a strong shelter so my grandson doesn't get wet. He will bring me peccary to eat so I don't have to beg for meat from these stingy people."

Ocelot and Coati looked at the ground as they ate their meat, and Ocelot moved his arrows from next to Vulture and leaned them against a tree by Turtle's fire. The other people looked at Vulture and each other and her pet, and were quiet. Vulture continued talking to her pet while she built a tiny shelter over the young coati. She knelt by the tree where her pet was tied, thrust sticks into the ground, and tied crosspieces to them with strips of green bark; then she covered the shelter with leafy branches. All the time she talked to the animal as if it were Lizard.

For a few moments, the entire camp was Vulture's audience. They watched her and exchanged glances and did not move. Vulture finished the shelter, took a burning stick from her fire and put it on the ground at the near end of the miniature house, and added a handful of sticks to it.

"Now we have a fire, Lizard," she said. "Now there is a fire, and you can warm this cold meat by it."

She took the largely uneaten piece of armadillo meat from in front of the confused coati and placed it by the smoking sticks.

"Don't be afraid; I will not burn you," she said. "This is our fire and our meat and our house, and I will take care of everything. When you go hunting and bring us peccaries to eat, we can cook on our fire and sleep under our shelter. We will be warm and dry, and we won't be hungry."

Vulture was oblivious to the rest of the people in the camp, and they looked at each other with confused faces. Soon there were whispers, and then they spoke as if Vulture were not there.

"She thinks the coati is Lizard," Parrot said. "She isn't going to eat the meat; she is giving it to her pet."

The coati backed away from the smoking sticks and voiced his fear with shrill, whistlelike cries. The two other pet coatis—one at Blackbird's fire and one at Anteater's—heard the cries and were afraid. They moved worriedly about on their tethers and also shrieked.

"Vulture is going to die," said Frog. "She is sick. She doesn't know that Lizard is dead. She doesn't remember that the Apa killed her grandson. Who is going to tell her? She has no close relatives in this band."

"I will tell her," Anteater said. "I will tell her that the coati is not her grandson."

Anteater rolled from his sitting position to his hands and knees and started to rise.

"Wait," said Grandmother Boa. "Wait, Anteater. We can't hear her pet talking. All we can hear is Vulture talking. She is talking to a coati, and she sees Lizard. We can't see Lizard, but Vulture does. Could Lizard be coming for Vulture? Is his spirit lonely? His relatives are all far away, and Vulture is the closest. Is Lizard's spirit speaking, speaking only to Vulture? Is the spirit coming to take Vulture because he is lonely?"

The camp was silent except for the screaming of the coatis. Vulture's pet was frantic, and it backed as far away from her and the tiny fire as it could get. It moved its head back and forth and tried to escape its restraint.

Anteater stopped and did not go to Vulture. He looked at Grandmother Boa and did not move. Catfish looked at his parents, and he looked at Otter, and Otter looked at him, and they were afraid. The coatis were making a lot of noise, the way they did when there was a jaguar near the camp, but there was no jaguar. Otter reached toward the coati tied near his fire to quiet it and then drew back his hand quickly, as if he thought there was something wrong with it. Vulture's pet was terrified of the fire; smoke from the fire was going in its face, and it pulled against its cord and was choking. Babies started to cry.

"Don't be afraid, Lizard," Vulture said. "I will not hurt you. Do you want to leave this band? I want to leave this band. Let's go live with my mother. Her band is near here, just by the Big River. We will leave these stingy people and go live with good Aché."

Vulture untied the string that tethered the coati to the tree and dragged the frightened animal toward her. She stood, lifted the coati by the string around its neck, and took it in her arms.

"Lizard and I are going to join the band of my mother," she said.

"We don't like it here, and we are leaving." She leaned over, picked up a burning stick from her fire, and prepared to walk into the forest.

Turtle stood and quickly went to Vulture. He reached out, grabbed the baby coati by the skin on the back of its neck, and took it from her. He held the string in his right hand and the coati in his left and turned toward the camp. Vulture tried to take her pet from him, but he kept her away with his elbows.

"Lizard's spirit has come to our camp to take Vulture with him, and she wants to go," Turtle said. "She wants to join her mother's band. Vulture's mother was dead before I was born. Vulture's mother is using Lizard's spirit to come for her. The spirit is speaking to Vulture. I do not want spirits in this camp, and I will send them away."

"Give me Lizard," cried Vulture. "Give me my grandson." The small old woman pawed at Turtle and grabbed his arms, but he kept turning slightly to keep her away from the coati.

"I will send Lizard's spirit away, and then we must leave this place so he cannot find us," he said.

Turtle turned his back to the obsessed old widow and threw the baby coati to the ground. Then he lifted his right foot and brought it down hard on the small black and white animal, crushing and killing it instantly.

Vulture ran around his legs and pushed on his foot. "Get off my grandson," she cried. "Get your ugly foot off my grandson."

Turtle bent over and pushed Vulture's hands away from his foot. He stepped aside and picked up the dead coati.

"This is not your grandson," he said. "This is not Lizard. This is a coati, and we are going to cook it and eat it, and then we are going to leave this place and go to a new camp."

Vulture looked at him and was very quiet. Her eyes stared straight ahead as if she didn't see him, and she turned and slowly went back to her fire and sat down. No one spoke, and Turtle went to his fire and dropped the coati in the coals. When it was singed and cooked, Turtle's wife, Parrot, broke the tiny animal in two and handed half of it to Blackbird. Quietly they ate the coati, which amounted to only a few mouthfuls, and the rest of the band resumed eating armadillo meat and prepared to leave. Vulture did not eat; she just sat and stared at her fire. Ocelot reached over and took the meat she had given her pet earlier, warmed it, and ate it.

9 ≡ MONKEY

The band moved through the forest in single file. Vulture was quiet and had not spoken since Turtle had killed her pet, but she packed her carrying basket and walked with the others. Everyone was certain that a spirit had been speaking to her and Turtle had sent the spirit away by killing the coati. They all wanted to leave the camp and get away from the spirit, and they were glad that the spirit had not lured Vulture into the forest. An old woman alone in the forest would surely die, and since the Aché would not know where or when she died, they would be in danger from her spirit as well. Spirits were lonely and dangerous because they could enter animals—not only tiny pets but other animals—and they wanted the living to join them. Most often they entered jaguars, and a jaguar spirit was the most feared animal in the forest.

Armadillo's basket was very heavy—still filled with the moist clay—and she was glad she did not have to carry Monkey. Monkey followed her mother without hesitation when they left camp, and shortly Snake picked her up and put her on his shoulders. They walked toward the peccary trail; they would follow it, and when they thought they had gone far enough to elude the spirits, the women would stop and make camp, and the men would try to catch the herd.

They walked for most of the morning, going north at first until they encountered the peccary trail; then they turned and followed it east. The trail was straight and easy to follow. Bushes had been flattened, and the earth was rooted up and disturbed. The hunters were impressed by the size and apparent proximity of the herd, and they became animated, talking excitedly about the hunt, pointing out signs to each other, and quickening the pace.

The forest was thick with vines and large trees—red trees, coati-leg trees, lapachos, and palms. The Aché had come here many times and knew this jungle well. The trail skirted the edge of a small swamp that smelled of decay and then moved out of an area that was thick with vines and into forest with heavy bamboo and *kwanto* undergrowth.

The Aché called this kind of growth ugly forest, and they did not like hunting in it because it was difficult to move through. Most of the bamboo was only finger thick, but it was very dense, and the leaves were sharp and made tiny slices in the skin like paper cuts. The kwanto grew in thick stands, and the swordlike leaves of each plant grew out from the center like the leaves of a pineapple and were edged with hundreds of needle-sharp spines. The Aché did not like the ugly forest, but much of the forest that was their home was ugly, and they accepted it. There was no choice. Besides, they would have followed a peccary herd anywhere.

They walked until the sun was high, and they stopped near the confluence of two tiny, milky trickles of streams that flowed though steep-sided, shallow gullies. They made their camp near a huge cedar tree that had fallen and taken several others with it. The fallen trees made an opening in the forest, and their camp was light and pleasant. By the time the women had lifted their carrying baskets from their backs and set them on the ground, the men had slipped into the jungle to pursue the peccaries.

Anteater stayed with the women, and he broke and pulled away the brush to clear the camp while they gathered wood. They laid mats on the ground and built their fires in a circle out of big dry logs fed in a little at a time from the outside; shortly their home was complete. The children played on the fallen cedar tree, walking along its huge trunk and climbing on its limbs. Monkey played with the other children, and Armadillo looked at her often because her ventures out of the camp were new. Armadillo smiled when she looked at Monkey, and she was glad to see that Catfish was staying and watching her.

The women made large fires that helped keep down the attacking mosquitos, which were usually worse in the ugly forest and were especially thick today. When the fires had burned for a while, the women raked some coals from them and doused them with water. They crushed the pieces of charcoal and reserved the black powder. They then each took some of the clay on their mats, kneaded it, and added the crushed charcoal for tempering. They added water and charcoal a little at a time and worked the clay until it reached the desired consistency.

Aché pots are simple, thick-walled vessels with no decoration, and the women formed them from lumps of clay using their thumbs and fingers and palms, squeezing and molding and patting until the pot took shape. Although they each needed only one pot, they made two apiece because Armadillo had brought sufficient clay and they knew some of the pots would break during firing. The pots were rough but sturdy and durable, and although they varied in size, most held about a gallon of liquid. The bottoms were rounded and nestled nicely in the ashes of a fire, holding without spilling the meat and palm broth and palm heart and grubs that were cooked in them.

Little conversation accompanied the work. Vulture did not make a pot; she sat quietly staring into her fire. She was thin and wrinkled, and she sat alone, moving slowly when she stirred at all, occasionally adding wood to her fire or waving at mosquitos with a leafy branch. Her body was streaked with dirt, and her hair was tangled and matted, and when she scratched her head with long bony fingers, she moved very slowly like a sloth.

Anteater prepared to go hunting, and before leaving, he went to Vulture and squatted beside her.

"Do you want some clay, Vulture?" he asked. "Do you want to make a pot? I will bring you clay. There is plenty of clay for you to make a pot. You make fine pots, Vulture; are you sure you don't want some clay?"

Vulture did not answer; she did not even acknowledge that Anteater was speaking to her. She stared straight ahead, but Anteater could see that she was not even looking past her eyes. He went to his fire and untied the pet coati from Deer's carrying basket, looking into his wife's eyes for a second before he returned to Vulture's fire.

"Here is a pet for you, Vulture. You love pets, and I will get another. Take this coati and keep it at your fire."

Vulture looked at the coati Anteater held in his hands, but she did not look at Anteater. She looked straight at the coati for several seconds and then reached and took it from him; then she leaned forward and tied its leash to a branch. She continued to look at the coati, and with one hand, she stroked the tiny animal from its head along its back, then withdrew her hand slowly when the coati moved away. She said nothing and did not look at Anteater; she kept her eyes on the coati the way she had looked at the fire. Her eyes pointed toward it, but she did not seem to see.

Anteater squatted by Vulture for a minute and then rose, still looking at her. He turned, looked at his wife again—opening his eyes wide—walked to his weapons, picked them up, and headed into the forest.

When the women had finished their pots, they set them out of the way to dry, but not near the fires because that would dry them too quickly and cause them to crack. Frog took the axe, and she and Parrot left camp to chop palms.

"I will go get bamboo to make water containers," said Deer, standing and adjusting her carrying basket and tumpline.

"I'm finished with my pots, so I will go with you," replied Armadillo. "Come here, Monkey," she called. "We are going to get bamboo."

Monkey heard her mother and stopped playing; she lay on her stomach on the trunk of the cedar tree and slid feet first to the ground.

"Monkey is walking and playing almost as well as my daughter, Rabbit," said Deer, "and Rabbit is much older. Rabbit was born before you were even pregnant with Monkey."

Armadillo smiled and watched as Monkey came running into camp. Catfish and Otter came, too, and picked up their bows and arrows.

"We'll go with you," said Catfish. "Maybe we can shoot some fish in the stream while you cut bamboo."

The boys were glad for the opportunity to go with their mothers into the forest. They were both a bit reluctant to venture out alone because they had been thinking about Berendy and the animal spirits, and the jungle seemed stranger and more dangerous to them than it had a few days before.

They followed the milky stream that flowed away from the camp, and the boys were disappointed that the women found good bamboo after less than a half-hour's walk. However, they were happy to find that the bamboo grew along a larger stream—four or five feet wide in spots—and they walked along it looking for a place to shoot fish while their mothers worked.

The women searched along the stream for bamboo of the proper size, bent good shoots at the base, and broke them off with their hands. They piled the bamboo in a grassy spot under a gnarled and twisted, thick, old sour-orange tree that had fallen once but continued to grow; its trunk now ran parallel to the ground, and new growth was coming out of it and heading toward the sky.

Monkey climbed on the splotchy green and gray tree trunk while the women worked; several times she called to her mother to look and see some small climbing feat she had accomplished. All Aché were excellent tree climbers, and it was an important skill to have. They often climbed to pick fruit or chop honey, and the men might climb several times a day to retrieve arrows or game that had lodged in a tree. When a jaguar threatened, the entire band would scoot up trees in a matter of seconds.

When they had gathered enough, Armadillo called to Catfish and Otter, and the women went to the pile of bamboo under Monkey's sour-orange tree and picked the pieces up to carry back to camp.

"Come down now, Monkey," Armadillo said. "It is time to go back to camp. Frog and Parrot were going to chop palms, so there will be palm heart and fiber to eat. Come with us; we are ready to go."

Monkey crawled along the trunk toward her mother and then got on her stomach to slide down a side branch to the ground. She wrapped her arms around the trunk and reached with one leg toward the branch. Her foot touched the branch, and she held on to it with friction and started to swing her other leg toward it, but just then her foot slipped, and her legs swung down. She held herself for a second and then fell, dropping about five feet and landing on a root that protruded above the ground. Her feet hit first, and she doubled over, falling hard on her buttocks and then hitting her face on her knees. The fall knocked the breath out of her, and she was silent for several seconds before she could get enough air to cry.

Armadillo dropped the bamboo she was holding, ran to her, and helped her to sit up. She hugged her crying daughter and tried to comfort her.

"You are all right, Monkey," she said softly. "You were being very brave and strong, and when you are brave and strong, sometimes you get hurt. Don't cry; you won't hurt long. You are a big girl. You will be all right."

Catfish and Otter and Deer stood by the bamboo and watched. Monkey cried loudly and did not stop. Armadillo was not able to soothe her, and the tiny girl screamed in pain and fell to the ground when Armadillo tried to help her to her feet. It was then that Armadillo noticed Monkey's left ankle. It was turned to the inside, and her foot looked as if it were not attached to her leg. The bones of her leg were visibly bulging under the skin where her foot should have been, and the sole of her foot was facing toward her other leg.

"Oh, Monkey," Armadillo said. "Your foot is broken. Oh, my poor baby."

She looked at the others who were still standing and looking. Catfish's eyes were squinting, and his mouth was drawn tightly, showing his teeth. His sister's ankle was not pretty.

"Her foot is in the wrong place," said Deer. "See if you can put it back where it should be."

Armadillo held Monkey's leg at the shin with her left hand and her daughter's foot with her right hand and started to move the foot, but Monkey screamed and pulled at Armadillo's arm, so her mother let go.

"Help me, Deer," she said. "You hold Monkey's arms, and I will try to move her foot."

Deer went to Monkey. She knelt behind the little girl, put her arms around her, and put her face next to Monkey's.

"Don't cry, Monkey," she said. "Your foot is in the wrong place, and Armadillo is going to fix it. Don't cry. You're a big Aché girl, and Aché don't cry. Armadillo will fix your foot, and then it won't hurt anymore."

Armadillo again grasped Monkey's leg and tried to move her foot. Monkey screamed and writhed, and Deer held her tightly, but Armadillo could not move the foot.

"It won't move," she said. "I can't get it to move."

"Pull on it first," said Deer. "Pull on it and then move it."

Armadillo pulled, and Monkey screamed so hard she ran out of air and kept crying, but no sound came out. Armadillo leaned forward and tried again; her muscles bulged as she pulled, and Monkey's foot slipped back into place.

"There, Monkey," she said. "Your foot is straight."

Deer relaxed her hold on Monkey, and Armadillo hugged her daughter. Monkey continued to cry, but her sobs were now softer, and in a few minutes, she began to calm down. Tears still came from her eyes, and she continued to whimper, but her breathing was easier, and Armadillo could tell that the pain was less.

"Let's go back to camp," she said. "Catfish, you and Otter help with the bamboo. Come on, Monkey, I will carry you."

10 ≡ SORES

Monkey rode uncomfortably on her mother's shoulders and sobbed quietly most of the way back to camp. She whined and grimaced each time Armadillo ducked under a low branch or vine, and she cried out sharply when they reached camp and Armadillo put her down near their fire. Her ankle was swollen, and the skin around it was puffed out, obscuring the normal contours of her tiny foot. Catfish sat by her and told the curious women and children about the injury and how ugly Monkey's foot had been when it was turned to the side.

"Monkey's foot came off her leg," he said. "It was in the wrong place, and the side of her foot was where the bottom of her foot should be, and the bottom of her foot was where the side of her foot should be. It looked like this."

Catfish grabbed his left foot with both hands and pulled it to the inside, trying to demonstrate the way his sister's foot had looked.

"It was ugly, and I thought her foot was going to fall off," he continued, "but Deer and my mother put it back in the right place."

"That's what happened to Caiman, a man whose band lives near the Little River," said Frog. "He fell from a kuri tree when he was chopping off branches so we could collect fruit, and his foot turned like that. He could never walk straight again, and everyone called him Short Foot."

"Yes, but his foot was worse than Monkey's," said Grandmother Boa. "His foot was turned, and there were bones sticking out of the skin. His foot stayed turned. Look at Monkey's foot now; it is straight. It is just swollen, and that will go away. She will heal, and her foot will be good again."

Monkey curled up by the fire and in a short time was asleep. She was tired but did not sleep well; she woke often and changed positions, and Armadillo sat by her and comforted her by putting her hand on the little girl's shoulder.

Armadillo and the other women sat by their fires, split the bamboo into long, slender strips, and began making baskets for carrying water. They worked with skilled, nimble fingers on the tight, deep, rounded baskets that would be waterproofed with a smooth covering of heated beeswax and charcoal powder. A twine net would be tied around the finished basket, and a string loop attached for carrying. The weaving and waterproofing took a day of work, and the women had just finished splitting the bamboo and begun coiling the strips around the foundation rods when Anteater returned, followed a few minutes later by the rest of the men.

They walked quietly into camp, empty handed, and went to their fires. Although no one in the camp had seen any game, there was no question about the success of the day's hunt: Snake and Turtle were both streaked from neck to buttocks with blood, and Blackbird and Coati had blood on their arms. The women and children pretended not to notice and were silent as the men relaxed after a punishing day.

The women continued working on their baskets and scarcely acknowledged the men's return while children sat by their fathers and quietly examined their backs and legs for ticks. Ocelot and Coati sat by their fire with Vulture, who stared hunched over into its embers. Ocelot and Coati had no children to groom them, and shortly they looked at each other, got up, and walked out of camp. When they returned, each carried a white-lipped peccary slung on his back, and the silence was over.

"Ooooh, peccaries," exclaimed Otter with wide-open eyes.

"Those are nice, fat peccaries," said Grandmother Boa. "We'll eat well tonight. We'll eat so much we will all look pregnant."

"I am hungry for peccary," said Parrot. "We haven't eaten peccary in a long time."

Wood was added to the fires in preparation for cooking the two eighty-pound pigs. Blackbird and Ocelot each took a peccary and began singeing it. They flopped the carcasses in the fires, producing billowing smoke from the crackling bristles, and scraped the burnt hair away with a flat piece of wood. Coati took the axe and went to cut saplings to make roasting racks. Despite the commotion and the peccary singeing only a few feet away, Vulture remained still, staring empty eyed at the fire; she had not even turned to look when the game was brought into camp.

Catfish knelt behind his sitting father and ran his fingers over Snake's scalp, pushing the hair against the grain, searching for head lice and their eggs. When he found one, he picked it out and cracked it with his teeth.

"Monkey hurt her foot today," he said. "She fell from a tree and turned her foot to the side."

Snake looked at his sleeping daughter, reached over, and gently touched her ankle.

"It is puffy and warm," he said.

"It looked terrible," said Armadillo, setting her partially completed basket aside and looking at her husband. "It was turned the wrong way, but Deer and I straightened it. It must have hurt her very much. Monkey cried almost all afternoon until she went to sleep."

"Can she walk?" Snake asked.

"She can't even stand. She screamed when I stood her up. Frog said that Caiman Short Foot broke his foot the same way, and you've seen how poorly he walks."

Snake drew in his breath in a slight gasp, indicating that he understood. He looked at Monkey as she slept and brushed his fingers lightly back and forth over her ankle.

Armadillo looked up and noticed that Turtle was watching her. He looked at Monkey, and then he looked at Armadillo. One eye was open a little more than the other, and Turtle looked straight at her. She looked back at him for a few seconds, and he continued to look at her, which made her uncomfortable. Snake rose, got some of the green sticks Coati had cut, and began building a cooking rack. Armadillo turned and watched him, but she still felt as if Turtle was watching her. When Snake had nearly completed the rack, Armadillo went to Ocelot, got a large blanket of peccary skin with a thick layer of meat attached to it, brought it to her fire, and put it on the rack. She adjusted its position and added more wood to the fire, and when she turned to look at Turtle, he was laughing and tickling his wife, Parrot.

The peccaries cooked all night, and the band was up late eating. They woke early, ate more, and left the uneaten meat on the cooking racks over low fires. The cooked meat stayed warm and did not spoil as quickly that way. Despite having a glut of meat in the camp, the men went out hunting as they nearly always did. The Aché never worried that there would be too much meat.

The women gathered wood for firing their pots and prepared a place for a large fire just outside camp. They cleared a small area and laid down a layer of wood. Then they arranged their dry, but unfired, clay vessels on the wooden pallet and piled more wood around and on top of the pots. They lit the fire with sticks from the fires in camp and let it burn all day. More wood was added from time to time, and the women turned and pushed the pots with long sticks to keep them in the fire and in even heat. Several times during the day— especially during the first hour—a low-pitched thud signaled that a bubble in one of the pots had caused it to break. Most of the pots survived the firing, however, and by evening they were finished.

During the day, the women also worked on their baskets, and the children played near camp. Catfish and Otter stalked birds in the forest but did not venture far beyond earshot. Monkey sat near Armadillo and played with strips of bamboo and pieces of wax; her ankle was still swollen, darkened now, and bruised. It was painful, and she was unhappy that she couldn't play. She was also embarrassed when she had to ask her mother for help when she needed to leave camp to defecate.

Vulture was quiet and continued to stare as if she were thinking about something important. She nibbled at some peccary meat when Deer reminded her but had no appetite. Grandmother Boa washed Vulture with juice from the *timbo* creeper to help cleanse her of the influence of the spirits, but Vulture seemed neither alive nor dead, and everyone wondered about her.

They moved camp the following morning; the women's carrying

baskets were now full with all of the baskets and pots and mats they usually had. The only piece of equipment still missing was axes, and the Aché were traveling north toward the mountains to get stone for axe making. Their baskets were heavy with meat, and Armadillo felt the strain of carrying Monkey on her shoulders atop her basket along with a full load.

With the task of replacing equipment lost in the Apa attack completed, the band returned to its customary flexible, mobile existence. They followed game, visited fruit groves, ate much honey, and enjoyed the early days of summer. The days were warm but not yet hot, and they moved slowly north and watched Vulture as life slowly left her.

The shrunken woman with sunken cheeks and pale, folded skin whose eyes had lost their white ate and spoke little. She cared well for her pet but she did not speak to it nor feed it meat. Her hair was tangled, and her fingernails grew long. She walked each day with the women and never complained, and she gathered fruit, but she no longer chopped palms. When she was in camp, she stared into her fire or out into the forest; she neglected her fire, and several times it went out and had to be restarted with sticks from someone else's. As the band prepared to leave camp one morning, it surprised no one when she asked to be left.

"I cannot walk," she said. "I am tired and cannot walk. Leave me here. I am too tired to walk."

Armadillo went to Vulture and bent over to speak to the slumping little woman with loose muscles and empty eyes.

"You can walk, Vulture; you walked well yesterday. You will not slow us down. We love you and want you to come with us."

Vulture did not look at Armadillo, and her body swayed a tiny bit the way a dead, naked tree does in a slight breeze.

"I cannot walk," Vulture said in a very quiet and cracking voice. "I do not want to walk. I want to stay here. I want you to leave me."

Armadillo stood and looked at the others, who were standing and waiting near the edge of camp. They paused a few seconds, and then Blackbird turned and walked away, and the rest, one by one, followed him. Armadillo took Monkey from her shoulders and swung her carrying basket off her back. She reached in, took a leaf-wrapped bundle from it, and laid it beside Vulture.

"I will leave this meat for you to eat, Vulture. There is plenty of wood for your fire; you can be warm and keep the animals away, and you will not be hungry. We will leave you now."

Armadillo lifted her basket, adjusted the carrying strap across her forehead, and hoisted Monkey back on her shoulders. She then walked quickly away from the camp and met Catfish, who had been waiting, and they hurried after the others.

The band walked north through leafy undergrowth along the sunlit banks of a sluggish, chest-deep stream. Armadillo stumbled once from her heavy load when they walked through a hundred yards of dark, leafy, organic mud that smelled of decay and sounded hollow as suction pulled at their feet. The men walked with the women for nearly an hour but left running when they heard monkeys in the forest.

Catfish felt good because he heard the monkeys, too, and recognized the sound and knew which direction it came from. He had learned much about the jungle animals from the young ones the hunters brought to camp and kept as pets. He knew their voices and could tell cries of fear from sounds of contentment or anger. He knew which foods they preferred, what their urine smelled like, and how their droppings looked and smelled. The Aché are keen observers of animal behavior, and they learn a significant amount from their pets. Knowledge of animals is very important in their beautiful, dangerous, and difficult jungle home, and they take advantage of it.

The women stopped in midafternoon beside an abandoned camp they had used two years earlier. The support poles of three shelters were standing in the old camp, and a couple of the crosspieces were still in place. Low to the ground and nearly obscured by the waist-deep vegetation that had reclaimed the small area was a tiny shelter that had protected pets from the rain. Catfish walked through the camp, and when he saw the scattered bones of a large snake, he remembered the stormy night they had spent under the shelters eating the moist, white meat of a fat boa constrictor.

Catfish and Otter helped clear brush for their camp while the women gathered wood. Monkey sat by her mother's basket and chewed on a small piece of paca skin left over from the day before. She held it with both hands and chewed and pulled and sucked on the skin, getting some flavor but almost no nourishment. Monkey's ankle was dark and not as swollen, but she still could not walk and fell to the ground in pain when she put any weight on it. She crawled in camp, but had to be carried anywhere else; as she was entering her fifth year, she was heavy and a burden for her mother. Armadillo did not complain, but others noticed the difficulty she sometimes had carrying the child and commented on how long it was taking her to heal; they wondered if she would ever be able to walk.

The women chopped palm hearts and fiber in the nearby forest, and Catfish and the other children played along the banks of a shallow, sandy-bottomed stream that flowed a hundred yards from camp. They took turns climbing in the red fruit trees that grew along the stream and shaking them so the cherrylike fruit with big pulpy seeds fell into the water. The rest of the children stood in the stream and raced after the fruit that sank and bounced along the bottom with the current. They ran in the shallow water, played tag, tackled each other, and screamed and laughed. When they saw a large fish swim under an overhang formed by the roots of a tree along a cut bank, the boys got their bows and arrows and waited quietly for a shot that never came.

Snake and Anteater returned to camp late in the afternoon, and the other men arrived soon after. They had not done well hunting, and the only game they had was an agouti Ocelot had shot while returning from their protracted and unsuccessful monkey hunt.

The silence that accompanied the hunters' return was broken when Monkey reached for a piece of palm heart by Deer's fire and twisted her hurt ankle. She cried out sharply and held her ankle, and when Armadillo went to comfort her, she noticed Turtle staring at Monkey and scowling. Armadillo quieted her daughter, and the camp was again silent for a few moments. People looked down at their feet or moved their heads very slowly and glanced at each other because they, too, had felt Turtle's mood and noticed his stare.

The uncomfortable stillness was broken when Anteater rose, got the agouti, and handed it to Deer to butcher and cook. He looked for cane to make a knife, and Deer showed him where it was by extending her lips, indicating that it was by Turtle's fire. Anteater reached next to Turtle, picked up the finger-thick cane, and eased down beside his wife. Turtle wrinkled his face.

"A man's back stinks," he said in a penetrating voice. "The sores on his back stink from the pus that always runs out of them."

Anteater glanced toward Turtle but said nothing. He peeled a strip off the cane and handed it to Deer.

"The sores make the camp smell like death. We shouldn't call him by his name; we should call him Sores."

Anteater's back did smell from the two open wounds that would not heal. Anteater knew it, and so did everyone else. It was not his fault that the sores would not heal, and no one knew anything to do about it.

"Sores should make his fire on the edge of camp," Turtle announced as if speaking to the forest, "so we don't have to smell the stinking pus."

No one spoke to rebut Turtle because they knew he was in a bad mood and was only saying things to provoke a confrontation. Otter stared straight at Turtle from across the camp, where he sat at Armadillo's fire with Catfish. He thought about getting his bow and arrows and killing the man who taunted his father. Anteater sat quietly and watched his wife gut the agouti and put the organs in the fire to cook. Nearly everyone watched Deer work, or looked at their fires and sat without moving.

Turtle stood and looked around; then he sat down but could not be still. He sat cross-legged and tapped the side of his right foot on the ground repeatedly.

"Sores's back stinks, and Armadillo's baby cries all the time and wants to be carried. She is too big to be carried, and she is getting bigger. This is not a band of Aché; this is a band of stinking, crying babies."

Snake and Armadillo looked at each other, and Snake put his arm around the little girl and looked past Turtle into the forest. Turtle stood again and took a few steps toward the edge of camp; then he walked back to his fire. He stood, shifting his weight from one foot to the other, pulling at the labret in his lower lip with his right hand.

"Vulture knew how to be an Aché," he said. "When she couldn't walk, she stayed behind to die. We should have left Monkey with Vulture. She will never walk, and an Aché that can't walk is not an Aché and should die."

He again strode to the edge of camp and then back to his fire and continued pacing. Snake pulled Monkey next to him and edged his feet closer to his body so they were nearly under him. He was taut, and his muscles were hard and flexed like a jaguar's when he is frozen and ready to spring.

"This is a band of weaklings who were afraid to attack the Apa when we had a chance." Turtle gestured wildly and spoke forcefully as if he were making a speech to the jungle or the air. "Crying children who can't walk, men who stink. We still don't have axes because this is a band of weak cowards."

Turtle stopped pacing and stood again by his fire. Points of perspiration sparkled on his forehead and nose, and he looked at Monkey and then at Snake, and then quickly looked away. The two strong, scarred men who were no strangers to violence kept each other in view but did not look directly at each other. They were tense, their muscles tight. No one moved, and the band all knew that something quick and terrifying and deadly could explode at any second. The silence rang in Catfish's ears; his heart beat very fast, and he was ready to run.

Snake rose slowly to his feet, looking close to—but not at—Turtle. He moved like the jaguar and had a focused look in his eyes that was not anger. When Anteater saw him stand, he knew Snake had decided to confront Turtle. Anteater looked at Turtle's brother, Blackbird, out of the corner of his eye and readied himself to help in case a fight started and Blackbird came to his brother's aid. Turtle's angry outbursts bothered everyone, but he usually calmed down if left alone.

When they saw Snake stand, the band knew one of the men must back down and that neither of them would. As Snake moved, so did all of the men—very, very slowly—and they prepared for a fight that would probably involve them all.

The women looked at their children and got ready to pull them out of the way. Both Snake and Turtle were motionless, and the seconds stretched out. Catfish was proud and scared; his heart beat loudly in his head, his back and neck tingled, and all life seemed suspended while the two men looked past each other with deadly eyes like dogs frozen with muzzles nearly touching before the violence explodes, and they tear at each other with deadly intensity.

A loud and sudden shuffling in the brush that was not caused by the wind startled everyone, and the camp jumped as if a compressed spring had just been released. The men dashed to their weapons, and the women and children crowded to the center of camp.

"It's a jaguar," cried Frog, pushing her young son behind her as she faced the forest from the scrambling, frightened, and crying group of women and children.

"Apa, Apa," screamed Duck, crawling over a fire toward the others.

The men drew arrows and faced the sound. A branch moved, and the men jumped into position to see. Seven long barbed arrows pointed into the brush, and the men held the powerful bows at full draw, waiting to spot a target. The leaves moved again, a twig snapped, and a dark figure moved from behind the vegetation. The men relaxed their bows, and the women strained to see. It was Vulture.

She was muddy and scratched, and blood was clotted along a cut on her forehead. She moved slowly and wearily to the edge of camp and fell to the ground as her leg muscles gave out.

"I didn't want the vultures to peck my eyes out while I was still alive," she said. "I didn't want the scavengers to eat my living flesh, so I followed you. Tomorrow you will bury me so the vultures don't eat my eyes."

She said no more; she stared into the forest, and the Aché returned to their fires and sat without speaking, and the evening was long and quiet.

11 ☰ VULTURE

They buried Vulture in the morning. They buried her in a grave Ocelot and Coati and Blackbird dug in the middle of the abandoned camp where the shelter had stood. The men unstrung their bows and used them to loosen the red sandy-clay soil. They took turns squatting in the hole and threw the dirt out by double handfuls over their shoulders. The men often dug for armadillos and other burrowing animals, and they moved the soft soil skillfully; soon a chest-deep oval grave was ready for the old woman.

"If we were like the other Aché, the Aché-who-eat-Aché, we wouldn't be digging this grave," Blackbird said, leaning on his bow while Coati cleaned the loose dirt from the bottom of the hole and Ocelot looked on. "We would hit Vulture over the head with an axe, roast her on the fire, and eat her."

"I don't think Vulture would taste very good," Ocelot said. "She is too old and tough and doesn't have any fat. It would be like eating a tough old monkey."

"The Aché-who-eat-Aché think they have to eat their friends when they die to make their spirits happy," continued Blackbird. "Then the spirits don't come looking for friends to take with them."

"It is not good to stay where someone has died," said Coati, putting his hands on the ground beside the grave and hopping out. "I would rather leave that place so the spirits can't find us. And I don't want to eat people. Especially Vulture."

"A man named Paca who married my cousin was from the Aché-who-eat-Aché," said Ocelot. "He said eating people was like eating peccaries. He said people have lots of fat, and the meat tastes good. He said babies were the best—nice fat babies."

"I'm glad we're not Aché-who-eat-Aché," said Coati. "I don't want to be eaten when I die. The Aché-who-eat-Aché are animals, and I don't want to be like them. They scare me because they don't eat only their friends; they eat anyone. If they shoot someone in the forest, they take him to camp and eat him. They probably eat Apa. They are frightening, and I don't like thinking about them."

Vulture lay on her side by her fire, and she looked small and thin. Her tired eyes were open, and they did not move; when she heard Blackbird say that the grave was finished, she sat up and tried to get on her feet, but she couldn't. She tried a second time and was able to stand, trembling slightly, and she looked across the camp to her grave. The red soil in the hole and mounded beside it was rich and bright in the cool, dappled, morning sunlight, and the grave looked larger than it was against the deep mottled greens and browns of the forest. Vulture walked toward the grave with small, weak, but certain, steps. She walked through the camp, hunched and frail, passing the fires and friends that she would never see again, and the women began to cry. When she reached the hole, she dropped to her hands and knees and backed in, lying on her stomach when her feet went over the edge, easing herself into her grave.

Catfish went to the grave and stood beside it looking at Vulture. The newly exposed earth was cool on his feet. He could smell the damp mineral odor of the ferruginous soil, and he thought for a second that it smelled like blood. Catfish was not afraid to be near the grave because Vulture was a woman and would be buried alone. Sometimes when a man was buried, he called for a companion— always a child, usually an orphan or sick one—to be thrown in with him. Catfish had seen it happen and knew that his father, Snake, had been thrown in a grave when an old man in his band had died, but Snake was big and had fought hard, so he managed to escape. They buried Snake's younger brother with the old man instead. Catfish watched as Vulture curled up on her side in the bottom of the grave and covered her face with her arms. The women's cries pierced the forest, and Catfish felt an empty tingling feeling in his stomach.

"Cover me," Vulture said in a stronger voice than she had used in days. That was all she said, and she lay without moving.

Armadillo and Frog brought mats to cover Vulture. Blackbird squatted beside the pile of dirt, scooped into it with both hands, and pushed it into the grave. The mournful cries rose sharply, and Vulture was still as the soil hit the mats covering her and scattered on both sides. The other men joined in, they covered Vulture with dirt, and Catfish watched with everyone else. When the grave had been filled, the Aché picked up their things and left camp quickly so they could elude Vulture's spirit. The women cried while they walked, and Catfish thought about what it would be like to be buried alive and wondered if he might find out some day.

The earth rose and fell beneath the band as they crossed the rolling hills that separated the drainages of the Big River and the Little River. The Little River was not far now; they would reach it in a couple of days. Just beyond the Little River began the uplift of the Mbaracayu Mountains, where they would find stone for the much-needed axes.

The forest was dense and dark, and the Aché moved through it in single file, accompanied only by the soft sounds of fallen leaves brushed by passing feet, the swish of leafy branches pushed aside and swinging back, and the occasional snapping of a twig. The women had cried for Vulture as they left camp and started walking, but before long the wailing began to subside, and then was over. The usual conversation that livened the band's travel did not begin, and the only words spoken were warnings when they disturbed wasp nests and broke file to avoid the angry insects. Snake carried Monkey and walked ahead of his wife, and they looked at each other several times without saying anything.

The quiet, monotonous walking through a dark forest that was dry and smelled of cedar bark made Catfish feel detached, and his eyes and body worked automatically while his mind rested. He stayed close behind his mother but saw only her feet and legs as she stepped over branches and vines. The air was cool and hung low in the vegetation below the broken, leafy canopy, and the jungle seemed endless.

Catfish's solitude was suddenly over when he left the comforting shade and walked into a patch of sunlight. His eyes watered, he could not see well at first, and he wanted to sneeze.

When his eyes adjusted to the light, he could see that the Aché were in the broken forest at the edge of a large meadow. The men advanced cautiously and surveyed the open area but remained concealed behind the brush and scattered, stunted, pioneering palm trees that marked the forest/meadow ecotone. The meadow was large—the biggest Catfish had ever seen—and sloped for nearly a half mile to a stream that meandered through its two-mile length. Beyond the stream, the land was level for a few hundred yards before the dark wall of the forest rose up again. The meadow looked smooth and was covered with gold and straw-colored grass that moved in waves ahead of the gusting, gentle breeze. Across the meadow, the forest stretched low and undulating for miles before rising slightly where rounded hills cut the horizon.

Catfish could see the jungle from above, and it seemed very big; he thought of all the animals that must be hidden there. The varying shades of green in the forest showed clearly and unbroken as mottled, circular clumps of light greens that were almost yellow to greens so dark they were almost black and many shades in between, and there was no space between them, as if master craftsmen had carefully shaped and fitted them together. Every hundred yards or so, a giant tree lifted its head high above the others, and Catfish wondered why some grew tall and others didn't; he was also aware that the tall trees were not all the same kind.

When the men determined that the area was safe, the band started walking across the grassy field. The meadow was not as smooth as it looked, and the grass was not continuous across it but grew in dense clumps a foot or two in diameter, separated by nearly bare patches of earth. When they were halfway to the stream, the ground became soggy, and the Aché stepped only on the bunchgrass clumps where the thick sod supported them. A step between the clumps meant sinking to their calves in the poorly drained soil.

When they were nearly to the stream, Coati, who was leading

the group, stopped and held his arm out to the side to signal the others. He turned quietly to Blackbird, who was beside him, and then pointed with his lips along the meadow to their left. Everyone stood quietly and looked.

"It's a giant anteater," whispered Blackbird.

Catfish could see the dark shape they were looking at. It was nearly a quarter mile away and had apparently not seen them. Coati, Blackbird, and Turtle split from the group and—crouching low—hurried toward the foraging edentate. Ocelot took the first place in line and led the group toward the stream, angling away from the hunters and their prey.

The band efficiently crossed the shallow, slow-moving meander and stopped when they reached the cover of the trees. While the women took off their carrying baskets and sat down to rest, Catfish stood in the shade of a young, bushy laurel and watched the hunt. The men and their prey were small and dark against the light-colored grass, and he could see that the men had surrounded the giant anteater and were moving in. He knew that they would try to get close to the animal without its noticing them and then rush it and club it over the head with a bow. He also knew that the giant anteater is a powerful and dangerous animal. When attacked, it strikes out savagely with long sharp claws on strong front arms designed for ripping apart concrete-hard fire-ant nests.

The men and boys and some of the women watched with Catfish as the hunt progressed. The three men closed in on the anteater, and the four figures merged momentarily before one split from the others, ran a short distance, and stopped. The men watching looked at each other to acknowledge that the first attempt had failed and then looked back. The figures again converged and stopped moving. The kill had been made.

Most of the others returned to the shade where the women had dropped their baskets and sat down. Catfish continued to watch as the hunters picked up the animal and started walking toward the band. They walked above the stream and stopped for a minute. They then went to the stream and crossed it, but instead of continuing toward the group, they walked straight to the edge of the forest and disappeared into the trees. When they emerged a few minutes later, they traveled along the edge of the forest to the waiting band.

Coati had the slain anteater slung across his back with one of its hind feet in his left hand. He carried his bow and arrows in his right hand at his side, and when he got close, Catfish could see blood running down his thigh from a three-inch-long diagonal gash. Coati paid no attention to the wound and did not even mention it when he reached the group. The cut was deep, and the skin was peeled back from it; Catfish could see the muscle under the skin that was cut and tiny white globules of fat sitting on the edges of the wound.

"We found an Aché trail," Turtle said as he joined the others and dropped to one knee beside his wife. "It was not very old, and we followed it into the forest. The trail heads into the meadow from the forest, so the people were going in the opposite direction."

"It must be Bushdog's band," said Anteater. "We thought they would be around here."

"Did you find a camp?" Snake asked.

"We didn't see one," Turtle replied. "We only went far enough into the forest to see the bent twigs so we could tell how long ago they had passed. It has been at least two days."

"I would like to visit Bushdog's band," Frog said. "My cousin is in that band, and she was pregnant when I saw her the last time. I'm sure she has had her baby by now. She was going to name it Rat."

"We'll have a clubfight with Bushdog's band when we next see them," said Turtle, and everyone knew that he was right. "We're hunting where they usually hunt, and if we stay in this area much longer, they will want us to leave and stop killing all of their animals."

"But we have no choice," said Deer. "We only came here because the Apa chased us from the place where we usually hunt."

"That doesn't matter," said Snake. "We are here, and we are killing their animals. They will know we are here soon enough, if they don't already. We don't hate them, and they don't hate us, but when we meet them, there will be a clubfight."

"The last clubfight—the one with Anaconda's band—was terrible," said Parrot. "Blackbird couldn't walk for days, and everybody was mad at Turtle because he almost killed Anaconda's son, Horse."

"I almost died, too," said Turtle, "because nobody fed me until they knew Horse wasn't going to die. I was hurt, too, and I couldn't hunt. I thought I was going to starve."

Catfish watched as Turtle spoke and saw the long indented scar along the side of his freshly shaved scalp that he had gotten in the clubfight with Anaconda's band. All of the grown men had clubfight scars, and Grandfather Jamo Paca had many. Catfish remembered the last clubfight and that he had had fun playing with the children from the other band before the fight. He had been amazed at the amount of meat the men brought in and left cooking over smoky fires for the days when few of them would be able to hunt. He had been awed by the size of the clearing the men had made in the forest for the clubfight and the showy paint and feathers the men had put on their bodies when they lined up in the clearing and shouted at each other. Everything about the clubfight had been fantastic and wonderful for the small boy until the fighting began. It started so quickly and violently when the men rushed each other, swinging long, sharp-edged clubs; then it became a free-for-all, not band against band but man against man. It had terrified him, and he still felt queasy in his stomach when he thought about it.

"I am ready for a clubfight," Turtle said. "We haven't had one in a long time, and I am ready." He looked at Snake as he spoke, and Catfish knew what Turtle was thinking.

Catfish looked at Coati, who was squatting beside him, and he admired the strong, quiet young man who was already known as an excellent hunter. He looked at the ugly wound on Coati's leg and the dead, giant anteater at Coati's feet. He studied the anteater's long head that was unlike that of any other animal, the long delicate mouth with its fused jaw, and the rough slender tongue that curled at the tip where it touched the ground in front of its mouth. The sharp claws were curled in tight death fists, and Catfish remembered that just a short time before, the giant anteater had been strong and beautiful in the grassy meadow and alive. He wondered if the giant anteater had a mate and family waiting for him somewhere. Then he looked at the long purplish indentation across the anteater's skull where Coati had clubbed him to death with his bow and thought about clubfights and how difficult and important it is to be strong.

12 ≡ BLACKBIRDS

The flock of blackbirds flew noisily from the sour-orange tree and with much chatter lighted in the bright and leafy lower branches of a mature chest tree. They blurted nonstop *trrrreeeps* and *errrrrts* and flitted from branch to branch in the tapering, thick-trunked tree as though they were discussing the potential danger they had just fled or the prospects of feeding on insects in the nearby forest. The crow-sized birds with curved beaks looked like black parrots and were not extremely concerned about the small boy who moved carefully and quietly through the vines and brush below them and sometimes surprised them by suddenly appearing too close.

When he was inside the distance that usually signaled them to flee approaching animals, they called to each other and flew to another tree. They flew straight and fast but not far, and the boy could always see which tree they were in. Had he walked boldly toward them making excessive noise, they would have flown a quarter mile or farther, and he would have had a difficult time locating them again. The boy was patient, and he never lost close contact with the flock.

Catfish had heard the blackbirds while sitting in the camp on a small elevated piece of land that jutted into the floodplain of the Little River. The small ridge was like a peninsula or spit and came right to the edge of the river, forming one of the few steep banks along its muddy watercourse. The dozen or so birds were feeding only a few hundred feet away, and Catfish listened intently. The thought of hunting them overcame his resentment for being left alone in camp to watch Monkey while his mother chopped palms and the other children played near the river. He listened to the birds' constant conversation that was not unlike Aché banter in evening camps and wondered if blackbirds could tell jokes. He imagined himself under the flock, seeing three birds lined up on a branch and killing them all with one arrow.

While the birds bickered in the background, he watched his sister intently peel strips from a discarded palm-heart sheath, searching for something edible, and he wished her ankle would heal. He loved his little sister, but she was too big to have to be cared for like a baby. He had been humiliated in front of the entire band the night before when he had balked at his father's instructions to help Monkey leave camp to defecate, and his father had spoken to him very sternly.

When his aunt, Deer, returned from the forest with a half basket of green philodendron fruit, she said, "Go ahead and play with the other children, Catfish; I will watch Monkey now."

Catfish stood, got his bow, and took one of his three arrows: the blunt-tipped one that would kill birds but not break when it struck branches. He flexed its shaft, looked along its length, and thumped the nock with his thumb to check the straightness; then, satisfied, he turned and walked toward the birds.

The prattle of the feeding blackbirds permeated the forest, and Catfish followed the sounds up the ridge and away from the river. He walked steadily but not carelessly until he could see the tree that held the foraging flock. They pecked and preened in the spreading branches of a red tree, and Catfish concealed himself behind the thigh-thick basal portions of a climbing vine that spiraled its way to the open sunlight high overhead. He studied the birds' position as compared to his own and planned the moves that would enable him to take a clear, clean shot. He nocked his arrow before he left his vantage point so he could minimize any movement when he was ready to shoot.

The birds were clustered on several sunny branches on one side of the tree, and Catfish first backtracked a few steps and circled quietly around the heavy vines. He positioned himself so the thick trunk of the flock's tree was between him and his prey and then moved directly toward them. When he was a dozen feet short of the tree trunk, he slowly stood tall and held his bow at arm's length with the arrow nocked in the string and held in place with one finger of his left hand where it gripped the bow. He then took the string and arrow between the first three fingers of his right hand, extended his left arm, and pointed it at a plump blackbird that was tearing at the sloughing bark of a dead branch. Catfish smoothly drew the string back and stopped when his right hand was even with his ear. He did not breathe as he held the bow and centered the bird above the hardwood knob that tipped his arrow.

The joints of the cane-shafted arrow clicked on the bow as he released the string, and the arrow flew straight and hard. It burst through the feathers on the back of the feeding blackbird, tearing two of them loose to flutter to the ground. The bird tumbled from the branch, opened its wings, caught itself, and flew frantically away. The arrow had been off by only an inch and had just brushed the bird's back.

Catfish took a deep breath, and his mouth tightened as he fought the disappointment of missing with a nearly perfect shot. His disappointment grew when he realized that he had watched the bird and not his arrow, so he had taken a shot that would make it difficult for him to find his arrow quickly. An arrow shot parallel to the ground does not go far and is easy to find, and one shot straight up falls close to the hunter, but an arrow angled up and away flies in a high arc that makes it very difficult to locate.

Catfish was still for a few seconds as he assessed his situation. Luckily the birds had not flown far, and they were nowhere near where his arrow had landed. He would have to be patient, find his arrow, and then attempt another shot. It was early afternoon, and he knew he had plenty of time.

The arrow had fallen in a patch of finger-thick bamboo, where yellowing dead and broken stalks looked like hundreds of arrows tossed in a heap. Catfish searched for several minutes before spotting it. The fletching was ruffled but undamaged, and Catfish smoothed the brown-and-white, vulture-feather flights between his thumb and finger. The blackbirds were out of sight, but he easily and almost unconsciously kept track of their position, movements, and excitement level from their calls.

As Catfish neared the birds for the second time, he was steady and didn't rush as young hunters often do. He negotiated the forest that separated him from his prey intelligently, using the vines, trees, and branches to his advantage to conceal his approach. He worked his way through the abundant undergrowth that choked the space between tree trunks and around and over the decaying detritus of the fantastic vegetation. He used the forest as an ally, incorporating its hard and soft, spindly and thick, and slender elements into his plan. He climbed and crawled more than he walked as he slipped this way behind a bush, ducked that way under a low branch, slithered under a silvery, barkless fallen tree, crouched and waited, then moved again.

When Catfish was almost directly under the birds, he moved surely, slowly, and single-mindedly, drawing his bow, holding, and releasing smoothly. The arrow struck an unaware blackbird squarely in the breast, and its wings fluttered spastically as it dropped to the ground. The arrow clattered on the branch, struck the tree trunk, and fell feathers first to the ground. The flock was gone by the time the arrow reached the forest floor.

Catfish went quickly to the fallen bird and twisted its head to be sure it was dead. He carried the bird in one hand and his bow in the other and retrieved his arrow. He then pulled a slender climbing vine from the tangle of dozens crawling their way up each other searching for light and bent, twisted, and broke it into a three-foot length. He wrapped and knotted one end around the bird's head, and the other around its feet. He slung the vine over his head and one shoulder and—with the blackbird riding low on his back—picked up his bow and arrow and resumed his hunt.

The birds had flown farther this time, but Catfish could still hear them, and he pursued the flock once again. Twice they flushed before he could take a shot. On his third shot of the day, the feather end of Catfish's arrow waggled as it left his bow, and—before the feathers could straighten its flight—it glanced off a branch and flew astray. It snaked up through the woody, leaf-poor midstory and stopped abruptly when it became wedged between close-growing vines and the trunk of a sour-orange tree.

Catfish studied the mottled, moss-green trunk trying to determine the best way to retrieve his arrow. The arrow was held in place too securely to be budged by a thrown stick, and he decided to climb most of the forty feet on vines and then cross over to the tree.

The vines grew about ten feet from the base of the tree and rose as a group, reaching and holding on to the sour-orange tree's branches about thirty-five feet above the leafy forest floor. Catfish stepped on the thick main stem that ran parallel to the ground for a few feet before it turned and angled upward. The vine was nearly a foot in diameter at the base, and where it began its ascent were the rotting remnants of the tree it had originally climbed and perhaps killed. Other vines spiraled up the large one and seemed to be merging with it.

Catfish climbed the first ten feet using the bulges of the vines that were twisted together like a huge rope as footholds. Higher up, where the vines were thinner, he climbed them like a schoolboy climbs a pole, pulling himself up with his hands and arms and holding the vines between his legs while he changed his grip. When he reached the branches of the sour-orange tree, he crossed hand over hand to the trunk with his feet dangling. When he reached the trunk, he pulled himself up, stood on the branch, and backed his arrow out. He held the arrow like a spear and tossed it gently, point first, to an open spot on the ground. He then swung down under the branch and crossed to the vines; holding on loosely with his hands and using the inside of his feet for friction, he slid smoothly to the ground.

Catfish could still hear the blackbirds, and he decided to try one more shot. The light was indirect now from the dropping sun, but there was still time for one more pursuit and a comfortable walk back to camp. Catfish was proud of the bird he had killed, and he hoped to be carrying two when he returned to the band.

He moved quietly along a low rise that overlooked the trickle of a stream that separated him from the flock. He decided to stay high and cross the stream at a right angle when he approached the birds. When he was opposite the flock, Catfish used the trunk of a towering cedar tree as a screen and crept carefully. As he reached the tree trunk, he peered around it to judge the distance and devise a route to follow to the birds' tree. Just then the birds called, left their perches, and flew rapidly away.

Catfish watched their flight, and while he was wondering what had spooked them, he heard voices. He moved quietly to the other side of the tree trunk, looked over the brush that covered the gentle slope, and saw two Aché standing close together near the edge of the stream. He felt something in his stomach when he realized that one of them was his mother, Armadillo, and Turtle was with her.

They stood in a tiny open place on the other side of the stream, and Catfish could see his mother's carrying basket lying beside her with palm fiber spilling over the sides. They stood close together, and Turtle touched Armadillo as they talked. Armadillo giggled, and Turtle smiled; he touched her again, and she touched him. Catfish watched as they sank to the ground in an embrace, and when he thought he was in danger of being seen, he ducked back behind the tree and was still. His thoughts were suddenly short and fast and jumbled. The mix of fear and anger at Turtle and love for his mother and father left him confused. Emotion welled up in him, and he didn't know what to think or do.

When Catfish looked again, Turtle and Armadillo were standing. They talked for a minute, and then Turtle left. Armadillo lifted her palm-fiber-filled basket, adjusted its tumpline, picked up the axe, and walked in the opposite direction from the way Turtle had gone. They walked at right angles back to camp, planning to circle around so nobody would know they had been together. Catfish waited for a few minutes and then hurried in a straight line to camp.

In camp Catfish sat by his family's fire and watched Monkey tease their pet coati by offering it tidbits of palm heart and then hiding them in her closed hand. The tiny, black-masked coati with his erect, striped tail squealed as he poked his long, flexible nose between Monkey's clenched fingers and tried to open them with his delicate front paws. Monkey laughed and relented, letting the pet have the morsel that he held with both front paws and ate quickly.

Catfish watched his sister's game and ignored everyone else in camp because he didn't feel like talking. Snake and the rest of the hunters had not yet returned, and Catfish was apprehensive, knowing how uncomfortable he would be when the camp was full.

The fire was burning down, and the logs feeding it were short, so Catfish left camp to gather wood. He found a dead, rotting tree trunk that was nearly a foot thick and six feet tall standing straight up. He leaned his weight against the snag, and it moved a few inches and creaked, then eased back to its original position. Catfish repeated the motion, each time moving the trunk a tiny bit more. Finally, it broke, and Catfish wrestled it back to camp. The log was large and heavy, and he worked hard to carry and drag it through the thick brush. When he reached camp, his father, Snake, was sitting quietly beside Monkey.

Catfish sat beside Snake and was grateful that hunters were silent after they returned to camp. He was uneasy because he knew something that he would rather not have known. He wanted to tell Snake what he had seen but was afraid of starting a fight. So Catfish and his father sat in silence, and a few minutes later, Armadillo arrived.

She seemed happy, and that upset Catfish. He hardly spoke to his mother, and when she saw the blackbird he had killed, she praised him and looked at him for a minute, so Catfish thought she suspected that he knew.

When Turtle arrived, the camp was silent. Women added wood to their fires, children groomed their fathers, and when the cooking started, everyone seemed to be in a good mood. Turtle joked with his wife and Blackbird, and Catfish watched warily when Turtle came to Armadillo's fire.

"How is Monkey's ankle?" he asked, smiling and rubbing the little girl's head with his rugged, thick-fingered hand. "It looks much better. I'm sure she will be walking very soon."

13 ≡ THE MOUNTAINS

Crossing the Little River was difficult because the water was high and the current strong from heavy rains upstream. The men found a place where a tree on the far bank had fallen into the river, bridging about three-quarters of the hundred-foot-wide stream. They cut another tree on the near bank to fall against the downed one and complete the span. Where the trees met was a tangle of spindly top branches, so the river crossing was like passing through a dense bramble patch while walking on a tightrope suspended over roiling muddy water.

There was no clear route to follow. As soon as a person passed, the branches sprang back, and there seemed to be no place better than any other. The women were encumbered by their bulky carrying baskets, and the men maneuvered with bow and arrows in hand, most of them carrying young children. Shouts and laughter accompanied the crossing, and it proceeded without major mishap until Frog, after passing the difficult portion, slipped on loose bark close to the riverbank and tumbled with a yelp into the waist-deep water. Most of the band had already crossed and laughed unmercifully when they saw her fall.

The band stopped and bathed on the north bank, and Armadillo walked back along the tree bridge and—when she reached the spot where Frog had fallen—waved her arms wildly, screamed, and fell off the log, splashing and gasping for breath when she surfaced. Everyone laughed, and the children took turns feigning clumsy falls from the tree trunk. Even Turtle joined in: he balanced on one foot for a long time while he pretended to try to regain his balance before falling headfirst into the river. Snake laughed loudly and seemed to enjoy Turtle's performance.

Soon they were ready to resume walking, and the men left in

two groups. Turtle, Blackbird, and Snake went west to hunt and gather arrow canes that grew straight and strong along the tributaries of the river. Jamo Paca, Ocelot, and Anteater walked north into the hills to find stone for making axes. Coati stayed with the women; they planned to walk toward the mountains and make camp in the foothills.

The land tipped upward on the north side of the river and climbed steadily toward the Mbaracayu Mountains, a low, but rugged, chain whose rocky outcrops broke the vast, undulating, interfluvial plateau. As the women moved up the steepening terrain toward the mountains, the streams flowed faster and had deeper channels, and the terrain was more rugged than in other parts of their territory. The rounded ridge they walked along was dotted with pebbles and chunks of rock eroding and washing down from higher elevations. White and red cherty pebbles and speckled metamorphic rocks occurred nowhere else in the region, and the uneven surface felt strange under their feet. The trees and understory thinned slightly as they climbed, and the Aché looked with much interest at the different surroundings. As they neared the rising mountains, they made camp just below the steep and slick outcrops that covered the craggy hills and made travel difficult.

Grandfather Paca led the way up the steep slopes toward the exposures that held the desired kinds of stone. The three men followed the edge of a steep-sided ravine, occasionally dropping to the bottom to examine the stream-washed stones in the dry bed, or climbing to look among the erosion-strewn cobbles where buried strata had been exposed. As they neared the head of the streambed, the ravine widened and opened into a bowl-like catch basin that fed the intermittent, but periodically raging, runoff that cut the arroyo. The slopes were spotted with dark green woody shrubs, lighter annual forbs and grasses, bare gray rock, and light tan sandy soil. The men spread out and searched for stones they could shape into axe heads.

They looked for sound, solid metamorphic stones with no flaws to cause breakage under hard use. To check for flaws, they hit two stones together and evaluated the sound: a dull thud revealed that small cracks or irregularities were present and had absorbed the shock, but a clear ringing sound indicated solid, homogeneous material.

The axe heads were shaped by pecking one stone with another, a long and tedious task, and the men looked for pieces that needed as little shaping as possible. The ideal stone was about as thick as a man's forearm, as long as his hand, and tapered at the end that fit into the handle. The axe handles were shaped like short, thick baseball bats, and the head fit snugly into a hole carved partway through the wider end. The socket for the axe head was carved with a rodent-tooth chisel, and when the tool was finished, the fit was so close that the stone and wood bonded tightly together with friction and needed no adhesive.

Along the river, Snake, Blackbird, and Turtle searched for game as they walked toward the place where they would get arrow canes. On the sloping branches of a partially fallen, but still living, chest tree, Snake spotted an opossum. Turtle and Blackbird waited and watched as he approached the animal, shot and missed, maneuvered for another shot, took it, and killed the gray animal.

"We will have meat for the grandparents to eat tonight," said Blackbird, "since only grandparents can eat opossum. I hope we find something else. I am hungry."

"There will be more game today," said Turtle. "We have plenty of time left to hunt."

"Snake has been very angry lately," Blackbird said. "I thought he was going to try to kill you the other night. Are you going to kill him?"

"I am not going to kill Snake, and he is not going to kill me. We are friends. We have hunted together many times. Our fathers hunted together. Snake is a good hunter, and he is strong. Snake is a good person to have in our band."

"What if Snake tries to kill you?"

"I don't think he will. Snake knows that would do no good. I don't think he is angry anymore. Did you see how he laughed at the river? Snake will not try to kill me."

"But Snake is afraid to fight the Apa," Blackbird continued. "And he might kill you. What good is a man who is afraid of the Apa and may kill another man in the band? I have always liked Snake, but he makes me nervous. Anteater and Coati and Ocelot all like Snake, and if there was a fight, they might help him. It makes me nervous."

"Snake knows that there is no reason to kill me. If he was angry enough, he would leave the band. And Snake is not afraid of the Apa. He was afraid to attack their house in the good forest, but he is not afraid to kill them. Don't you remember when Snake and I killed those Apa who were chopping trees near the big shallow lake? Snake was not afraid. He ran right up to an Apa and smashed him in the face with an axe. Snake is not afraid of the Apa, and I'm not afraid of Snake."

Catfish and Otter roamed the ridges and slopes searching for small animals and exploring the varied terrain that was new to them. They saw rabbits and plants they did not recognize, and they shot without success at small fish in a clear, fast-flowing stream. The pebbles and rocks that littered the ground hurt their feet, and late in the afternoon, they stopped on the crest of a ridge near camp to rest.

From the rocky point, the view to the south and west was unobstructed. The forest below the toe slopes of the mountains ran for miles, and Catfish and Otter sat quietly, surveying the diverse forest from above; it appeared green and wavy and continuous, stretching to the horizon and beyond. They saw cruising vultures with slender wings designed for gliding being buffeted by even moderate gusts of wind. A harpy eagle rode smoothly through the same shifting currents on wings powerful enough to lift prey equal to its weight to a tree-top nest. From their promontory, the boys could see farther than they had ever seen before. To eyes accustomed to views blocked by chaotic, confining, almost-claustrophobic vegetation, the panorama was captivating and a little disconcerting.

Tall clouds that were scattered randomly in front of them

appeared individually at the horizon and coalesced as they moved toward the mountains. The late afternoon sky was nearly covered as the clouds marched north and east and congregated above the boys. The huge cloud bank slowed as it neared the mountains, and some of it slipped over the hills behind them and grew very dark.

Low in the sky to the west, the sun shone orange between the forest and the clouds, and its rays hit some clouds and colored them pink and missed others and left them light on the bottom and dark higher up. The soaring harpy eagle looped over the valley below and west of the boys; as it neared the crest opposite them, two small, fast birds darted after it, and it flapped its wings and turned sharply to avoid their ire. As the boys watched the avian confrontation, a glint in the sky to the south caught Otter's eye.

"Look, Catfish, over there," he said, pointing with extended lips. "A light in the sky."

"It's Berendy," said Catfish, his eyes wide and heart beating fast.

They watched closely, and the glint disappeared; where it had been, they saw a dark, winged shape. It banked slightly, and the sun again reflected from it and was bright in their eyes.

"Berendy looks like a huge eagle," Otter said, watching intently.

A low droning sound drifted toward them on the shifting wind. At first it was very faint; then it faded and disappeared, then came back louder, disappeared again, and returned, steady and increasing.

"It isn't Berendy; it's one of the giant bees that fly over the forest, and it is coming straight toward us!" exclaimed Catfish, standing and holding his bow and arrows.

The boys quickly ducked behind a large, thick, woody shrub and squatted low, still watching. They were quiet and afraid.

The small, polished, aluminum Cessna with high wings flew steadily up the valley toward a pass in the mountains. It was not far from Catfish and Otter when it passed, and they could see a face in the window. The boys were so frightened they almost broke cover and ran, but they were too scared even to do that. They watched with relief as the plane continued up and over the mountains and disappeared under the dark blanket of clouds.

"That wasn't Berendy, and it wasn't a giant bee," said Catfish almost in a whisper. "That was the Apa. That was the Apa hunting like the eagle."

"Did you see the face?" asked Otter. "I could see a face, an Apa face."

"I saw it," answered Catfish. "I was afraid it was going to pick us up the way an eagle snatches a monkey and carry us away."

"Do you think it saw us?" asked Otter.

"I don't know," said Catfish, "but I hope it never comes back."

The two boys stood for some time, looking north over the mountains. The clouds grew darker and obscured the contours of the peaks above them. Lightning flashed in the clouds beyond the mountains, and for a second, their tops were backlit and silhouetted. When the light was gone, all they could see was the darkness of clouds and mountain.

"Let's go back," Catfish said, and they hurried down the ridge toward camp.

In camp Coati and a couple of the older boys were busy making shelters for protection from the coming storm. The smell of rain was strong, and the sky was growing steadily darker. Lightning flashed in the clouds over the mountains, but they could not yet hear the thunder. Catfish and Otter joined the construction effort, and when Jamo, Ocelot, and Anteater returned, they helped also, and soon the camp was well roofed. Just as the first small raindrops reached the forest floor and made the dry, fallen leaves dance from their impact, the hunters returned, laden with game and arrow canes, and everyone sat quietly and watched and listened as the storm developed.

The rain started softly and steadily, and a short while after the hunters arrived, Snake sent Catfish to retrieve the game they had brought so the cooking could begin. The men had killed the opossum, two pacas, and an armadillo, and processing began immediately.

"We saw a giant bee today," said Parrot as she cut into the armadillo with a cane knife. "First we heard it, and then it flew by, and we could see it. It was shiny and bright."

"We saw it, too," said Otter, "but it wasn't a giant bee. It was the Apa."

"*Taaa*," said Blackbird, his mouth open wide. He looked around incredulously as if to mock the boy. "The Apa can't fly. They are people like us. They don't have wings."

"It was the Apa," Catfish said quickly. "Otter and I both saw it. It had an Apa's face and looked like an eagle. We thought it would come down and pick us up and carry us away. It looked at us."

"How would you know an Apa's face?" asked Blackbird. "You've never seen an Apa. I've seen them, and they can't fly."

"We saw it, too," said Ocelot, "when we were coming down the mountain from getting stones. It wasn't a bee. And it didn't have one head; it had two. They weren't bee's heads; they were people's heads."

"The boys and Ocelot are telling the truth," said Jamo Paca. "I don't know what it was, but it had two faces—people's faces. It had big wings and feet and looked like a huge shiny bird."

"We thought it was hunting for Aché to eat," said Catfish.

"I don't know what it was, but I don't want to stay here," Ocelot said. "The forest is better. The Apa birds don't come and hunt there and try to carry us away. The mountains are too steep. It is hard to hunt, and we are not used to it. We have stone now, so we don't need to stay here any longer."

Conversation kept coming back to the Apa bird for the rest of the evening. The men worked into the night pecking the stones against each other to shape the axe heads: a hundred pecks, blow away the dust, check for evenness and straightness of the edge, a hundred pecks more, and on and on. They also trimmed the arrow canes and sat under the shelters listening to the tropical storm. That night they all thought about the big, two-headed Apa bird and wondered.

14 ≡ THE RED FLOOD

Rain fell throughout the night—sometimes hard and sometimes soft—and lightning flashed all around them and struck and split a tall fig tree less than a hundred yards from camp. The storm continued into the morning, and the weak daylight came gradually. The Aché pulled their fire logs close together and blew and fanned and encouraged the struggling embers, repeating a task that had been reenacted a dozen times since the rain had begun. They heated leftover meat and ate quietly, accompanied by the percussive whisper of the rain and the plaintive moans of cramped, damp children.

Hunting is no good in the rain, and traveling is difficult and dangerous, especially in the mountains where the rock outcrops are slippery even when dry, so the band remained under the shelters. The men pecked at the stone axe heads, slowly forming the thick-edged blades that felled trees more by bludgeoning than cutting. The older men were more experienced at working the stone because the Aché had been stealing and using metal axes with increasing frequency in recent years, so they made and used stone axes only when there were no others available.

Grandfather Paca made the best axe heads, and Catfish watched as he pecked and rubbed the stone and sculpted from it the most useful tool. He held the elongate cobble between his wide, calloused, cracked, and scarred feet, and he sang as he worked. He sang in a low husky voice, and Catfish could catch only occasional words of the refrain that was more spoken than sung. His lips moved only slightly, and the thin beard that grew in the shape of a goatee obscured the old man's labret hole beneath his lower lip. Jamo wore his labret rarely—only when the band met another—and Catfish could not really remember how the grandfather whose front teeth had long ago fallen out looked with his monkey-bone lip ornament in place. The singing and tapping complemented each other, and Catfish was glad to listen, for all morning he had been uneasily awaiting the sound of the big, two-headed Apa bird.

A trickle of water from outside the shelter cautiously invaded the ground at Catfish's feet, searching for some slope in the nearly level, leafless, and now compact floor. Catfish poked his finger into the earth ahead of the water and watched as it found his hole, filled it up, and continued its journey. He made a furrow across its path and hummed with Jamo Paca as he sang, "Ey, eey eey ey eeeeey; ey, eey eey ey eeeeey."

When Jamo's song was finished, he stopped abruptly, but Catfish did not notice and kept on humming, sitting on the ground with his right elbow on his knee, scratching at the ground between his feet, watching the tiny stream try to escape his several diversions.

"Catfish likes to sing and has a good voice," said Jamo Paca. "Maybe one day he will sing for us and make us happy."

Catfish looked up and saw the wide, wrinkled, gap-toothed smile of the old man, and he smiled, too, somewhat embarrassed because he hadn't been aware that he had been singing along with the grandfather.

"The penis is making a flood in the house," Jamo Paca said. "The water is red with mud and is making a lake by his feet."

Catfish looked down at the water between his legs that had begun as a tiny trickle—fed a few drops at a time from the edge of the palm-frond roof—and was now growing and filling a depression he had scooped from the soil. The rain came hard and steadily, roaring as it pounded their house and the forest.

"Take a stick, Catfish; take a stick from the fire," said Jamo Paca. "Put it in *timbo* water to keep the Big Flood from coming again."

Catfish had seen adults and older children perform the small and almost casual ceremony, but he had never been asked to do it. He stood and went to his mother's fire. Selecting a burning branch about as big as his arm, he pulled it from the fire and shook it to dislodge loose embers. Deer leaned forward and pushed toward him a ceramic pot that contained timbo water she had used to cleanse Anteater's back. Catfish squatted and plunged the end of the stick into the water. It sputtered and sent up a puff of ashy steam, and Catfish splashed the special water onto the stick with his hand to extinguish all sparks and flame. When it was out and no longer steaming, he returned to the fire and replaced the stick. With the ceremony completed, he went back to his place near the puddle and sat down.

"The Big Flood came when my grandfather's grandfather was not yet born," Jamo Paca said, slipping easily into the rhythmic, lilting speech pattern used when telling stories.

"The red water came and filled the rivers and the streams, and it was full of mud and foam, and it bubbled and grew until it wanted to fill the forest. The red water came to the Aché, and there was no forest to run into, and there were no hills to climb. The Aché were afraid, and the red water came into the camp and went into the fires and put them out, and the red water grew. 'What shall we do?' cried the Aché, and they ran to the trees and climbed them.

"Some Aché climbed a sour-orange tree, and the red water grew and grew, and the Aché climbed to the very top. They stood on the tiny branches at the top of the tree, and after the blood-red water grew some more and washed at their feet, and there was no place to go, they cried, '*Aiiiieeee, aiiiieeee*,' and the red water took them away." Jamo paused as he reached above his head and tucked a loose palm frond back into the thatching.

"The red water kept coming, and it grew and grew, and it took all the Aché until only one man and one woman were left. They were in the top of a palm tree, and all of their friends were gone. The red water came and pushed their tree, and it fell against another palm tree, and they climbed higher. Soon their tree was the only tree left, and they could see nothing but water—thick red water.

"They climbed to the very top of the tree and sat on the palm fronds and didn't know what to do. Trees floated by, and the red water was everywhere. They reached down and picked some palm fruit from the tree and threw it into the water. *Ploosh, ploosh* went the palm fruit. *Ploosh, ploosh, ploom.* One hit a log that was sticking up. The log moved and broke open a hole in the bottom of the red water. The red water went away, and all the Aché that the water had taken away became capybara, and that is why they always want to be near the water."

The old man rocked back on his buttocks and tucked his right leg under him. He held the nearly completed axe head in his left hand, turned it over, and rubbed its surface with his thumb to clean the dust from it and examine the edge. Taking the spherical hammerstone in his right hand, he resumed pecking.

When the story was over, Catfish looked down at the puddle he had made. The water was gone, and the small pit was lined with smooth, reddish-brown foam from the bubbles that had ridden on it. He touched the foam with his finger and heard the *fsssss* of the tiny bubbles bursting. The water must have run into the ground, he thought, but he knew that there would be no hole. He dragged his finger across the muddy, foamy depression and listened closely for the sound. When he heard it, he realized that the roar of the storm was gone. The rain had stopped.

The end of the storm brought a change to the camp. The men put down the stones and axe handles and began sharpening and straightening their arrows, which were especially prone to warping when it rained. They lay back and restrung their bows by holding one end against the trunk of a tree, grasping the other end, and flexing the bow with one foot. They carefully rewound the twine and tested the spring and were careful not to make them too tight because the strings would shrink as they dried.

The women wrapped the leftover meat and packed their carrying baskets, which would be heavier now with the new axes. Grandmother Boa pulled from her fire a piece of wood as thick as her thigh but not as long and poked it with a stick to expose the glowing embers, blew on them, and loosely tied a broad leaf around the burning end with a vine to protect it from the wetness of the jungle as she carried the fire to their next camp.

Catfish straightened his arrows and—when he had finished—looked for something to eat. The meat was already packed away, so he searched the ground near his feet until he found a paca foot that had been discarded but still had some bits of skin and meat attached to it. He brushed it with his hand to clean it and then bit at the toes and pads with his incisors. When the meat was gone, he used his molars to gnaw at and disarticulate it, and he ate the entire piece, swallowing those small, but robust, phalanges and podials and metapodial bones that he could not crush. He spit out only the claws.

They walked quietly through the forest, chilled by the rain-drenched leaves that hung heavy with water and sprang up lightened when an arm or leg touched them. As they moved from the rocky slopes to the more rounded lower hills, the men went into the forest to hunt, and the women and children continued walking. They walked west along the river, and the women pounded much palm fiber each day with the new axes. The hunting was good, and they continued moving west until they were past the usual hunting range of Bushdog's band.

Anteater's back was strong, but his sores still drained clear fluid that smelled bad, and Monkey's foot was less swollen so she could walk a step or two at a time without help. Turtle's remarks about Anteater's back continued, but he said no more about Monkey, and Catfish noticed the times when his mother and Turtle were both absent from camp, and he thought Snake noticed, too. The days were like each other, and the way of life that was Aché and had been Aché since before Jamo Paca's grandfather's grandfather had heard the story of the Red Flood went on.

And then they found the Apa trail.

15 ☰ STRANGEHORN

Seferino Cueva de Perez draped the reins loosely over his knee and examined his cigar. It had gone out some time ago and had begun to unravel. He held the reins against his leg with one elbow and carefully rerolled the dark blistered leaf that he had brought from his small farm near Caaguazú. He had not seen his family since he had come to the *monte* to cut fence posts several months before, but the money he made splitting and hauling the hardwood poles was his only income, and he enjoyed the solitude. The work was hard, but Seferino had always worked hard, whether hoeing his gardens in the hot sun or splitting trees in the forest. He rolled the small cigar tightly and moistened it with his lips so it would hold.

Two thin, humped, flop-eared white nelore oxen pulled the loaded, two-wheeled cart through the forest. The six-foot-high, spoked wooden wheels groaned with the weight but rolled smoothly enough along the deep-rutted, red narrow road to allow the two younger men to doze. *They've worked hard,* thought Seferino as he searched the deep side pocket of his once-white pullover shirt for matches. *And they're just boys. They don't like the forest the way I do. They are only here to make some money so they can go to the city and buy nice clothes. That's the difference between a young man and an old one.*

He dragged a wooden match across the coarse sandpaper striker on the matchbox and puffed on the cigar until the thick blue smoke came. The cart passed from shade to sun to shade again, and the leaves of the forest were so close that they brushed its sides. Sometimes Seferino reached out to lift a low-hanging branch and keep it from waking his young partner beside him.

The first arrow entered just under the bullock's right scapula. The daggerlike hardwood point slipped silently in to nearly half of its three-foot length, piercing the animal's heart. The bullock slumped immediately to the red dusty roadbed, a bright flow of blood coloring its white flank that was pockmarked and blistered from numerous botfly larvae just under the skin.

"*A la pinta,*" cursed Seferino as the cart lurched and listed to the right, unaware at first of what had caused the draft animal to fall.

Seferino's nephew, half sleeping as the older man guided the cart toward their camp, awoke as the bed tilted. He slid off the side of the cart to the ground and landed on his feet. As he fell, he saw the arrow and the blood, but before he could speak, a heavy, barbed arrow shot from a powerful bow at very close range pierced his back. The force knocked him forward as if someone had shoved him from behind, and he fell against the stationary wooden wheel and clung to it for a second before dropping slowly to the ground.

The volley of arrows that followed the first shot buzzed like deadly bees and filled the small corridor carved through the forest. The second young man was hit in the shoulder before he was fully awake. He leapt from his seat atop the neatly piled fence posts and was running as he reached the ground. A second arrow hit him in the buttock and a third in the abdomen. He stood in the middle of the tiny road like a wounded deer sometimes waits when he has no more fight while the jaguar patiently approaches for the kill.

The Aché showed no patience, and the young barefoot laborer was quickly pierced twice and then twice more before he collapsed. The six-foot arrows that impaled him slowed his fall the way branches impede a collapsing tree. The arrows bent and twisted as he fell but did not fully break, and when the only remaining movement was the foamy blood trickling down the hardwood and cane, the man was partially suspended, held above the ground by the numerous shafts.

Seferino, too, jumped from the cart and was hit twice before he could take a step. The gray-haired man with a gap in his teeth that showed each time he smiled fell to his knees and sat back on his heels. The remaining ox pulled frantically at his traces, trying to escape the hot flashing pain that came again and again, but the weight of the cart and his dead partner beside him prevented him from jerking the load more than a few inches at a time. When a final well-placed arrow ended the animal's agony, the shooting was over.

Snake was the first to leave the cover of the trees. He looked carefully along the road and surveyed the results of the attack. Seferino looked at Snake but could not rise or even move. Snake walked toward him and looked at the kneeling man. Seferino extended his hands toward Snake, palms up, and pulled back his lips in a weak smile—an expression of fear and a timid plea for mercy.

Snake and the woodcutter looked at each other for a few seconds. Without rushing, Snake leaned his one remaining arrow against the cart. He grasped his heavy black palm-wood bow with both hands and swung it like a baseball bat, striking Seferino in the forehead and sending him straight to the ground. The old man moved, and Snake struck him again and then a third time; then there was silence.

Turtle, Coati, and Blackbird stepped quietly from the cover of the forest. They looked up and down the road, and then they looked at the slain oxen and the dead Apa and the cart. They moved cautiously but quickly and were alert to the tiniest detail their senses could detect. They moved as they moved when combing the forest for a wounded jaguar—searching and pursuing but ready at any instant for a startling and deadly attack.

They retrieved salvageable arrows, first spinning them to release the barbs and then pulling them free from the flesh. On the cart, they found three axes, two machetes, a plastic bleach bottle half full of drinking water, an enameled cooking pot with two partially eaten pieces of boiled manioc, and a small cloth sack of sugar. They took everything but the sugar, which they would have loved, but they didn't know what it was and were afraid of it. They took a bone-handled knife from its sheath on Seferino's belt but were puzzled by the crucifix that hung from a string around the youngest man's neck, so they left the cross behind.

Turtle took an axe and went to the largest ox. He didn't bleed or gut it but began chopping at its tail, working his way forward through the pelvis, hacking at the bone until it split free. When he reached the vertebrae, he cut through the flank, lifted the leg, and chopped it loose. When he had finished, he handed the axe to Blackbird to carry, picked up his bow and arrows in one hand, dragged the ox's hindquarter behind him by the hoof, and led the way into the forest.

The men disappeared quickly in the vegetation. They hurried and ran when they could, and they did not even think about the clear trail made by the dragged hindquarter. The Aché were such adept trackers that they could follow a deer or a single man through the forest with ease. They had no reason to think that the Apa were less able to follow signs in the forest, and they made no attempt to disguise their trail. An Aché child could have tracked the hunters through the forest, even without the crushed and blood-stained path carved by the ox leg. They did not realize that the Apa could never follow them if they simply carried the leg back to camp.

The men fled south through the forest as they might have fled another Aché band or the Chiripá, not attempting to hide their tracks but trying to put as much distance between them and their pursuers as they could. They used the strategy of their favorite game—the white-lipped peccary—whose herds left wide, easily followed trails, but whose speed enabled them to escape predators less able to run through the dense forest. The Aché had more respect for the tracking skills of the Apa than they perhaps deserved, but the men also ran from the terrifying animal the Apa kept and controlled; an animal the Aché did not understand; an animal that could follow Aché through the forest, attack them, and lead the Apa to them; an animal the Aché feared as they did the spirits of the dead: the dog.

The warriors hurried through the long still evening, moving at a pace no one but an Aché could match, keeping together but not in a line, not stopping to talk or rest; at dusk, when the sky turned orange and the bright colors around them faded to shades of gray, they reached a wide swampy floodplain lying in a flat, low, narrow valley. Turtle handed his weapons to Blackbird, hoisted the leg to his shoulder, and carried it into the water. The men waded through the channels that were like a flooded maze with hedges of grass and cane rising above their heads where the water was shallow. On the other side of the main stream, the bank rose gently, and thick cane and thorny bamboo crowded the water's edge.

Turtle continued to carry the hindquarter as the men pushed their way through the wall of vegetation the way ants might try to pass through a broom. Two days later, when a small group of men, armed with machetes and old military swords left over from the Chaco War, and rusted pistols and shotguns held together with wire, reached this spot, they could not pick up the trail on the south side of the swamp and gave up the chase.

When night came, the Aché men slowed their pace. They had no fire and could not make torches, and walking in the forest at night is almost impossible and extremely dangerous, but they were wary and kept moving. As the deepening darkness closed about them, and they could see no more than obscure dark shapes that disappeared when they looked straight at them, the men took turns leading and walked in a tight line, navigating by the slope and evenness of the ground beneath their feet toward the camp they had left two mornings before. The men, who were now *bayja* from spilling blood, felt their way through the jungle, pushing and parting the vines and branches with their hands and the bows and machetes they carried.

The jaguar that hunted the dark forest replaced the Apa in their minds. They knew that to encounter the slashing, brutal predator that would be drawn like a magnet by their bayja condition and that could see in the dark meant certain death for one or more of them, so they listened and felt for sound and smell and presence that were not theirs and pushed on. When the light of the rising half moon softened the darkness, they smelled and heard the camp, and before they could even see the light of the fires, they called and were answered. In a short while, they entered the small cleared circle that glowed warmly and smelled smokily of home.

The women and children and the three men who had stayed with them looked with happy, but anxious, eyes at the returning warriors, making certain that all who had left had returned. The children sat near their mothers and were still to allow the men the distance and quiet they always received when they came back to camp.

"We have axes," Snake said after a few minutes, ending the silence. He reached down, picked up the axe at his side, and pushed it along the ground toward Armadillo.

She looked at the axe with mouth and eyes open wide, for she had never seen one so new. It still had some patches of blue paint along the sides of its blade, and the handle was smooth and clean.

"*Taaa*," she exclaimed as she picked up the axe and spun it in her hands before handing it to Deer.

The camp came quickly alive as the men showed their booty. The axes and machetes and bottle and pan were passed from hand to hand, and everyone commented on their strength or sharpness or size. When Turtle's son, Puma, dragged the draft bullock's hindquarter into the circle of fires, the excitement grew. Jamo Paca began building up his fire, and Armadillo made a roasting rack; the others examined the leg and hoof and spoke with amazement about how huge these animals with the strange horns must be to have legs and feet this big.

"We haven't had strangehorn in a long time," said Parrot. "Most of the children have never eaten strangehorn."

"I want to eat strangehorn," said Monkey, tugging with all her weight on the hoof but not able to budge it. "I will cook it and eat it."

The children playing near her laughed at Monkey, and so did Snake and half the camp.

"Her foot must have stopped hurting the way she is pulling on that leg," Snake said to Armadillo. "Soon it will be all healed."

Catfish looked at his little sister and was glad that her foot was better; when he looked at Turtle, who had been laughing loudly, Catfish was not surprised to see him stop and look quickly at Monkey when he heard Snake speak.

The party lasted late into the night. Anteater and Ocelot had killed a paca and an armadillo while the other men were away, and the roasted meat was already cooked when Jamo took the haunch, singed it, and cut it into several pieces, some to roast over the fires and some to boil in the new metal cooking pot. The roasting beef dripped fat, so around the roasting rack was a constant flow of people, dabbing at the meat with palm-wood brushes so they could taste the savory juices that were otherwise lost to the fire.

The men told and retold the story of the raid and choreographed parts of it for an attentive audience. Blackbird acted out the part of the young woodcutter who was so full of arrows that he could not fall; he stood in the center of the camp with a half-witted look on his face, moving in slow motion as he reacted to each of the imaginary arrow strikes, gradually slumping toward the earth, and holding himself above the ground with one arm extended while he pretended to die the death of a soft, stupid, cowardly Apa. The camp roared at his portrayal.

Even more entertaining was Coati's imitation of the old man's death. He puffed out his stomach and indicated where the arrows hit, saying "*tu, tu*" to duplicate the sound of the arrows piercing his belly; he let out little cries and looked at his stomach with such an exaggeratedly sad and pained face that the band howled. Turtle and Snake and Blackbird interjected minor additions and corrections to Coati's enactment, standing to show their positions relative to the old man's and indicating exactly how the arrows had entered his abdomen. In Coati's version, the post cutter cried and wailed and pleaded and squirmed, and Snake fussed with his arrow for several minutes before he finally dealt the death blow. Coati created a very convincing death scene, mimicking rather precisely the way the first blow from Snake's bow (pantomimed in slow motion by Snake) had brought a whining exhalation from the doomed man, followed by a noisy and gargling inhalation, and then the second and third blows had finished him, ending with the slow and familiar-to-all-Aché, last, long and rattling exhalation of a dying man. Coati even made sounds with his cheeks when his portrayal of the death ended with the old man losing control of his bowels.

The women prepared *timbo* water and bathed the warriors to ward off the *bayja*. The Aché felt strong, and even the thought of bayja did not destroy their elation. The entire band—from Jamo Paca and Grandmother Boa to little Monkey—felt relieved of the anxiety that had been with them since their camp was attacked and replaced it with feasting and night-long giddiness.

In the morning, the band was up and off more quickly than usual, despite having gotten little sleep. Catfish was the last to leave camp, and before he stepped into the forest, he turned and gazed across the small cleared and trampled area that was ringed with still-smoldering fires and nearly roofed over by the green leafy branches of towering trees and leaning saplings. Bones and palm-heart sheaths littered the ground, and among them were three still-new stone axes, not yet dulled, discarded as unceremoniously as fruit pits or chewed palm-fiber quids. There was no use for them now, and carrying them would have been a waste of effort. Still, Catfish looked at them for a moment, reflecting on how important and costly they had been, and now they were no more than trash.

The band walked in line as a group away from the Apa and their trails. A long day's walk would take them to the kuri fruit groves— a place rare in the jungle—where numerous trees of the same species grew, and where they often camped for days, eating the delicious yellow fruit and hunting the many animals that came to forage there. They had talked about going to the kuri groves for weeks, and now that they were heading there—despite the necessarily steady pace—they thought about what was ahead, not what they were leaving behind.

The pace was slow enough that when Monkey asked her father to let her walk, he dropped her from his shoulders. The child walked ahead of him, just behind Catfish, limping some but not complaining. Snake watched proudly as she picked her way over and under and through the obstacles of the forest. He had always been impressed by how well the little children—once they decided that they could—were able to walk in the jungle. He was especially glad that Monkey was walking because anyone—particularly a child—who was lacking in any way was at risk in the forest, as well as from Aché like Turtle.

Monkey walked behind Catfish, and he helped her, pulling her over a fallen log, holding vines so she could pass before they sprang back. When he held a spiny *kwanto* blade and waited for Monkey to catch up, he heard a rustle in the leaves near his feet. Looking down, he saw the glistening side of a large bothrops snake sliding along the base of the kwanto. Catfish let go of the blade and—still looking at the coiling snake—pushed Monkey with both hands, knocking her off her feet. Snake saw instantly what was happening, and he stepped forward, grabbed Monkey by one arm, and flung her out of the way. In the same motion, he slapped Catfish aside with the back of his other arm, sending him tumbling, and as the boy fell backward, Snake saw the viper strike, hitting his son's foot.

As soon as Monkey hit the ground, she shrieked and then kept crying. Snake edged forward, his eyes on the viper, and when he saw his target, he struck quickly with his bow and drove the triangular, horrid-looking head to the ground. He held it there for a second before lifting his bow. The fer-de-lance continued to move, and Snake spun his bow and pushed the blunt tip through the head of the deadly *membo*.

Armadillo was ten yards behind Snake when she heard the scream and—as every mother can—recognized it as her daughter's. She rushed ahead, bumping Parrot and Frog who had stopped to look, and ran to Monkey. The snake's mottled yellow and brown body writhed in the brush and leaves at Snake's feet, and Armadillo dropped to her knees and enveloped Monkey in her arms, swinging her away from the dying reptile. Monkey wailed even more loudly when her mother spun her around. Catfish stood quietly a few feet behind Snake. He did not even know that he had been bitten. Armadillo shouted over the cries of the panicked child.

"Is she bit? Did the membo bite her?" Armadillo held Monkey under the armpits and lifted her off the ground to look at the girl's legs and feet. Monkey writhed like the snake, not knowing what was going on.

"A membo bit Monkey," Frog cried to Parrot, and everyone hurried to see.

"*Aiiiii,*" said Parrot, her teeth clenched as she turned her head to look at Frog.

Snake kept his eyes on the viper's head as he withdrew his bow. He backed sideways toward Catfish, reached out, and found the boy with his hand. "Monkey's not hurt," he said. "She did not get bit." He turned and laid his bow next to his arrows on the ground beside him.

Armadillo pulled Monkey close and held the little girl's face against her cheek. "Don't cry, Monkey; the snake is dead." Armadillo swayed a little with her daughter in her arms, and she began to hum. Monkey squirmed and looked toward her father, not quite able yet to understand; she had not even seen the snake, and when her mother said that it was dead, Monkey thought that her father had been killed. She calmed down quickly when she saw her father standing above the dying membo.

Snake bent over and looked at Catfish's foot. "The membo bit your foot," he said, running his thumb over the marks. "The bite is here, but I don't think it is bad. I saw the snake strike, and there was kwanto between your foot and its mouth. The teeth didn't go in straight; they just scratched your foot. I've been bitten like that before, and it may swell up and hurt, but you won't die." Snake stood and looked at his wife. "The membo bit Catfish, but it is just a scratch. He will be all right."

Snake got a machete from Ocelot and severed the membo's

still-dangerous head. The jaws were wide open, exposing the dripping fangs. He dug a small hole with his hands and buried the head. He then picked the snake up by the tail and held it for the others to see. It was nearly as long as he was tall, as thick in the middle as his forearm, and would make a good contribution to the evening meal.

Catfish sat on the ground by his mother. Armadillo held Monkey in one arm and rubbed Catfish's foot. Deer came with milk-creeper vine, and Armadillo crushed it in her hand and rubbed the juice on Catfish's wound. She took a short length of twine from her basket and tied it around the boy's leg just above the calf, not as a tourniquet but an amulet for healing. She built a small fire to heat his foot and blew smoke over it to drive the poison out.

Catfish was quiet as everyone in the band crowded around to see his foot, and he was very glad to hear that they all agreed with Snake that the bite was not bad and he would not die. Catfish felt good, very good, because he had just come close to death, a common way of death for an Aché, the way he had seen Parrot's sister die. But he would survive. He felt like a man, rather than a boy, because now he could tell the story that he had been bitten by a membo, and he could laugh.

They found the first kuri tree in the late afternoon. Otter ran to it and hollered back to the rest that the fruit was small and not yet ripe, and they continued on. In twenty minutes, they found another tree, and this time the fruit was good. Otter and Puma and Duck climbed the tree before the rest of the band reached it. High above the others, the children clambered out on branches and shook the fruit loose. The plum-sized citrus fruit with large seeds rained down and sounded like the first raindrops of a summer thunderstorm on the undergrowth and leaves on the forest floor. Much of the fruit would not fall, and as the others scoured the ground for it—eating as they went and collecting some in baskets—the climbers picked the stubborn pieces from the branches and threw them toward a small clear spot on the ground. Normally Catfish would have been in the tree with the other children, but his foot felt warm and was beginning to throb, so he sat under the tree, peeling and eating the yellow fruit that tasted like sweet grapefruit.

When the only pieces of kuri fruit left in the tree were out of the children's reach, and no more were obvious on the ground, the band moved on. They were not yet in the thickest part of the grove, and they wanted to find several more trees before they made camp. In a short while, they spotted a very large kuri tree, and as they were heading for it, the men heard coatis.

The foraging coatis—a troop of a dozen ring-tailed animals with raccoonlike masks and delicate, dexterous front paws—feasted on the ripe fruit of a tall, spread-limbed kuri tree. The small omnivores moved easily about on the arching branches, eating, calling to each other with shrill, whistlelike cries, looking, always looking and listening, a dozen pairs of scanning eyes and ears, alert to the bending branch or moving shadow that signaled approaching danger. With paws like hands, they picked and peeled and held the yellow fruit while they ate, and when they finished one piece and dropped the pit to the ground, they looked about before seeking another.

The coatis first heard the Aché men approaching when the hunters were spreading out to encircle the kuri tree and cut off possible escape routes. Only one tree—a leaning lapacho—was close enough for the coatis to cross to it without going close to the ground, and when two females bolted along the heavy limb that was their only avenue to freedom, Blackbird ran to a point directly ahead of them, yelled, and rapped his arrows against his bow, frightening the coatis and turning them back toward the main trunk of the tree.

Blackbird stayed where he was in case any others attempted the same crossing while the other men put down their weapons and calmly began bending saplings and breaking them, dragging away fallen limbs, and pulling up shrubs and brush and vines, clearing the area under the coatis' tree. The men did not speak, and as they worked, they made low groaning sounds—"*uuunnnhhh, uuunnnhhhh*"—which sounded like the growls of a prowling jaguar and kept the coatis from trying to flee. Some of the coatis paced back and forth on the tree's thick limbs, nervous and confused. Some clung tightly to the tree, peeking around or over a branch, watching the activity below.

When the women arrived, they dropped their baskets, left the children just beyond the reach of the tree's branches, and went to work with the men. They moved carefully and quietly, and soon the area under the kuri tree was clear of most of the brush and branches that had cluttered the ground. The children watched as their parents and grandparents and aunts and uncles spread out around the tree. They each found a place and looked up at their prey, and when the movement stopped, there was a pause, an instant of silence shattered immediately by shouts and shrieks and waving arms and kicking feet and shaken branches.

The sudden explosion of sound and motion terrified the coatis, and they ran through the branches seeking to escape, but they could not get away, for the horror was everywhere and seemed to have them already in its grasp. And so the coatis leaped. They leaped for freedom because they knew no other way. They leaped to escape swooping eagles and pouncing tayras and striking boas, so they leaped to escape this new terror with a fear that only one in the grip of a predator can feel. And they leaped into the arms of the waiting Aché.

The first coati hit the leafy jungle floor in front of Jamo Paca. He had watched it plummet and was bent and ready as it thudded on its belly and bounced from the impact. The animal's legs were clawing for traction as it tried to regain its footing, but before it came into contact with the earth for a second time, Jamo had it. His right hand grasped one hind leg, and his left grabbed its tail, and he swung the coati in an arc over his shoulder. The force of his swing kept the reaching head with drawn lips and exposed canines away from his body, and he slammed the coati to the ground, stunning it. Jamo then repeated the motion, this time swinging his prey higher and with greater force and precision, slamming the coati once again to the earth and ending its life. He then let go of the limp body and looked up, searching for another coati to intercept.

The melee under the tree lasted only a few minutes, and when it was over, not a single coati had escaped. Each one had been slammed, slammed the way Turtle had killed Otter's little sister, slammed the way a wounded monkey was sometimes finished, a method of killing that had its own name. Slamming a coati was dangerous and had to be done quickly and forcefully because the coatis could twist and strike at their attackers with catlike coordination, and their small, but sharp, white teeth had left lacerations on many an Aché arm. Today Blackbird acquired an open gash on his thumb because he had not reached a cascading coati soon enough, and when he had grabbed it, there had been time for the animal to whirl and sink its teeth in his hand before he could slam it into the trunk of the tree, breaking its back. Coatis sometimes escaped if only the men were hunting because they could not cover the entire area under the tree, but with the women helping, there had been no holes in their coverage.

The coatis were gathered and carried to the spot where the children waited. The women put them in their baskets, and the older children vied for carcasses to carry. "Let me carry one," they cried. "I want to carry one." They walked in line to the large kuri tree they had headed for earlier and gathered more fruit. When the tree was exhausted, they continued on and made camp on the side of a long gentle slope just above a small spring in a place surrounded by thick undergrowth and dozens of fruit-heavy kuri trees.

They ate that night until their bellies were distended and tight, feasting on leftover strangehorn and paca, kuri fruit, coati, and snake. The women peeled the yellow kuri, put the large fruit-covered seeds in waterproof baskets, and mashed them with palm-wood brushes. The pulpy liquid was sweet and slightly tart, and families gathered around the baskets, dipping with their brushes and sucking them dry. They cooked, tended fires, and joked, and ate more slowly as the evening passed.

A big armor-plated beetle careened over the camp, attracted by the light of the fires. When it dived low over Catfish's head, he reached up swiftly and snatched it out of the air. He leaned forward and opened his palm slowly in the flickering orange light, inspecting the two-inch beetle. Still holding it captive in his partially opened hand, he picked off its legs and tossed the beetle into the ashy embers in front of him. The wings buzzed for a second and curled from the heat. In a minute, Catfish nudged the beetle with a stick, pushed it farther into the coals, stirred it around for a moment, and then flicked it out of the ashes. He let it cool for a few seconds and then broke open the carapace with his fingers and extracted a lump of white meat nearly the size of his thumb. Despite having bones all around him from the meat he had consumed and no shortage of food in camp, he ate the tender, but firm, morsel that was like shellfish in a single bite, then dabbed a brush in the kuri juice, and sucked noisily.

"Catfish doesn't have enough to eat," said Anteater, chuckling. "He is hunting beetles right here in camp."

Catfish looked up at his uncle and smiled around the sides of the foot-long palm-wood brush that was still in his mouth.

"Well, I'm getting enough to eat," said Otter, rising to his knees, arching his back, and puffing out his stomach. "Look at my belly. It feels like an armadillo had made its nest there."

"Otter looks like he is pregnant," laughed Blackbird. "Maybe a giant armadillo made him pregnant, and he'll have a bunch of baby armadillos."

"It did," yelled Puma, leaping to his feet. "A giant armadillo made Otter pregnant. It got him in the ass." Puma went to Otter and pretended to mount him from behind.

Catfish laughed with everyone else at the sight of Puma humping Otter, and he started to get up, but when he stood on his foot, it hurt, so he sat back down.

"It got him in the ass; it got him in the ass," squealed Monkey, clapping her hands and grinning. "It got him in the ass."

"What will you name the babies, Otter?" taunted Puma.

"I'll name them Puma," Otter shouted, turning toward him with his mouth open wide and teeth bared, "because I'm going to eat Puma tonight." Otter grabbed Puma's arm and tried to bite it, but the bigger boy pushed him away and danced to the edge of camp. Otter stood in the middle of the ring of fires for a moment, still laughing, but he knew from the way the adults had stopped laughing and were

watching that the silliness had gone far enough. He returned to his
fire and sat down.

When the commotion had died down, Armadillo finished the
piece of fer-de-lance she had been eating, sucking the last bits of
meat and juice from a segment of vertebrae before taking it from her
mouth and throwing it into the fire. "Otter may be naming his babies
Puma," she said, loud enough for the whole camp to hear, "but I am
going to name my baby Snake."

The band was quiet for a second. Frog looked at Armadillo and
said, "*Taaaaaa*," and grinned, acknowledging the good news.

Jamo Paca hadn't heard Armadillo, and when he looked with a
puzzled face at his wife, Grandmother Boa, she repeated the revela-
tion: "Armadillo is pregnant. She is naming the baby Snake."

Jamo acknowledged the announcement with a smile and a nod.
The band was excited by the news, and the camp was full of chatter.
Duck, Frog's oldest daughter, said loudly, "She'll name the baby Snake,
the same as its father."

Catfish realized from the reaction in the camp that he wasn't the
only one who knew about Armadillo's relationship with Turtle. He
understood that Snake might not be the father of Armadillo's child
and that Snake knew that, too. Catfish could not understand why
Snake did not say anything; he just kept eating. Why did he do nothing? Was he afraid?

The band left the kuri grove when the number of fruiting trees began to diminish. There was still plenty of kuri fruit, but it was getting more difficult to find and pick, and they were ready for something else. They headed south toward the Little River. On its south side were the groves of scattered palm trees where they had spent many days recovering from the Apa attack, and where now there would be many fat and nutritious palm-beetle larvae feeding on the fermenting wood of the felled trees.

The Little River was easy to cross; its water was low but still moving strongly in the main channel. The water in the deepest spot only reached Armadillo's waist, so she had no trouble carrying Monkey perched atop her basket across to the southern bank. Catfish and the older children laughed and teased each other as they braved the current, which came to their chests and pushed against their bodies and legs. They held their arms above the silty brown water, leaned upstream, and ran when they broke free of the current in the sandy shallows.

When they were safely across the river, the men left to hunt, and the women walked into the trees and took off their baskets. Deer piled dry leaves and sticks on the smoldering branch she carried and blew on it until flames appeared. She put more sticks on the fire and blew and fanned, and the smoke drifted and thinned and kept some of the mosquitoes away.

Parrot and Armadillo and Grandmother Boa left the resting group and waded into the sluggish, warm water of a nearly isolated, horseshoe-shaped lagoon that had once been the main river channel but had been cut through. In high water, the lagoon filled, and the center was an island, but in very low water, it was cut off from the river. The women moved quietly and steadily through the water, feeling the bottom with their feet.

In a few minutes, Armadillo stopped, steadied herself, took a breath, and ducked under the water. Before the ripples had smoothed above her, she burst to the surface—arms outstretched—gripping with both hands a thick black-and-brown catfish. She waded with the fish held tightly in front of her, and when she neared the bank, she held it above her head and threw it high up onto the dry, leafy ground. Otter was watching her, and he went to the flopping fish, took it by the tail, and slammed its head against the thick buttress of a towering chest tree.

Had the water been lower—cutting the lagoon completely off from the river—they might have tried to roll for fish by piling brush in one end and pushing it completely through the lagoon, trapping some fish and forcing the rest into a confined area at the other end, where they all could be caught. They would have needed at least a day to cut enough brush, and this lagoon was too large for a single band, so they could not roll for fish here.

Armadillo waded back into the deeper water and rubbed her hands together. She splashed water on her face and her chest and breasts and washed off the bits of debris that had come with her from the river bottom and stayed when the water ran off. She leaned back, dipped her head in the water, and stood up again, slicking her short, almost-spiky hair back with her hands. The women continued fishing for half an hour longer, and Parrot caught another catfish. Sometimes small caiman could be caught this way—felt first with the toes and then wrestled out of the water—and occasionally someone lost part of a finger or a grape-sized piece of flesh to a hungry piranha, but today they encountered none.

The band turned southeast after crossing the river and traversed forest that was foreign, but not unknown, to them. Thunderstorms followed them in a series, swirling over the low-lying, rolling jungle, and the gray puffy clouds that covered the sky between storms kept the air heavy and damp. The jungle smelled of moisture; the rich woody, clean decay of the innumerable trunks and limbs of fallen trees; and slightly sharp, acrid, white mold and fungus. When rain fell, it came down hard, and when it stopped, the air was still and hot. Mosquitoes and gnats clouded the air around the band, and when they stopped walking, they quickly kindled fires and swished and swatted leafy branches. The irritating insects relented only during the cool of night and when it rained. The biting pests were worst when the band was in camp or resting, so they kept moving when they could and never camped twice in the same place.

The palms they had felled six weeks earlier had not yet lost their fronds, but bacteria had invaded their orange wood, which softened it, consumed the sugars, and fermented them; when opened, the palms exuded a strong smell like silage or sour mash. The long, needle-nosed palm beetles, from whose thorax the Aché sometimes made hard, shiny black beads to string alternately on necklaces with the white incisors or canines of monkeys, had completed their task. In the hollowed-out cavities where Aché had pounded the palm wood into fiber, and in small notches they had cut especially to facilitate the insects' desires, they had laid their eggs. When the eggs hatched, the larvae bored into the softening wood, eating their way deeper and deeper into the moist trunks.

Armadillo sunk her axe into the decaying wood of a felled palm. She remembered cutting this tree herself weeks before because it had caught in the crotch between the rising trunks of two young cedar trees, and she had had to cut one of them to get the palm to fall to the ground. She chopped three times across the grain of the fallen tree, then split it lengthwise for several feet; dropping the axe, she pulled the tree open with her hands. Inside were the tunnels made by the palm-beetle larvae, and she ran her fingers along them: feeling, inspecting, taking the larvae if there were any. She broke off pieces of the wood, looked at them, and felt for larvae in the fibrous balls lodged in some of the tunnels. The larvae were long and fat—the size of her thumb—and yellow with hard, reddish-brown heads and massive pinching jaws for chewing their way through wood. They moved with wavelike ripples running through their waxen bodies when she pulled them from their sanctuary. She pinched each one's head as she found it and threw it to the side in a pile.

Monkey played as her mother worked, and Armadillo let her eat a larva when she was tired or grouchy from being bitten by the predatory insects. When Armadillo had searched all the cracks and tunnels in the opened section of the tree, she took her axe and opened another. When she reached the end of the tree, or a place where the larvae had not yet penetrated, she stopped, gathered her bounty, put them in a bamboo basket, and moved on.

Armadillo went to another downed palm, knelt beside it, and put her ear to the bark to listen for the sounds of larvae chewing through the wood. Satisfied with what she heard, she had just started chopping to cut the palm open when Deer walked up. Her daughter, Rabbit, ran to Monkey and tumbled to the ground beside her. The little girls played with their arms draped around each other, laughing and happy.

"The larvae are nice and fat," Deer said as she leaned her basket against the fronds of Armadillo's palm. "I wish we had cut more trees when we were here before. We will finish the larvae by tomorrow."

Armadillo worked her axe free from the wood and straightened up. She took a slow breath and let the axe slide through her hands until the head rested on the ground by her feet. She raised one arm, wiped her forehead, turned to her sister, and smiled.

"If we had had these sharp Apa axes, we could have cut all the palms," she said, reaching across her shoulder to scratch her back. "We had only that sad old stone axe when we cut these palms, and we still cut many of them."

"We will cut more this time so we can have palm-fiber broth to cook these good larvae in, and the children of the larvae that escape will be our food when we return," Deer said.

"We don't need to worry about having enough axes," Armadillo said, swinging hers up and cleaning the bits of drying wood from its face. "The axes we have now are the best I have ever seen or used. They cut cleanly and quickly, even in hard wood."

"I'm not worried about axes; I'm worried about my sister," Deer said. "I'm worried that someone will hurt her."

"I am in no danger," Armadillo said. "Snake will not have the rage. He will not hurt me."

"I thought he would have the rage when you told the band you were pregnant," Deer said. "I thought he would try to kill Turtle and then you. Anteater thought so, too. He reached for his bow."

"Snake already knew. So did everyone else," Armadillo said. "Snake knew a long time ago. He saw me in the forest alone, and I told him. He was angry, but he didn't have the rage. He knows why I did it. He is angry, but he understands."

"Why is he so nice to Turtle?" Deer asked. "He acts as if he would be happy to let Turtle have you. Yesterday I heard him say that he was tired of being married. He said he wished some man would take his wife so he could look for a new one."

"All men say things like that," said Armadillo, laying the axe on the ground and sitting on the log beside her sister. "He pretends he doesn't care so no one will think he is weak."

"I know that," answered Deer, "but I know Snake. If he really doesn't care about losing you, if he is tired of competing with Turtle, then he may beat you. And if he wants to keep you, he will end up fighting Turtle."

"Snake wants to keep me; I know that," Armadillo said. "I don't think he'll beat me, and I know he won't hurt Monkey or Catfish. But Turtle may, and that's why I am nice to Turtle."

"But Snake is strong," said Deer. "Anteater thinks that Snake will either have to lose you or fight Turtle. Snake is a good fighter. He may beat Turtle. Anteater thinks he should fight him. Anteater would help him."

"Snake is strong," answered Armadillo, "but Turtle is the strongest Aché. All Aché know about Turtle, and they all listen to him. Turtle's band is strong, and we need a strong band."

"But Turtle is so mean," said Deer, looking at her hands. "He is mean to Anteater and Monkey and Snake."

"Snake doesn't want a fight," said Armadillo. "He knows our

children may be hurt. He knows the band would be destroyed, and we need a good band, a strong band."

Deer looked down at Armadillo's feet. "The band would be strong without Turtle. Snake is strong; Aché listen to him. The band would be stronger without Turtle, better without him."

"The band would die without Turtle," Armadillo said, reaching to brush a mosquito from Deer's shoulder. "Snake knows that. If Snake killed Turtle, Blackbird would kill him. Anteater would kill Blackbird, and Jamo Paca would kill Anteater. Then we would all die. Snake is angry with Turtle, and he is not afraid, but if he killed Turtle, he knows he would kill the band, kill his family."

Deer sat on the palm log and picked at a scab on her ankle. She was afraid of Turtle. He taunted her husband by calling him Sores for the wounds on his back that would not heal. He had killed her daughter, and yet she deferred to him, was nice to him, flirted with him. She knew why Snake didn't kill Turtle, but she wished he would. The band was alive and strong—held together by kinship and common needs—but also by fear.

"We should leave the band," Deer said suddenly. "We should leave Turtle's band. We don't need Turtle."

"I don't know," said Armadillo, slowly scratching her leg and looking at the ground. "I don't know."

The invitation to clubfight came that evening at dusk, just after the men arrived, and it was unexpected because they thought Bushdog's band was south of them. The larvae cooked in the metal pot and the earthen bowls with palm-fiber broth, concentrating into a thick lumpy stew, and the children tasted it with palm-wood brushes; they also took larvae that were not in the stew and roasted them. They pinched off the heads, threw them away, and ate the larvae that were soft and sweet inside with tough and rubbery skins. Their mothers told them not to eat too many because their teeth would turn brown and fall out.

Mosquitoes were everywhere, and the Aché made smoky fires, sat close to them, and swatted themselves with leaves. Despite having lived with the annoyance of biting insects every day of their lives with no real relief, they were irritated, and the babies cried more than usual; the children ran when they played and sat close to the fires when they stopped.

The men arrived from hunting, and they were tired. They had run a long way after peccaries and gotten two. Then they had come upon a jaguar and her cub feeding on a freshly killed peccary; when they approached, the jaguar ran away, and the cub climbed a dead, broken tree, and Coati pierced it with an arrow. As they carried the two peccaries, the baby jaguar, and a leg from the jaguar's peccary back to camp, Jamo Paca angrily told Coati that he shouldn't have killed the baby jaguar if he couldn't kill the mother, too, because she would look for her baby, smell it with the Aché, and come to the camp and kill someone. The men carried the game to camp through thorny, slashing, ugly forest, and they were weary when they arrived.

The quiet of the camp while the men wound down from hunting made the rising breeze seem loud, and when the quiet time was over and the cooking was about to begin, Blackbird stood and took a machete.

"The rain is coming," he said, turning toward the forest. "We should make a house."

Before he reached the forest, they heard the call:

"Hoo, hoo, Aché. The time has come to clubfight. Bushdog is ready to clubfight. Rat is ready to clubfight. The clubfight will happen. The place to clubfight will be made. The Aché will clubfight."

"My brother, Peccary, who was called Big Beard and is now dead, killed two baby jaguars in the forest near the Big Lake—tiny baby jaguars that still had their milk teeth. He did not need to pierce them with an arrow because they were so small; he clubbed them with his bow. When he found them, he called me, and when I got there, they were dead, and he was sitting by the hole between the roots of a dead red tree where the jaguar had its house." Ocelot paused while he reached across his chest and scratched the back of his arm.

"'You shouldn't have killed the babies,' I told him, 'because the mother will be angry; she will come and cut you open with her claws, and bite the back of your neck, and kill you.' Big Beard just laughed. 'Those are stories the grandfathers tell because they are afraid of jaguars,' he said, and he tied a vine around the baby jaguars' heads and carried them over his shoulder.

"In the camp, he skinned the jaguars, rubbed ashes on the skins, and built a rack over a small fire to smoke them dry so he could make a hat. He wanted a jaguar hat like the one Short Anteater wore when he was a famous man. Big Beard talked about the hat while he skinned the jaguars, and we ate the meat; it was juicy and good, and Big Beard worked until past dark smoking and drying the jaguar skins. He had his son hold a burning stick so he could see what he was doing, and when he was finished and the fires had burned down, it was very dark. There was no moon, and there were no clouds to make the sky lighter; everything was dark.

"While we were sleeping, a sound came from the forest, and we all heard it. The sound was not a jaguar calling but a branch breaking and leaves shaking. We listened and were ready because we had heard the stories about jaguar mothers, and we could all smell the smoking skins of the baby jaguars.

"There was silence in the forest, and we sat listening and trying to look, but the only thing that we could see were the coals glowing in the fires. I tried to see a tree that was near my fire, and I could not even see that far; that's how dark it was. I held my son, Coati, between my legs." Ocelot looked for a moment at Coati, who was now taller and stronger than his father, and continued.

"When the jaguar came, we heard it pounce, and we knew what it was because it growled as it jumped, but we couldn't see it. I heard it behind me on the other side of camp, and then I heard Toucan scream. He screamed, and we could hear him fighting the jaguar. Then everyone in the camp was yelling and crying and trying to get away, and we could hear the jaguar and Toucan wrestling in the brush; the sound got farther away, and Toucan stopped screaming, and the forest was quiet except for the children and women crying and the men yelling and trying to find their bows and arrows. We built up the fires, and all night we sat together in the middle of the camp. The jaguar came back twice, and we could hear it walking around the camp. We heard it coughing—'*unnhhhh, unnhhhh,*'—all night, and it didn't go away until the light came.

"In the morning, we found Toucan and his belly was open, and his guts were eaten; his face was also eaten along with part of his legs and his ass. Toucan was a strong man, but he was no better at fighting a jaguar at night than a baby would have been." Ocelot finished his story, brought the piece of roast peccary he held in his hand to his mouth, and resumed eating.

Catfish looked through the rain dripping from the roof of the shelter, but he was not worried about jaguars coming into camp. The baby jaguar was gone—eaten—and the rain made him feel safe.

The call for the clubfight surprised the band, coming when it did, but when the voice sounded—high pitched and diffuse through the forest—they knew who was calling and what he would say. They knew the changes the call would bring, and the first cry hit each of them quickly and hard in the chest with adrenaline. The violence and fear and pain of a clubfight came to them without warning as they thought of roast peccary, baby jaguars, and shelter from the rain. The men listened with cold eyes and frozen, tight bodies and faces while the women drew their breath, looked at each other, and shared their concern. The older children sat quietly and fidgeted, and the younger ones squirmed and turned to their mothers.

When the forest was again filled only with the cries of birds and insects and the soothing noise of the wind, Jamo stood. He cupped his hands by his mouth, faced the caller, and answered the invitation. "We are ready to clubfight," he called. "Turtle is ready. Blackbird is ready. Snake is ready. Turtle's band is ready to clubfight. When the place to clubfight has been made, we will come. We are ready."

The rain began as Jamo finished his call, and he remained standing. Blackbird stood where he had stopped at the edge of the camp, holding the machete. The band was quiet, but everyone's heart was racing. When Blackbird turned and walked into the forest, others followed; the men attacked the palms and saplings with uncalled-for savagery, and the shelter was constructed quickly and without conversation. The band made roasting racks and butchered the game mechanically, and the rain was heavy and cool and loud. Each Aché worked alone and was insulated by the sound and the wetness. When the storm weakened, Ocelot told his story, and when he had finished, thunder sounded all around them, lightning strobe-lit the dark forest for a second or two at a time, and the Aché alternately saw smooth, empty darkness and a brightly lit jungle sharper than daylight in the clear white electrical illumination. Ocelot's story did not take their minds from Bushdog and his band, and the storm further swept away fears of jaguars.

The Aché faced daily the possibility of death and pain, and they faced it the way they had to—taking each step as it came, fighting battles when they had no choice, running when flight was the best alternative, killing when it was necessary, and controlling fear, for fear can cripple, fear can defeat. The most constricting fear—greater than the fear of a painful death from snakebite or quick and savage butchery by a jaguar—was fear of those like them: the unknown and powerful Apa, but more than that—much more than that—fear of those most like them, those who lived the lives they did, who shared their strengths and matched them, the most respected enemy, their friends, their relatives, the masters of the forest: the Aché.

A young boy looked forward to becoming a man, a hunter, with anticipation and relish, for despite the hardships, rigors, and dangers of the hunt, there were also praise, esteem, and the exhilaration of hunting: the straining, pumping abandon of pursuit and the pride of success. He faced the prospect of his lip piercing and scarring ceremonies with acceptance and a sense of challenge, certainly with slight weakness and a shudder when he thought of the pain he would face, but he knew it would bring freedom—this graduation to adulthood—freedom to be an adult, sexually active, and fully and finally Aché.

His journey to adulthood was also one to the clubfight arena, where he would be most severely tested; where even the greatest and strongest were beaten and scarred; where prestige was gained and as easily lost; where men were tested against men; where the goal was to survive, beat, and punish but not to kill; where more pain was inflicted in a short time than in any other endeavor. A boy watched his father and uncles and men he knew and respected, men who ran toward jaguars and killed them at close range, men who abandoned fears of pain daily to survive in the jungle; he saw these men grow quiet and serious when they spoke of a clubfight. He heard the terror in their voices, thinly disguised, and he knew that of all of the trials an Aché man faced, the clubfight was the greatest, for it tried him against his peers, his greatest competitors.

When the Aché spoke of clubfights, they talked of the spectacle or visiting Aché they had not recently seen, of the food they gathered and hunted in quantity, and of the recuperation of the fighters. But they rarely talked about the fight itself, for each had memories that were less than pleasant: a man fighting poorly, a brother's eye hanging on his cheek, a cousin's severed ear, deep bleeding scalp wounds that would not stop, fractured skulls and damaged brains, those who were never the same and those who had died. The clubfight was central to the interaction among Aché bands and the competition among men, and it terrified them all.

Catfish snuggled closer to his father. The family nestled together against the chill on Armadillo's twilled, palm-frond mat. Snake lay closest to the edge of the shelter with his feet toward the fire, and Armadillo lay with her head near the smoldering logs, over which a blanket of peccary skin with attached meat slowly cooked. She tended the fire to keep it going in the spattering rain. Between them were Catfish and Monkey, pressed on both sides by the warm and protective bodies of their parents. Catfish put his head on his father's thigh and felt Snake's easy breathing. Snake rested his hand on Catfish's hip, and he felt secure and safe.

Catfish knew that Snake had never known that feeling of security. He had had no parents to shield him from the cold on rainy nights, no mother to groom him and hold him close, no father to make him a bow and teach him to hunt, no loving knees to huddle between when a jaguar stalked the camp or a man savaged the band with the rage, no strong and solid barrier between him and the world who would allow no harm to come to a child. Catfish knew that not many orphans survived and that his father was exceptional.

He knew his father was two people, as all Aché must be. The warm and gentle man to whom he went for comfort could in an instant unleash fantastic, furious energy that could not be diverted, single-minded abandon necessary for being a good hunter, and even more, evolutionary reserve needed to fight with everything. It was the same reserve that enabled a crippled coati to drag herself to attack a hunter taking her young, a reserve honed to razor sharpness by necessity in those who live in the jungle and stropped to even greater intensity in an orphan like Snake. Snake had proven himself as a hunter and a clubfighter, and Catfish knew that each time the men entered the forest to pursue game or faced each other—painted and adorned in the clubfight arena—Snake was still an orphan and, ultimately, alone. In hunting and fighting, brothers and cousins counted more than strength and cunning. Catfish knew that Snake would be alone in the clubfight arena, and he was afraid.

Catfish felt Snake's deep, easy breathing change and his muscles tense and then relax. He could feel in his father the planning, the imagining, and he knew Snake was clubfighting. Snake had told Catfish that when he sat quietly before a hunt, he saw the jungle and the game, and he took himself there and hunted in his mind; when the men rested after hunting, he saw the hunt again and remembered what had gone well and what had not; then he went there in his mind and changed the mistakes so he would not make them again. Catfish could feel Snake going to the clubfight in his mind, and Catfish went there, too, a little boy lying on the forest floor in a rainstorm—painted and strong—being the brother his father didn't have.

19 ☰ PREPARATION

When Jamo Paca went each evening to the ridgetop at the head of a gently sloping valley to call to the grandfathers of Bushdog's band, Catfish and Otter and Puma went with him. The boys stayed close to the wiry old man and were quiet when they neared the ridge. They pointed out places where someone had passed, and they felt the excitement of being near other people—other Aché. They were careful but not afraid.

When they reached the ridgetop, Jamo called toward Bushdog's camp: "Is the clearing ready? Is it time for the clubfight?" They listened quietly for the response, wondering if the time had come, hearts beating too loudly for them to hear perfectly, believing that the men from Bushdog's band would need more time to cut and clear a spot in the forest big enough for the clubfight. Clearing the dense hardwood forest is a formidable task—nearly impossible with stone axes—a characteristic that had kept the farming Guaraní away for hundreds of years. Only with metal tools, increasing prices for lumber, and land scarcity was the home of the Aché becoming attractive to outsiders.

For days the boys followed the grandfather to the ridge to call to the elders of Bushdog's band, knowing that each day the likelihood that the clearing would be ready increased. Turtle's band moved camp only three times while they waited, and they did not travel far, only enough distance to escape the gnats and mosquitoes and foul smells that infested a longer-term camp. The men hunted to the south so they would not interfere with the hunters from the other band, and they ranged a long way, hunting peccaries. Often they arrived after dark, carrying game slung over their shoulders, game they would not have ordinarily transported this far since the band could have moved to the kill site.

After a few days, they intensified their efforts, and what meat they brought in addition to what was eaten they kept suspended on racks over smoky fires, preserving it as best they could in the humid jungle. The band needed to carry as much meat as possible to the clubfight both to impress Bushdog's people and also have food when the men were tired and injured after the contest.

The men also worked hard making the special fighting clubs they would wield when they faced Bushdog's band in the arena. They cut long staves from the same hardwood they used for the heads of their arrows, and they shaped them carefully with punctured land-snail shells, holding the wood against the flat of one foot as they sat cross-legged on the ground, planing the wood with even, repetitive strokes, and accumulating great piles of fine shavings in front of them. The clubs were five or six feet long, as thick as a man's wrist, flattened from midway up the shaft, sharp on the edges like a long-handled wooden sword, and pointed at the tip. The men spent long hours each evening working on their clubs—shaping them, heating them in fires to harden and straighten them, and decorating them with lines and dots and stripes of beeswax and charcoal. When a man stood in the camp and tested his weapon—holding it with hands spread and swinging it down onto the scalp of an imaginary opponent—the club flexed and whistled through the air, drawing everyone's attention.

The women were busy, too. They chopped palms and gathered fruit, and they tended the meat piled high over smoking fires. They also looked for *genipa* fruit, which when ripe was sometimes cooked in a pot or an armadillo carapace and eaten but was now reserved for painting the bodies of everyone in the band. The necessities of life in the jungle had to be attended to—as they were every day of every Aché's life—and the added tasks of preparing for an important event kept everyone very busy.

The boys smeared themselves with charcoal and staged clubfights of their own in a small open spot near the creek that wandered quietly through the forest below the ridge that temporarily separated the two bands. They made clubs from finger-thick bamboo that grew along the banks of the stream and chanted and yelled and fought with great intensity. Catfish earned his first clubfight scar when Puma rapped him hard on the scalp after he had swung at the older boy and was off balance. Catfish saw a flash, and for a moment could not see at all; then Puma struck him again, and he went down. Catfish rose quickly and began swinging wildly, but he could not find Puma, and the other boys stopped fighting, and the girls who had been watching laughed. Blood trickled into Catfish's right eye, and he stopped when he heard the laughing and laughed, too.

"Don't hit him again, Puma," Otter cried, joking. "You might kill him, and we would not feed you, and you would starve."

"I won't kill him," Puma said. "I'll just show him how strong a real Aché is. I will teach him how to clubfight."

Puma raised his club as if to strike Catfish again. Catfish was still slightly dazed, and when he saw Puma raise his club, he swung his own in a counterattack, striking Puma across his cheek and ear. Puma whirled away, dropping his club and holding his hands to his face. Catfish lunged toward the taller boy and raised his club to strike again, but Otter and Duck rushed and grabbed him.

"Stop, Catfish," they cried. "Puma was joking; he wasn't going to hit you. Stop."

Catfish stood still, and Puma turned to face him. A welt across his face and a few drops of blood on his ear marked the spot where the blow had landed. Puma scowled at Catfish, and for the first time since starting their game, the younger boy was afraid.

"I thought you were still fighting," he said. "I thought you were going to hit me again."

Puma grinned. "It doesn't matter. We both have scars. We are both clubfighters. When the penises in Bushdog's band see our clubfight scars, they will know we are Aché, and they will be afraid of us. They will know we are strong and *chija*."

The children left their clubfight arena, went to the stream, and made knives from the cane that grew there; then they carefully shaved their heads, leaving a strip of erect hair along the crest of the scalp with a tuft of longer hair falling over their foreheads like very short bangs. All the while they talked excitedly of meeting the boys from Bushdog's band.

≡

The light, intermittent rain that fell on the ninth day after they had received the invitation to clubfight was not enough to keep the band in camp. The men left early to hunt capybara along the banks of a large stream not far from the meadow where they had killed the giant anteater and seen the tracks of Bushdog's band weeks before. The women and children stayed close to camp and spent much of the time under the shelters, catching drippings from the smoking meat in pots to mix with charcoal and honey to decorate themselves before they went to the clubfight. They painted each other with the juice of the genipa fruit, drawing lines and swirls and spots on their faces and bodies with the clear liquid that gradually stained the skin a deep black color that did not wash off and remained for weeks.

Armadillo painted Catfish with genipa from just below his eyes down to the center of his torso, including his neck and upper arms. She covered his stomach, back, and legs with large round dots. When the juice had stained his skin, Catfish looked as if he were wearing a black mask that covered his mouth and a black turtleneck that stopped short of his belly. She painted Monkey with thin vertical lines on her face, arms, torso, and legs. The children loved to be painted because it made them feel different, larger, stronger—more Aché.

Late in the afternoon, the boys stole away and went to the place where for days they had heard the axes of Bushdog's band chopping. The forest was silent today, and the boys crept quietly through the wet vegetation. Well before they reached the clearing, they knew it was large from the light ahead. Bushdog's band had begun in a small natural open area and cleared away from it. They had removed all the brush and smaller trees from an area fifty yards on a side and had cut a number of very large trees on the perimeter so they fell away from the center and took other trees with them, opening up the forest and allowing light to penetrate as if it focused on the arena. Not even a stump remained in the barren arena, and what most impressed the boys was the bare earth: cleared of every branch, leaf, and stem, it showed naked and red, surrounded by the gradually rising forest like a bowl cut in the jungle. In the center of the bowl was the arena—stark to eyes accustomed to the forest—where soon their fathers would compete in a deadly display. When the boys saw a man stepping over a log on the far side of the clearing, they turned and slipped back into the dark, damp protective cover of the forest and returned to camp, where they told their mothers what they had seen, and everyone knew that the clubfight was imminent.

Shortly before dark, Armadillo went to the stream for water, and as she stood after filling her beeswax-covered water basket, she heard a noise in the brush and saw Turtle step from behind a branch. He smiled and went to her. He touched her breasts and put his hand between her legs. Armadillo did not look at him but allowed him to continue, and shortly she lay down on the bank of the stream and raised her legs. Turtle covered her, and they made silent, harsh love. When he had finished, they stood, and Turtle faced Armadillo, but she looked away.

"You should leave Snake and be my wife," he said. "I am strong; I am chija. I want you for my wife. Your children will be safe if you marry me."

"Snake is strong," Armadillo said, still looking away. "I want Snake for my husband. I don't want to be your wife."

"Turtle is the greatest of all Aché, the strongest of all Aché. I want you. Leave Snake. You are not happy. Your children are not happy. Leave Snake and be my wife."

"I love Snake. He is a good father and husband, a strong man. I love Snake, and I do not love you."

"Snake will find another wife. He will leave our band and find another. I do not want Snake in my band, and I want you for my wife. Marry me, and I will not have to punish Snake."

"I don't know," Armadillo murmured.

"If you try to leave this band—to run away with Snake—something may happen to your children."

"Go walk in the forest, Turtle. I do not want to be your wife. I want to be Snake's wife."

"When we have the clubfight, you will see who is the strongest man. I will smash Snake's head. I will put him on his knees. I will pound Snake and make him bleed, and you will know who is the best husband. Then you will marry me. You will see. I will pound him the way women crush palm fiber. I will smash your husband, and then you will marry me."

He turned and disappeared quickly into the forest.

Armadillo reached camp slightly before Turtle, and they were both quick to notice that only two band members were absent: Snake and Turtle's wife, Parrot. When the two arrived only minutes apart, Armadillo was slightly amused to see the expression on Turtle's face, as if he had had a thought that had never crossed his mind before—an idea he was not prepared for and didn't quite know what to do with.

When Jamo Paca arrived in camp after calling to Bushdog's people, he confirmed what the band already knew.

"I have spoken with the grandfathers of Bushdog's band," he said. "The clubfight arena is ready. We will move our camp there tomorrow."

"My cousin's baby should be big by now," piped Frog. "When I saw her last, we were both pregnant. Her baby should be as big as . . ."

Frog ended her half sentence with a whimper and looked at the ground as she remembered her baby that the Apa had stolen.

"The clubfight will be large," said Jamo, interrupting the silence. "Short Foot's band will be arriving. Caiman Short Foot's band will clubfight, too."

"*Taaaa*," said Blackbird, wide eyed and wordless as he often was.

"Caiman Short Foot's band is big," said Turtle. "There will be many men in the clubfight. This will be a good clubfight." Turtle stood, walked out from under the roof of the shelter, and picked up his fighting club. He raised it above his head and swung it down hard onto the palm-frond thatching above Snake's head. He swung again and again, striking the fronds just enough to make a slice where his club hit before pulling back. "There will be many Aché, many heads to split." He stood, looked for a brief second at Snake, and returned to his fire.

≡

Preparations for their arrival at the clubfight consumed the band's next morning. The Aché decorated their bodies with shiny black paint made of finely powdered charcoal mixed with honey, water, and grease, and each person's adornment was unique. Snake was painted the way Catfish had been stained with *genipa:* his chest, shoulders, neck, upper back, and lower face were blackened, and dots covered his limbs and lower torso. Armadillo was painted with straight lines arranged as chevrons, converging at her midline. Turtle's body was quartered with opposing solids and stripes. Jamo was painted nearly solid black with only a few small circles of unpainted skin showing. Little Monkey was covered with large spots, and her cousin, Rabbit's, arms, legs, and torso were encircled by rings of numerous stripes.

The paint shone glossy and wet, and although the men would create even-more-resplendent adornment just before the clubfight, everyone was finely decorated. When every person's designs had been checked, touched up, and approved to his or her satisfaction, the band packed food and belongings and crossed the short physical, but great social, distance to Bushdog's camp.

The sun shone brightly and heavily on the painted band as they crossed the open arena. They could feel the assessing eyes of those who watched from the shadows, and they walked stiffly like children on a stage, sometimes forgetting to move their arms; their joints appeared to have become arthritic, and the clearing seemed immense. Drifting smoke in the trees at the far end directed them to the camp, and once within the wall of the jungle—free from the heat and the unobstructed view of others—they felt more at ease.

Dappled light illuminated the smoky camp set a dozen yards back from the edge of the clearing. Members of Bushdog's band converged near the camp and watched passively as the arriving band chose a spot adjacent to theirs, lay down their burdens, and began clearing away the brush. The boldest of the hosts were the children, who came close and whose uninhibited stares and smiles were irresistible to Catfish and his friends. Leaving their parents even before the work had begun, the boys and girls went grinning and excited to meet their peers. The children approached each other with little trepidation, eager to satiate their curiosity and indulge in the social interaction they so rarely experienced.

At the edge of the camp, a pudgy, three-year-old boy beamed at the arriving band. He struck absentmindedly at the trunk of a slender tree with a stick, swaying awkwardly with each stroke. From his shaved head bulged a golf ball–sized bump that housed a growing botfly larva, and he reached every few seconds with his free hand to touch the tender spot. When Monkey saw the boy, she turned to face him, and he shyly stepped backward on his baby legs that had not yet learned to bend properly. As soon as his foot touched the ground, he collapsed, screamed, and rolled on his back, holding his foot in his hands.

From behind him, a girl quickly darted to his aid and announced that he had been stung by a velvet ant, which is not really an ant but a flightless wasp. To the girl's short-cropped hair clung a young capuchin monkey that rode her head like a furry cap. She comforted the boy while she coolly picked up the stick he had been playing with and smashed the fast-moving orange insect, whose sting is twice as painful as a bee's. When the child's mother arrived, his cries began to subside. The children from Turtle's band crowded around and watched closely, and soon they were joined by other children from the camp. The girl whose pet monkey clutched her hair the way it would have its mother's was named Margay, and Catfish could not turn his eyes from her.

Soon the children of both bands were off in the forest playing noisily. Several women of Bushdog's band approached the new arrivals, and after a minimal amount of clearing had taken place, the women of Turtle's band left their belongings and joined them. Frog's cousin was there cradling her baby, and so were some women who were distantly related to Turtle's wife, Parrot. The women all knew each other, or had at least seen each other, and they had many common friends and relatives by blood and marriage; they quickly erupted in conversation that only stopped for short interruptions until they parted after the clubfight.

Of great interest were the new axes and machetes, and when the tools were retrieved from burden baskets and passed around, the men of Bushdog's band came to look. After some initial shyness, the men retired to the edge of the clubfight arena, where they stood close together and touched when they talked; they discussed the Apa, hunting, women, battles, hunting, the big, two-headed Apa bird, women, and hunting.

In the middle of the afternoon, several children sprinted to the edge of camp. "Short Foot's band is arriving," they cried. "There are very many people." Conversation broke off as the men and women, who had fragmented into small groups, craned their necks to view the arriving guests. As the band entered the camp—painted and walking quietly in line, emerging one-by-one from the curtain of vegetation—there seemed to be no end to them. With nearly fifty people, Caiman Short Foot's group was one of the largest Aché bands, and their arrival pushed the population of the gathering to one hundred. Rarely did so many Aché gather in one place, and it was, especially for the children, a very exciting time.

Catfish watched from the branches of a sour-orange tree, where he had climbed with Puma and Margay. He recognized some of the people, not because he remembered seeing them but because of the stories he had heard, tales that often emphasized a peculiarity or distinctive characteristic of a person and provided a source of nicknames. Caiman Short Foot walked with a severe limp and was well known among the Aché because—despite his broken and twisted foot—he was a good hunter who was especially talented at locating and digging armadillos from their burrows.

Catfish also recognized the White sisters, three Aché women who had exceptionally light skin and were considered beautiful. He knew that two women in Short Foot's band were related to his mother's father, but Catfish had never seen them, so he looked at each woman as she passed to see if he could tell which were his relatives. He instantly recognized the man called Bearded Paca, a man whose beard was unusually thick for an Aché and who distinguished himself by carrying not a bow, but a burden basket; he did not hunt with the men but stayed with the women and children, gathering fruit and pounding palm fiber, and had never taken a wife. Catfish watched him closely because Bearded Paca was tall and strong, and to see him walking like a woman and carrying a basket seemed incongruous and strange.

The members of Turtle's band enjoyed a certain celebrity as a result of their recent dealings with the Apa and particularly because of the bounty they had reaped in their raid on the logging cart. Turtle had a reputation as a strong and combative man, and he was one of the best-known Aché, even to bands that had never encountered his. Turtle relished the opportunity to tell of his exploits and impress new people with his tales of daring. For much of the afternoon, an attentive audience seated on fallen trees and beside fires followed his bold gestures and excited, creative descriptions of his war with the Apa.

"Some men in my band are afraid of the Apa," he said, glancing briefly at Anteater. "They want to run and hide in the forest. They think the Apa will go away. They think that hiding in the forest like the deer will keep their families safe. They are afraid to fight the Apa. They want metal axes but are afraid to take them from the Apa. There are many Aché who are afraid, who wish the Apa would go away." Turtle looked at those gathered around him, pausing for a moment when he faced Short Foot, who was as well known among the Aché for his reluctance to confront the Apa as Turtle was for his violent zeal.

"When we attacked the Apa and pierced them with arrows and killed their strangehorns, they cried like babies. They died fast like soft rodents. The Apa are not strong like the Aché, and they will run if we hunt them. We are Aché; we are *chija*; we are strong, and we can kill the Apa. We will kill them and take their thunder. We take their axes and machetes, don't we? We will take their thunder, and then they will run from us. We will take their thunder and chase the Apa from the forest. We will chase them from the good forest, and the mountains, and the rivers, and the meadows. Turtle will chase them. He will take their thunder, and then every Apa will fear Turtle."

Turtle picked up an axe and pointed the handle at the forest. "*Choooom*," he shouted, mimicking the thunder. "*Choooom, choooom, choooom*." He ran around the camp, shooting the axe into the air, pointing it at people, and shooting it at them. When he came near the fat boy with the botfly larva on his head, the baby screamed and ran crying to his mother. Two teenage boys giggled at Turtle's antics and were silenced by a stern look from Jamo Currasow, a grandfather from Bushdog's band. The men who had been listening began to get up and wander off, and each of them knew that Turtle had reestablished himself as an Aché to be taken seriously, an Aché who played hard, an Aché who could dominate others and loved doing so.

In the forest, the penises and premenstrual girls played chasing and climbing games with great energy, squealing and laughing. They greatly enjoyed the pleasures of their age, when boys and girls are close in size, strength, and shape while all are keenly aware of the attractions that are beginning to grow between them. They knew that the older boys—those who would soon have their lips pierced—and the girls who had begun menstruating were playing their own games, spending much of their time in the forest away from the adults who would try to curtail their fun. Catfish and Margay had silently watched Coati—already a marriageable young man—and a young, nearly adult girl named Macaw slip away together into the thick ferns near a slow place in the creek, and they had looked at each other and grinned when they had seen the ferns shake back and forth.

Near a shallow, sandy-bottomed stretch of the stream, the children stopped their play to forage in a purple-fruit tree. When they had eaten and their hands and faces were streaked with juice, they went to the stream and splashed and washed. Some of the boys took their bows and arrows and began following the stream bank to look for fish. Catfish saw the glint of scales in a shaft of sunlight near the far edge of the stream, crept high on a log for a better angle, and pierced a foot-long, golden-sided fish with his first arrow. Otter and the other boys congratulated him and put their fingers in the arrow hole, and Margay wanted to carry it.

Not wanting to be outdone by a younger boy, Puma and a boy

from Short Foot's band named Dove challenged the other boys to a shooting contest. "We'll go to the sour-orange tree where we ate the purple fruit, and we'll show the little penises how to shoot," they said, and they led the way back along the stream to the tree. Puma shot first at a sour orange hanging only ten feet above the ground. Sometimes a very close shot is more difficult than one just a little bit longer, and Puma confidently drew his bow and pierced the green orange. Dove impaled a second orange, and the other boys followed, all successfully.

Otter was the first to miss. Aimed at an orange twenty-five feet above the ground, his arrow glanced off a low-hanging twig, clattered as it was deflected back and forth among the higher branches, and fell, scattering the children. Otter smiled and shrugged. As he retrieved his arrow, Dove neatly placed his between the guarding limbs and brought the orange down.

Puma's next shot was at a large orange that was well protected by foliage. For a moment, Catfish and the others could not see the orange he was aiming at. Puma's arrow flew true through the foliage but only brushed the orange. He snorted through his nostrils in disgust as he went to find his arrow. Dove was not able to repeat his previous clean shot, and he, too, missed, as did Otter and the two boys from Bushdog's band. When Catfish stepped forward to shoot, he noticed that Margay was watching him closely and smiling. He felt warm and slightly uncomfortable; he knew he wanted to impress the girl who was so dominating his attention. Catfish nocked his arrow, looked back at Margay, and noticed Dove standing beside her, frowning at him. The young monkey—still perched atop Margay's head—screeched loudly, and she laughed.

Catfish smiled, and when he looked up at the green sour orange—barely visible in the cloaking leaves—his mind cleared. He saw only his target and stepped forward, then edged to his left; when he drew his bowstring past his ear and held it there—adjusting for the angle—he did not quiver. His arrow clicked on his bow, and before it reached the lower branches of the tree, Catfish knew his aim had been good. The barbed arrow pierced the orange with the sound of a kiss, pulled it cleanly from its stem, and traveled in a steep arc unimpeded to the ground, where the arrow stuck, pinning the impaled fruit to the earth. Catfish looked at Margay, and she grinned at him, showing her teeth and squinting her eyes, still holding the fish. Dove and Puma looked at each other with disappointed faces and turned to leave, and the other children followed.

Catfish and Margay did not hurry. They walked toward the camp but took every opportunity to investigate a hollow log or the cry of a bird, or follow the meander of a dry streambed. When they stopped to drink at a hillside seep that filled a tiny basin and then trickled slowly into the ground, Margay sat and washed away the pieces of leaf and soil that now coated the fish.

"If we had fire, we could cook this nice fish and eat it," she said, dripping water from her hand onto the plump, large-scaled fish.

"I couldn't eat it," replied Catfish, "since I shot it. You could eat it, but I couldn't."

"I won't eat it," said Margay. "You should carry it to camp and give it to your mother. She will be proud to have a good hunter for a son."

"You keep it," said Catfish. "When you are my wife, I will bring all my game to you."

Margay smiled and took the pet monkey from her head to let it drink. "You will be a good father for our children," she said, and Catfish grinned. They moved together and touched each other—running their hands over each other's smooth skin—and they felt very close. Catfish touched Margay's still-boyish nipples very lightly with his fingertips, and she touched his. They lay quietly in the leaves, gently exploring each other's bodies, and they were very happy. They laughed when Margay's monkey leaped to her shoulder and cried shrilly as he pushed Catfish away with a dainty hand, and they left their hiding place when they heard the sound of children playing nearby.

21 ☰ STORYTELLING

"I'll have some of that meat," Howler Monkey said as he squatted by the fire.

Snake cut a hand-sized piece from the peccary shoulder he was carving and tossed it to Howler Monkey, who took it and began eating, slurpily sucking the juices. Snake distributed the rest of the meat to Turtle's camp, tossing or handing a large piece to someone at each fire, to be further divided among those who gathered around it. He kept a piece for his family and cut and tore it into five sections, one for each person in the family and one for Margay, who had been with them since the children had returned from playing. Armadillo put the fish Catfish had killed in the ashes and began eating. When Howler Monkey finished, he stood and stretched, looked around, and ambled toward the fires of Bushdog's camp.

Turtle's band had more meat than the others; Bushdog's men had been busy clearing the clubfight arena, and Short Foot's band had only learned of the fight two days before and had traveled directly to the gathering. Turtle's band shared its meat and enjoyed the prestige and attention that brought to the camp. They would share meat with any Aché who wanted it and asked because it was Aché to ask and Aché to give, and there was no Aché way to refuse a request.

The clubfight would not take place until more meat was brought into the large camp, and the men of all the bands planned to hunt in the morning. Most of the women were going to chop palms in a grove an hour's walk from the camp, and arrangements were already under way to form foraging groups. Women from Bushdog's and Short Foot's bands were anxious to attach themselves to those from Turtle's band so they could use the sharp steel axes. The two women from Short Foot's band who were Armadillo's relatives had already asked if they could go to the palm grove with Armadillo and Deer.

The evening fires of the three camps that were so close that they were actually one lit a greater expanse of the forest than Catfish had thought possible. For a boy accustomed to spending each night in a camp no larger than a room in a house, walled by the jungle, lit by low fires, and surrounded by thick, dangerous darkness, the open, clean, well-lighted place that was his to move around in, to visit, to play and listen in was wonderful. He ate at his parents' fire, and went with Margay to her parents' fire to eat palm fiber. When Jamo Currasow told the story of the Red Flood, Catfish went to Bushdog's camp and listened and was surprised to hear a version that was not exactly the same as the one he was familiar with. When Catfish heard Turtle describing the attack on the Apa logging cart, he followed the others who flocked to Turtle's camp to hear the famous man speak, and as he lay with Monkey between their parents, he thought of the Apa rising like the thick red water, driving the Aché from their camps, away from their home in the forest.

When Turtle finished, Frog told the story about losing her baby in the Apa attack on their camp. She described how frightened she was when she heard the thunder, and that when she ran, an Apa jumped from behind a bush, snatched her baby, and tried to grab her; then Anteater had shot an Apa in the mouth with an arrow and gotten shot in the back by the thunder. When a woman from Short Foot's band wanted to see the holes in Anteater's back, he turned so the light from the fire shone on them, and several people gathered to look.

"Anteater is a brave man to have shot the Apa," the woman said. "Frog is not even related to him, and he tried to save her baby. Anteater is *chija,* and he is the only man I know who has lived after being shot by the thunder."

"He is weak, and his back stinks," snorted Turtle. He is called Sores."

Those who had been listening turned and looked at Turtle, and he folded his arms and looked away.

"Only one man calls Anteater Sores," said Snake, angrily looking past Turtle into the forest. "No one else does."

Anteater turned to face his fire. He looked at his wife, Deer, and then into the fire. The sudden tension made him uncomfortable.

"Anteater went to help Turtle's sister-in-law," continued Snake, rising up on his elbow. "Anteater could have been safe, but he went back to help Frog. Others could have helped Frog, but they ran. Anteater could have run, but he didn't."

"I killed an Apa that morning," Turtle said loudly, getting to his feet. "I killed the first Apa, the one that shot Lizard."

The listeners were silent, and most of them looked at the ground.

"A man did kill an Apa that morning," Snake said. "And then he ran."

"Snake ran, too," said Turtle. "Snake didn't even shoot one arrow. He ran."

"Everybody ran," said Snake as if he were speaking to the low flames of the fire in front of him. "We all ran. But Anteater went back to save Turtle's sister-in-law and her baby, and he got pierced, and now Turtle calls him Sores."

Turtle appeared to be swelling because his anger was so great. He looked around at the faces in the camp, and when he saw his father, Jamo Paca very discreetly motioned with his eyes for Turtle to sit. Turtle clenched his teeth, making the muscles at the side of his jaw bulge. He sat down quickly and awkwardly, and Catfish thought he looked like an angry, but dangerous, child. Those listening were suddenly very uncomfortable because Turtle's silence meant that this was not a simple argument but a deeper, more serious conflict.

"The things that fly in the sky—those things we call giant bees—are not bees," Jamo began, retelling the story that had been related a dozen times already that day. "They are big, two-headed Apa birds, and they swoop down like eagles to catch Aché and carry them away."

Jamo's story brought calm to the camp, and when he had finished it, he began another. Catfish worried about what would happen between his father and Turtle, and he thought about the clubfight. He snuggled close between Snake and Monkey, and the warmth made him drowsy; soon he fell asleep. He woke several times to hear bits of the stories that were told long into the night, and he listened when men took turns singing the old songs; the sounds were good ones, and he slept well.

The morning dew was heavy and sounded like rain on the leaves of the jungle as it condensed and fell in drops from high branches. The Aché felt the moisture as fine, floating mist, and they sat close to their fires on a morning that reminded them that the cold season was coming. Meat from the racks that was becoming dry and tough was warmed, shared, and eaten, and the men and women prepared for a day of foraging. The men sharpened and straightened their arrows, and the women removed from their burden baskets those things they would not need on a short day trip into the forest. Babies cried, and their mothers comforted or nursed them. Fathers played with their children and laughed while they waited for others to finish their tasks.

Turtle came to Armadillo's fire and squatted beside Snake, and the two quietly discussed the day's hunt as if there were no tension between them. No one thought that strange, for whatever the problems between them, they were hunters in the same band, and the cooperation that kept a band together and strong and good for its members and their children was a way of life for these men. There were times and places to differ or fight with—perhaps to kill—another band member, and other times that required other approaches.

Snake and Turtle enjoyed hunting with each other because they were both superior hunters who brought success to those who were with them. Today they would return to a spot where they had tied down spoiled monkey meat in hopes of attracting vultures that they could kill for meat and the fine white down on their breasts that would decorate the men when they entered the clubfight arena. Turtle rested his hand on Snake's shoulder, and they talked into each other's ear; Catfish could hear them. They would also hunt tapir.

Hunting parties left the large camp in groups of two to five men, heading in different directions and departing when they were ready. Coati and Ocelot went with Ocelot's cousin, Rat, from Bushdog's band, and Anteater hunted with Howler Monkey and his brother. Two men from Short Foot's band wanted to hunt with Snake and Turtle, but when they asked, Turtle said, "I don't know" and looked away, which is the only way to say no in Aché. Snake and Turtle took only Blackbird and Bushdog with them, and when they were ready, the four slipped quietly away.

The women, like the men, made little effort to coordinate their foraging. They left in small groups, some to chop palms, some to gather philodendron fruit, and some to chop grubs from spiny palms; the rest would stay in camp. Armadillo and Deer unloaded their carrying baskets and hoisted them, adjusted the tumplines on their foreheads, took axes, called to their daughters, and walked into the forest. Their cousins met them near the edge of camp, and they headed together for the palm grove. Monkey and Rabbit walked close to their mothers, and the women from Short Foot's band followed, each carrying an infant in a sling and one with a toddler on her shoulders. Catfish and Otter ran after their mothers.

"We'll go with you," Catfish called, running slightly off balance as he tried to gather his arrows and grip them more tightly.

"Without Margay?" Armadillo exclaimed, turning and looking at her son. "My little penis would leave camp without bringing his wife?"

The women laughed, and Catfish smiled and looked at the ground. Then a branch cracked behind him, and Margay emerged from the vegetation. She stopped when she saw everyone looking at her and was uneasy when the laughter increased. She looked behind her to see if they were laughing at something she had not seen, and she straightened the strap of her newly made carrying basket with both hands when she once again faced the women. The monkey riding atop her head shrieked and looked about wild eyed when Margay shifted the tumpline to which he clung.

"We're not laughing at you, Margay," Armadillo said. "We're laughing at the penis who acts like your husband."

Margay looked at Catfish, and they smiled at each other with the corners of their mouths.

"That's the way all men are at first," said Deer. "They act the way husbands should until they are married, and then they act like penises."

The women laughed and resumed walking. The children fell into line behind them, and they walked with little talk to the palm grove.

The palms were thick and sweet, and the four women kept the axes busy felling trees, trimming fronds from the sheathed palm hearts, opening the trunks, and pounding great quantities of palm fiber. Guan and Tayra, the women from Short Foot's band who were cousins and both related to Deer and Armadillo through the sisters' deceased father, were astounded by the steel axes and asked to use them each time Deer or Armadillo stopped chopping for longer than a few seconds. Margay pounded palm fiber with Guan's stone axe from a tree that Deer felled, and she filled her basket while the little girls played near a small smoky fire, and the boys hunted.

When all the women but Tayra had filled their baskets, they rested by the fire and snacked on crisp, white palm heart. Tayra continued chopping, and they could also hear the sound of other axes working in the distance. Margay played with the little girls and made them laugh by propping her eyelids open with tiny strips of bamboo, giving her a bug-eyed look that thrilled Monkey and Rabbit and made them roll screaming on the ground each time they looked at her. When Tayra finished chopping, she joined the others, took a palm heart from her basket, and began stripping it.

"Your band brought a lot of meat to the clubfight," said Guan, picking a bit of crusty deposit from the corner of her baby's eye. "The men in Turtle's band are very good hunters."

"They hunted many days for that meat," said Armadillo. "Your band was walking, and the men couldn't hunt."

"We're hungry for meat," said Tayra. "We don't eat enough of it."

"There's never too much meat," said Armadillo, laughing.

"Our men don't bring enough meat. Our children cry for it," said Guan.

"But Short Foot's band is very large," said Deer. "You must have plenty to eat with so many men hunting each day."

"The band *is* large," replied Guan, "too large. We don't get enough to eat. With so many people, even a peccary doesn't fill us."

"The camp is so big that by the time meat reaches our fires, there isn't much left," added Tayra.

"With so many men hunting, there should be lots of game," said Armadillo, thoughtfully munching.

"Some of the men bring in much game," said Guan, glancing at Tayra, "but some provide less. Short Foot only hunts armadillos, and we hardly get any, and Bearded Paca doesn't hunt at all."

"Our husbands have been talking," said Tayra, looking back at Guan. "They were talking about joining your band, becoming part of Turtle's band."

"Your men are all good hunters," said Guan. "They bring much meat, and our husbands are good hunters, too. We are trail happy like you. Short Foot likes to stay in one place too long, so the men don't find enough game."

"We want to be with our cousins and their mother," said Tayra. "We don't want to stay with those stingy women in Short Foot's band." She spoke quickly and stopped short, as if she was afraid she had said too much.

Armadillo looked at Deer, slowly stripped the sheath from a piece of palm heart, and handed the sweet white center to Monkey. "Give some to Rabbit and Margay," she said to her daughter.

"We may be leaving Turtle's band," Deer said after a moment of thought. "We are not happy, and we may leave Turtle."

"Don't you get enough to eat?" asked Guan.

"We eat well," said Deer. "The men in our band bring much meat, and we are not hungry."

"Why do you want to leave?" asked Tayra. "If you leave, we won't have relatives in Turtle's band, and we don't know the others. We can't join Turtle's band if you leave."

"You have seen Turtle and Snake and Anteater," said Deer, almost crossly. "You were there last night. Turtle is angry almost all the time, and he is mean to Anteater. We are tired of being in Turtle's band."

"But Turtle is a famous man," said Guan. "He is chija, and he has a strong band. You could join Bushdog's band, but you have no relatives there. Short Foot's band is too large. You should stay with Turtle, and we will come, too. He is a famous man, and famous men are loud and strong. It is better to live with a loud man who is a good hunter like Turtle than with one who isn't even a man, like Bearded Paca."

"Anteater and I want to leave Turtle's band," said Deer, "and we want Armadillo and Snake to come with us. If we leave, you can join us."

Armadillo leaned back and took a slow breath. She brushed a mosquito from Monkey's shoulder and reached for another piece of palm heart.

"Do you want to leave Turtle's band," Tayra asked Armadillo.

Armadillo was silent for a moment and did not look up. "I don't know," she said.

"Turtle is angry at your husband, Armadillo." said Guan. "I heard him say he will pound him in the clubfight. Everyone is talking about it. If you and Snake leave Turtle, we can start a new band, a strong band. Why don't you leave?"

Armadillo used her teeth to start peeling a strip of sheath from the palm heart. As she peeled, she stared at her work and didn't look at the other women.

"I don't know," she said quietly. "I don't know."

"Are you afraid to decide until after the clubfight?" Guan asked. "Will you stay with Snake if he beats Turtle and leave him if Turtle defeats him?"

Armadillo slowly chewed the palm heart and neither looked up nor spoke. Deer put her hand on her sister's shoulder, and Tayra shot a very sharp look at Guan before rising to pick up her basket and begin the return trip to camp. The others followed quietly.

22 ≡ TAPIR

The call sounded just as Armadillo and Deer entered camp. Snake and Turtle had killed a tapir. Word spread rapidly to all the fires, and the forest was filled with animated chatter. Tapirs were less common than they had been in years past, and a kill was noteworthy. The three-hundred-pound tapir is the largest land animal in the jungle, and the meat, along with what the other men brought in, would be enough. The men would fight in the morning.

Deer and Armadillo dropped their baskets when they reached their fires, and—leaving Monkey with Deer—Armadillo went into the forest for firewood. When she returned, carrying an eight-foot log balanced on her shoulder, a small group of women from Short Foot's band passed, returning from the palm groves, and Bearded Paca was with them. Armadillo watched as he walked by. He carried an axe in one hand, and a full basket hung from the tumpline that crossed his forehead. Armadillo was reminded of the time Snake had carried her basket when she had an infected foot and could not manage the burden. Snake had managed the basket easily but had looked odd, standing with the wrong posture, not like the women.

Bearded Paca handled his basket without awkwardness, unselfconsciously, and he carried it the way a woman did, with that pigeon-toed, short-stepping gait that guaranteed the best balance. A person who spent years bearing heavy loads made minor adjustments in stride and posture that compensated for the weight, and the coordinated way Bearded Paca moved made the basket seem like part of him. Armadillo's gaze followed the man as he walked past the camp and went to his fire.

"My daughter must think the unlucky one is good looking," said Grandmother Boa to Grandmother Agouti, the old woman sitting next to her. "She finds him so interesting that she is going to step in her fire if she isn't careful."

The old women laughed, and Armadillo felt foolish, standing with the huge log on her shoulder, staring at the man who seemed so strange to her.

"I was just thinking that it is too bad he is unlucky," she said, lowering the log and placing one end in the coals of her fire. "With one as big as his, he could make a woman very happy. Especially an old woman." She glanced at her mother and her wizened friend and grinned.

"Don't think he hasn't used it," cackled Grandmother Boa. "People say he is the father of that sick ugly child of Green Lizard's. Even her husband thinks so. He says such an awful child couldn't have come from him."

"Men like that don't want women," said Armadillo. "And no woman would want him. Look at the way he walks, just like a woman. He didn't father that baby; that's just gossip."

"I don't know," said Grandmother Boa. "A man is a man, and a woman is a woman. Some men prefer other men, but I have heard the stories about Bearded Paca. I think he is more of a man than he appears."

"He won't be a father for long, even if that ugly baby is his," interjected Grandmother Agouti, kneading palm fiber in a pot of water to make broth. "That baby will be killed. One of the men will kill it. Green Lizard's husband, Peccary, looks at it as if he wants to kill it, and I think he will before long."

"Turtle would probably kill that baby if it were in this band," said Grandmother Boa. "That baby will never be right. Its legs are too thin, and its head is too big. It cries all of the time. It should be killed. Green Lizard should kill it herself and get another baby."

"I heard Peccary say he wanted to pound Bearded Paca," said Grandmother Agouti. "He thinks Bearded Paca carries a basket so he can stay with the women and have sex with them when the men are hunting."

"Why doesn't Peccary hit him?" asked Grandmother Boa. "Peccary is a strong man. Why doesn't he pound him?"

"Bearded Paca has two brothers in the band, don't you remember?" answered Grandmother Agouti. "Peccary tried to make Bearded Paca fight in the clubfight like a man so he could hit him, but Bearded Paca wouldn't fight."

"I wonder if it is true," mused Armadillo. "He does have a big one, and he is not ugly."

"He is just like a woman," said Grandmother Agouti as she scooped a large wad of the spent palm fiber from her pot. "I think Peccary is the father of that ugly child, not Bearded Paca. No woman I know would let him touch her, not even Green Lizard."

Armadillo watched the old woman as she threw the fiber over her shoulder away from the mat, and she knew from the way the woman had spoken that there was some truth to Peccary's allegations.

When the men carried the tapir into camp, Catfish knew that his father had been the one who killed it. Turtle arrived first, carrying a hindquarter that was as large as a peccary. Blackbird and Bushdog and Ocelot, who had helped chase the wounded tapir, carried the rest of the body, and Bushdog's son, Little Fish, trailed behind carrying three vultures. Snake carried the head. It rested on his right shoulder, and he held it in place with his right hand over its soft, curved snout. The long, broad head was immense, and blood ran in wide streaks down Snake's back and buttocks and splattered his calves and feet. He carried his bow and arrows in his left hand, and—despite his strength—he staggered the last few steps before heaving the massive head to the ground in the center of the ring of fires. The commotion that had rocked the camp died as soon as the men emerged from the forest, and the constant din of the birds and insects and frogs was once again heard.

The women and children stopped what they were doing and watched the arriving hunters. The men went to their fires after dropping their burdens and sat quietly. Monkey crawled between her father's spread knees and cuddled against his chest, and Catfish softly stroked Snake's scalp, searching for ticks and lice. They sat quietly for a long time as three other groups of hunters entered camp, all with game. Soon the activity in camp began to increase, and Monkey left to play with Rabbit at Deer's fire.

The tapir's eyes were half open and starting to wrinkle. Fat, gray, blood-gorged ticks hung like soft growths at the base of its ears, and as Snake leaned forward to move the head into the fire and singe it, Catfish reached out, plucked three of the ticks off, and tossed them into the coals. He watched as they slowly browned, blistered, and burst; then he left to join the other children playing in the club-fight arena. Snake slung the head onto the coals, and a cloud of acrid smoke crackled into the air. He rolled it, turned it, and scraped it until it was singed evenly and was naked and black.

When Snake dragged the head from the fire, Armadillo added wood, and Anteater helped him lift the head onto the roasting rack. The two men squatted by the fire and watched the flames rise nearly to the meat and free the first droplets of fat. Anteater reached for a palm-wood brush and leaned forward to drag it along the line of drops forming at the ragged edge of flayed skin where the animal's head had been severed.

"Howler Monkey wants to join us," he said, almost in a whisper. "So do our wives' cousins from Short Foot's band. We can leave after the clubfight."

Snake drew in his breath, affirming that he had heard, and stared into the fluttering flames.

"Ocelot and Coati may come, too," Anteater said. "It will be a good, strong band."

Snake rolled back off his feet onto his buttocks. He examined the sole of his left foot and rubbed his arch with his thumb.

"What is the matter?" asked Anteater. "Have you changed your mind?"

Snake leaned to his left and reached for a small, pointed monkey bone lying on the mat. He looked up at Anteater and pointed with his lips toward Armadillo, who was sitting at Frog's fire and chatting while Frog wove strips of palm frond into her burden basket, repairing a separation near the seam.

"She wants to stay so she can be with Turtle," sneered Anteater. "That is the main reason to leave."

Snake dug into his foot with the pointed bone. He widened a tiny hole in the calloused side of his foot until it was a quarter inch in diameter, and from it he pried and squeezed a whitish firm ball. He held the egg sac in his fingers for a second and looked at it before tossing it into the coals.

"Make her leave," Anteater whispered. "I will help you. Deer will help you. If you don't leave this band, Turtle will kill your children and steal your wife."

Snake drew in his breath and turned to replace the bone tool. "I won't make her, but I think we'll leave," he said. "I think Armadillo will change her mind." He breathed out heavily. "I hope she will."

Snake and Anteater ended their conversation when Howler Monkey and Short Foot arrived at their fire. Others followed, and soon the camp was filled with talk of the tapir hunt. Snake and Turtle and Bushdog recounted every detail of the way they had searched along the banks of the stream, how the tapir tracks had looked in the moist soil, and how the sounds of the tapir bird had led them to their prey. They mimicked the sounds of the tapir and acted out the way it had entered the water and Snake had pierced it with a dagger-bladed arrow, turning the water red. The men discussed whether the tapir had a mate, and if they might kill it, too, following the clubfight. Talk of the hunt led to talk of other hunts, and the evening went by quickly; the men felt very good and very Aché.

Catfish climbed gracefully up the sloping, moss-shagged trunk of a slender, leaning red tree. He scaled the trunk the way a quadruped might—walking on his feet and hands—and stopped when he reached the first vertical branch that had become the main trunk when the tree reorganized its growth pattern after being toppled by some past mishap. He sat in the tree's crotch with one leg dangling on each side of the trunk, and he had an unobstructed view of the clubfight arena.

The dry, sunny weather of recent days, following the rain that had soaked the clearing, had baked the orange soil hard. The men, decorated with sharp, carefully applied, glistening black designs, were now flecked with neatly arranged fluffs of white down, and they were magnificent. Each man's hair was freshly cut in a crisp pattern with a row of erect, inch-long hair running down the crest of his scalp and the rest shaved, except for one or two thin bands of short stubble encircling his head just above the ears. A labret protruded from each man's lower lip, and some of them wore loops of string around their arms or legs, tied tightly above the calf or bicep; the strings accentuated definition of the clean musculature most of the men displayed. Each man held his fighting club—its butt resting on the ground in front of or beside him—and each was a study in intensity.

The time for the clubfight was very near, and Catfish remembered that the start of the last clubfight—the one with Anaconda's band—had startled him with its sudden violence. He felt the uneasiness of anticipation and dread that often precedes contests, and he could see the men preparing for the greatest trial an Aché could face. Some rocked from one foot to the other, holding their clubs in front of them. Others remained quiet and erect, breathing deeply, looking at nothing. Some were standing beside other men as if to gain strength. Snake stood alone. Catfish knew that Snake had been preparing himself for this moment for weeks, and he had felt the strain in his father. In just moments, he could lose his father, and the thought made him feel tight and light and almost dizzy.

His stomach began tingling almost as if he were going to fight himself. He knew that Turtle wanted to hurt Snake and that Blackbird and Jamo would help Turtle if he needed it. Other men would also probably side with Turtle because he was strong and powerful. Anteater would help Snake, but he was still weak from the Apa thunder. He was expected to fall early in the fight.

From his perch in the tree, Catfish looked down into the open arena at the men who waited nervously while others finished preparing themselves. Snake looked large and strong, and Turtle, standing nearby, looked—for the first time to the boy—less of a man. Snake was one of the biggest men, and Turtle was smaller than most; Catfish wondered why he had never noticed the size difference; until this moment, he had, in fact, thought that Turtle was larger than Snake. Snake had looked especially strong last evening when he had carried the tapir's head, huge and bloody, into camp on his shoulders with blood streaking down his back and buttocks and legs; when children had flocked around him as he arrived, Catfish had been proud.

The sun was nearly straight overhead as the last few men left the shade of the forest and stepped into the arena. The men stood near the other men from the same band, but there was no order to their placement or that of the bands. The men made a rough circle around the arena, and there was no more human noise in the forest. Birds shrieked, and cicadas buzzed; tree frogs bleated love songs, and the jungle was saturated with its sounds, but the Aché were silent; even the babies seemed to sense the seriousness of the moment.

Then the men were no longer still. They strode forward, shrinking the circle; they walked with high, bent-kneed steps, and their backs were stiff. Each man held his club with both hands now, and their eyes were sharp like the hawk's as they stared across the circle. The men seemed to grow, and then they stopped.

"Break their heads!" came the cry. "Show them how Aché men fight! Break them! Pound them!" The old woman ran into the arena, screaming and gesturing wildly to the men. She shrieked and ran to the edge of the loose ring of fighters. "Split them! Break them! Pound their heads!"

A chorus of cries rose from the edges of the clearing, and several more women dashed into the open, exhorting the fighters. Grandmother Boa danced along the fringe of the arena behind the men of Turtle's band, arms flailing, inciting them to smash the cowards with their clubs, to teach the other men to be Aché with blows to the head, to bring honor to themselves by maiming opponents. Parrot swung wildly with a leafy branch, whirling and stumbling, screaming incoherently. Some of the women were brave enough to shove or push their husbands and brothers from behind, grabbing their arms, shrieking, and adding to the frenzy.

The men began moving, little by little, and some raised their clubs. Soon fierce cries came from the men in the shrinking circle, and the women retreated to the safety of the trees. Turtle raised his club high and shouted. His face was contorted, and Catfish no longer thought he looked small. He held his club high above his head with spread hands and swung it forward, almost striking the ground. Blackbird ran to his side and swung his club wildly through the air. Other men did the same, and the circle shrank some more. Snake was near Turtle, and he raised his club and yelled, brandishing his weapon.

Soon the cries became one, drowning out any one voice, obliterating words, overrunning the clearing, and covering the jungle with chaotic sound. The women watched from the edge of the arena as the men advanced, closing the circle until only twenty feet separated the fighters from those they faced. The clubs danced above the heads of the advancing men, pointed and sharp, painted and deadly, their light color contrasting with the glistening black, white-flecked bodies of the fighters who held them. Turtle spun just ahead of the others, waving his club back and forth, and when he faced the center of the circle, he hesitated for an instant, raised his club as high as it would go, and charged across the opening. The fight had begun.

The ring of men instantly closed. The center of the arena was now completely in chaos, a moving, swarming melee of bodies with clubs thrashing, flailing, striking, and cracking against each other, against heads and faces and bodies. Shouts and cries of attack mingled with the screams and shrieks from the women and children, who were safely hidden in the forest from the frenzied madness of the men who struck wildly at anything that moved. A man near the outside of the cluster fell and staggered to his feet, only to be struck again and go back down. The throng quickly colored from blood spurting bright red from scalp wounds, and the pack thinned as fighters dropped.

Snake charged with Turtle when he sprinted across the open center of the ring. They were met from the front and sides, and they struck out savagely with their clubs, not able in the wild free-for-all to choose a single target. Nor were they able to duck and dodge and defend themselves. Snake felt a blow glance off his back, and he swung at a man in front of him, only to see the man fall from another blow before his connected. He saw Anteater fighting beside him and heard a club crack against his skull and send him down. Snake turned and attacked the man who had struck Anteater and knocked him senseless with three rapid blows before sending him face down on the baked red clay with a glancing, slanting swipe to the temple.

Snake stumbled on a fallen man's leg and was struck on the shoulder by a numbing blow. He swung from a crouch and caught a grandfather in the ribs. The old man's air blew out with a deep grunt, and he toppled to the side. Snake regained his footing and spun so his back was to the outside of the battling throng. Half of the men had fallen, and most of those still fighting were bleeding, bruised, and broken. Snake raised his club and stepped forward to face the clos-est man, who swung before Snake realized that he had been seen. The blow glanced off Snake's club and sliced the knuckles of his right hand. He brought his club down over his attacker's and forced its tip to the ground at his feet. For a second, the opponents' eyes met; Snake was fighting Turtle.

Perhaps the fighting continued around them. Perhaps all battlers stopped and leaned on their clubs to watch. Perhaps the women and children held hands and danced about them on a carpet of flower petals. They would not have noticed. They could not have cared. The world spun with them as they circled each other, slowly, to the right. The jungle enclosed them, reached across the clearing, and blotted the sun. They followed each other with their eyes, looking not into the person's eyes but at his center, the top of his stomach, the base of his sternum, seeing the opponent with the coordinated completeness and heightened peripheral vision that comes to a fighter.

Turtle struck with a half swing, and Snake blocked it with the handle of his club. Snake responded with a quick short stroke and gave Turtle a light blow on the neck. Turtle did not recoil but took a full stroke at Snake, swinging hard at his head. Snake stepped to his left and tipped his head forward. He felt the club blade graze the erect hair on his scalp. Before Turtle could recover from his swing, Snake rapped him sharply on the crest of his scalp, and Turtle was jolted backward.

Blood from Snake's hand wet the handle of his club, and he tried to find a dry place to grip. Turtle attacked with many rapid blows, and Snake backed up, fending most of them off with his club. Twice Turtle's blows connected, once caroming off the side of Snake's head, flattening his ear and making it ring, and once on the forehead just above his left eyebrow. Blood trickled into his eye, and the salty sting partially blinded Snake, who turned so he could see Turtle with his good eye. When Turtle gathered himself and brought his club down toward Snake's head with full force, he danced to the side and struck a counterblow that thudded into the muscle of Turtle's shoulder, low-ering it. Turtle swung again, and Snake once again dodged and landed a retaliatory stroke, this one angling across Turtle's scalp. Turtle stepped back, and over his lowered shoulder, Snake again connected with the famous man's head. Turtle raised his club high and swung, but it came so slowly that Snake easily avoided it and struck a very hard blow onto his other shoulder.

The accumulated blows had slowed Turtle, and Snake now controlled him. He chose his strikes, each one punishing the bleeding man whose frenzy was now matched by his inability to move quickly, to see well, to coordinate his movements. Snake's bleeding hand and head, ringing ear, and deadened shoulder seemed to go away, and he used his advantage to pummel his nemesis, bringing his club at will to Turtle's ribs, his forearms, his head, his neck, his shoulders that now were stooped. Turtle held his club low and waved it at Snake—unable to move but unwilling to leave his feet—and Snake measured his attack, damaging the man, avoiding the blow he could easily have delivered, the heavy blow to the head that might have killed the man he would like to have killed.

Snake's club splattered blood with each strike, and he floated around the staggering Turtle, oblivious to his surroundings, reveling in his victory, determined to take as much from Turtle as he could. He was only vaguely aware of the shadow that crossed Turtle's body before the flash that seemed to blot out all sight popped in his head, and Snake realized in that less than an instant before he knew no more that he had been struck and his clubfight was over.

Snake awoke laughing. He did not know why he was laughing. He shot to his feet as if to show that he was not hurt, but he could not keep from slumping to his knees when darkness swirled about his head, and he almost passed out. He knelt for a moment, smiling, and the light gradually returned. A few yards in front of him, he could see Turtle on his knees and elbows, his head resting on his hands. He was retching. Blackbird sat next to Turtle, his club lying beside him, holding his hand on his head. Parrot ran to Turtle and bent over to look at his head. Snake felt a hand on his shoulder and turned to look at Anteater.

"You pounded Turtle," Anteater said. "You split his head and beat him."

Snake could not remember. He grinned, looked around, and immediately forgot what Anteater had said. He felt Anteater's hand on his head, and he reached up and touched blood. It ran down the side of his face, and he wiped his hand across his brow and cheek; when he looked at his palm, it was covered with red.

"It is just a small cut," said Anteater. "Not as bad as Turtle's."

Snake looked at Turtle and saw a pool of blood and vomit under the famous man's face.

"Blackbird hit you," Anteater said. "He could barely stand, but he hit you when you were looking at Turtle. He swung hard, and he fell down when he hit you and still hasn't gotten up."

Snake looked around the arena. A few men were standing, but most were sitting or lying on the red ground. Women were starting to come into the area. An old woman ran up to a man lying on the far side of the arena and started wailing. Blackbird stood and leaned on his club when Frog came to him. He swayed and leaned on Frog's shoulder. Blood streaked his forehead and shoulder and ran from a gash on his cheek. Snake smiled at him, and Blackbird looked at Snake as if he were insane.

Snake heard voices behind him that sounded far away, and he felt hands under his arms lifting him to his feet. He rose slowly and felt the darkness coming back, but this time it wasn't as bad, and he stood still until the light returned. The hands steadied him and then let go. He turned slowly and looked at Armadillo.

"Come into the shade and sit down," she said. "You should get out of this hot sun. I have *timbo* to wash your head."

The old woman continued to wail, and Snake looked back at her. Several people were with her now, and they were looking at the man on the ground.

"Did someone get killed?" he asked.

Armadillo turned, looked for a minute, and replied, "He's not dead. His legs are moving." She started walking toward the shade of the forest.

Snake followed her, and they walked past Turtle, who was still unable to rise. They saw Jamo Paca and Caiman Short Foot standing in the shade near the edge of the arena. The two old men were laughing, and Grandmother Boa was rubbing timbo creeper juice into a cut on the side of Jamo's head. Snake grinned as he passed, and the two men looked at each other and laughed some more.

When they reached camp, Snake sat near the fire, and Armadillo peeled the bark from a length of vine, crushed it between her hands, and sponged the blood away from his eye and forehead.

"Did Turtle hit me?" Snake asked. "What happened?"

"You beat Turtle," Armadillo said. "You beat Turtle and were pounding him when Blackbird hit you from the side."

Snake could still not remember.

The afternoon and evening were very quiet. Many of the men slept, and few were able to do more than lie beside their fires. The women fed them meat broth and palm-fiber broth, and what conversation there was focused on the fight. Anteater was not badly hurt, and neither were Jamo Paca or Coati. There was much talk about how well Coati had fought in his first clubfight, and the old men said that he would be a famous fighter.

Bushdog's and Short Foot's camps were full of talk of the fight between Snake and Turtle, and people spoke in hushed tones about the way Snake had split Turtle, pounded him, and would have beaten him even worse if his brother hadn't saved him. Turtle was unable to speak more than a few words, and no one in his band was ready to talk about what had happened. No man complained, and no man cried, and everyone was thankful that no one had died.

The children were quiet and sat near their parents. Catfish and the older children spent most of the afternoon in the forest searching for timbo, which was being used in great quantities to wash the many wounds and purify the men, who were now *bayja*—attractive to animals and spirits because they had spilled blood. Snake slept most of the afternoon and woke only for a short while after dark to ask for a drink of water. Armadillo gave him water and broth, and he took them quietly. He asked about the other men and once again who had hit him, and then lay back down and closed his eyes.

After Snake went back to sleep, Anteater leaned over from his fire and spoke softly to Armadillo.

"As soon as Snake can walk, we should leave," he said. "We can go to the forest by the place where the Little River meets the Big River. Howler Monkey says Bushdog's band never goes there and that there are no Apa. We can leave before Turtle is better, and he won't try to stop us."

"I am afraid to leave," Armadillo whispered, staring into the coals.

"Snake can't stay in Turtle's band," said Anteater. "Not after he pounded Turtle today. Turtle will kill him. And if Snake leaves, Turtle will be mean to your children. He will try to kill Monkey."

"But if I leave, Snake may kill my new baby," Armadillo answered, looking at her still-flat stomach.

"You would lose your husband and endanger your children to save a baby that isn't even born? You should come with us. Do you really want to be Turtle's wife?" Anteater turned back toward his fire and resumed chewing on a piece of roast tapir.

Armadillo continued staring into the fire. When she noticed that Catfish had been listening, she put her arm around him and held him close.

24 ☰ A NEW BAND

The days following the clubfight were ones of recuperation and relaxation, days when conversations were free of the tension and worry that had preceded the event. The children played from first light until fatigue drew them to their mothers' fires, for they knew the opportunity to be with so many friends would soon pass. The adults were more comfortable with each other now that they knew the outcome of the contest. The confrontation of the moment was over—the debts settled, the scores recorded and known. Until the next time. And the clubfight had gone well. There had been no deaths, no grievous wounds, no breaches of etiquette to mar the occasion.

The most noteworthy event had been Snake's momentary triumph over Turtle. Nothing changed as a result of it, for although man to man Snake had proven himself better, the outcome was the way everyone had expected. Snake was strong, brave, *chija*, a superior fighter, but he lacked family, and for that reason, he had fallen. For that reason, people suspected, Armadillo still was unwilling to leave Turtle's band.

Snake recovered rapidly, but Turtle was slow to mend, and an infection set in, giving him a slight fever. When the fever came, he ceased being strong. He whined and whimpered and lay on his wife's mat complaining. He was not considered weak because of his actions, for all Aché can combat pain, but none can effectively deal with sickness. A man who will not flinch when sliced open by a blow from a club will cry or moan because of a fever or bellyache. Turtle was cut, bruised, and broken, and he did not let these things bother him; he acted like a whiny child because of his fever, and people worried. They said to each other, "Turtle is dead," which was the only way to say that he was sick in the Aché language. Sickness often led to death in the jungle, and there was apparently little need for a different word.

On the second day after the clubfight, Snake was strong enough to hunt, and he went with Anteater to find capybara near a large creek several miles from camp. They went alone and hunted quietly and deliberately, searching the banks of the sluggish stream for tracks and signs of the large rodents. When they encountered no capybara, they began a long looping return to the camp, searching for whatever game they might find. In a small opening at the top of a low rise, they stopped and looked across the valley they would cross on their way back to camp.

"The animals should be flocking to us, but we haven't seen any," said Anteater, adjusting the wrap of his bowstring. "We both drew blood in the clubfight and are *bayja*. I thought we would kill animals all day, and we haven't seen any. Not even a monkey or paca."

"Sometimes even bayja men don't see animals," said Snake. "The animals still come to us, but they don't want to be seen."

"We will find something in the valley," said Anteater.

Snake sat down in the leaves and leaned back against the rough trunk of a lapacho tree. "There is still some meat in camp," he said.

Anteater raised his bow and pulled back on the string to test it. "The others are ready to leave. They want to leave in the morning."

Snake swept his gaze across the treetops below them. "I don't think Armadillo will leave," he said softly.

Anteater lowered his bow and leaned it against the tree trunk next to his arrows. "She will come if you make her. You can pick her up and carry her with us. When we get far enough away, she can't run back."

"I don't want to make her come."

"If she stays and you come with us, there will be no one to protect your children if Turtle has the rage and wants to kill them. She has to come."

"Armadillo says her cousins want to join Turtle's band. She will have more family. She says it will be better for all of us." Snake rubbed the inside of his arm on his knee and then looked at it. "I would rather leave, but if she won't come, I'll have to stay in Turtle's band."

"Her cousins will join us in the new band. We will be a better band without Turtle. Being in Turtle's band is bad for all of us. We must leave." Anteater slumped to the ground and sat with Snake. "We want you to come with us," he said. "But even if you don't come, the rest of us are leaving in the morning."

Despite the attraction of being bayja, Snake and Anteater encountered no game on their return to the camp. When they arrived, Armadillo and Deer were away, and the men sat silently. Monkey and Rabbit sat between the fires and played with a large beetle, pushing it back and forth between them with twigs. Turtle was sitting up and appeared to be feeling better. His head was swollen, and his eyes looked tired, but he was not moaning. He was eating a piece of fish, gently chewing a big mouthful at a time and pausing every few seconds to take some of the numerous tiny bones from his mouth.

When Deer arrived, she went straight to her fire and stooped to talk to Anteater even before she dropped her basket from her back. She was smiling.

"Armadillo is ready to leave," Deer whispered. "She will go with us."

Anteater turned to look at Snake. Snake raised his eyebrows; he had heard.

When Armadillo arrived a few minutes later, she walked lightly and smiled at Snake. Monkey got up and ran to her, and Armadillo lifted her high and twirled her around in a circle. The little girl squealed, and Armadillo laughed.

Snake looked at his wife and remembered when they were younger, before they were married. Armadillo had always smiled, and Snake had thought she was beautiful. He still did, and it made him feel very good to see her happy.

"My cousins will go with us, and so will Howler Monkey and his family," she said. "We will have a good band, a strong band with good hunters and generous women. We can leave in the morning."

"When did you change your mind?" Snake asked.

"This morning after I talked to my mother." Armadillo settled to her knees on the mat beside Snake. "I have worried for so long that Turtle would kill Monkey and Catfish. When Turtle started being nice to them, I was afraid to leave because I thought they were finally safe. I was also afraid to leave because I feared for my new baby." She looked down at her stomach and then raised her head slightly to look at Snake. "My mother told me that I should leave. She said that Turtle was being nice to Catfish and Monkey because I was being nice to him, but the only real reason he didn't kill them was because of you. He was afraid to kill them because he feared you. If you left and I stayed, Turtle would kill them so I could spend all my time being his wife and raising his children." Again she looked down at her stomach. "My mother said she didn't think you would kill my new baby, but even if you did, it would be better than losing Catfish and Monkey."

Snake put his hand on her shoulder and smiled. "I am glad you are going with us. I love you. I couldn't leave if you didn't go. Our new band will be good."

"I am so happy," Armadillo said. "I love you, Snake. Our life will be better when we are away from Turtle."

"It will be very good. Let's go tell the others."

The new band walked through the forest in single file. Guan and Tayra and their families came from Short Foot's band, and Howler Monkey and his family came from Bushdog's. Ocelot and Coati also joined the group, and Coati brought his new wife, Macaw, the girl from Bushdog's band he had spent nearly every moment with since arriving at the clubfight camp. The trail leading west disappeared a short way from the large camp, and they continued through a relatively open forest with tall, great-trunked trees and many vines; through cane- and bamboo-choked ugly forest; and through poorly drained lowlands. They headed for the jungles beyond the Shallow Lake, where the Little River and the Big River approach each other and eventually converge. They headed for country that was new to them with a new band, new people, and they were ready.

On the fourth day after leaving the other bands, they neared the Little River, territory they knew, that they called good forest. When the men left in midafternoon to hunt, Ocelot stayed with the women and children. He went ahead carrying a machete and cut an occasional branch or vine to mark the way. Catfish and Otter followed closely behind Ocelot, and soon they were far enough ahead of the women that they could not hear them as they moved through the forest.

The boys pretended they were grown men, hunting away from the slower-moving band, and they felt good. Turtle seemed to Catfish to be a dark spot in his past that he was leaving farther behind with each step. Catfish pretended Margay was his wife, walking with the others, and that he would see her and sleep with her at their fire that night. They had not said good-bye when the new band had left the big camp because there is no Aché way to do that. They had looked at each other for a long time and smiled, and Catfish knew he would think often of Margay. He would remember her smile and the monkey on her head that was almost permanent.

When Ocelot stopped and stood quietly with his ear cocked, the boys paused, too, and listened. Catfish thought for a second that Ocelot had heard monkeys because he heard rustling in the treetops. Then the cry came—high pitched and full of alarm—and Ocelot turned and sprinted back the way they had come toward the women; the boys ran after him.

"Someone is calling. We hear someone calling," Armadillo whispered to Ocelot. "The voice is coming from over toward the meadow—away from where the men went to hunt."

They all sat quietly, and Ocelot and the boys fingered their arrows and tested their bowstrings. Then it came again, high pitched and rapid.

"Hoo, hoo, Aché, call to me," the voice said. "I want to visit you."

"Everyone be still," Ocelot said quietly. "Catfish, run and try to find the men. Go quickly and quietly. They should be near the palm grove by the Little River, not too far from here. Otter, go with Catfish. Toucan, I need you to stay here with me. Now go!"

Catfish and Otter raced off toward where they thought the men were hunting. This was the most responsibility they had ever been given, and they tried to be men, moving quickly and without fear, but it was always just a step or two behind them.

Toucan—only a boy like Catfish and Otter—got ready to help Ocelot in case they were attacked.

"Does anyone recognize the voice?" Ocelot asked.

No one responded. They all stood—tense and alert—and listened intently.

"Hoo, hoo, Aché," came the cry, much louder and closer this time. "My name is Monkey, and I am called Withered Hand. I was in Big Armadillo's band."

"*Taa*," said Ocelot. "He was one of the people the Apa captured when they attacked Big Armadillo's band. He could be bringing Apa here to attack us. Everyone remain quiet and start moving toward the place where the men are."

The women and children started hurrying in the general direction that Catfish and Otter had taken earlier. Ocelot and Toucan brought up the rear and stopped occasionally to listen and look, to determine if they were being followed. They were certain that they were and hoped that they would meet the hunters before Withered Hand and whoever was with him caught up with them.

Catfish and Otter could hear the hunters well before they saw them, and they knew what was going on. The men had a troop of capuchin monkeys isolated in some trees and had surrounded them. The men made a lot of noise trying to frighten the monkeys back when they tried to escape and startle the small primates into exposing themselves to a whistling arrow.

The boys called to the men from a short distance, "Fathers, the women and children need you. Someone is calling to us, and we are afraid."

Snake ran to the boys and asked them what had happened. When he understood, he called to the other men. "We must go. Our families are in danger."

When the hunters reached the women, they gathered everyone together. Ocelot told them that Withered Hand had been calling to them and they were worried because the Apa had captured him and he might be leading Apa to the Aché, to capture this band the way Harpy Eagle's band had been caught.

"Let's go toward the Little River and make camp. We will post sentries around camp and be ready for Withered Hand," Snake said.

As light was fading, the band made camp. The men scattered in the forest surrounding the camp, and everyone was alert. Shortly before dusk, another call came.

"Hoo, hoo, Aché. I would like to visit you. I am your friend Withered Hand, and I am with my brother, Piranha. No others are with us. We are your friends."

Snake called the other men to the spot where he was standing. "If they had Apa with them and wanted to attack us, they would try to surprise us, not call out. They know where we are, so I think we should have them come to us, and we can be ready."

The men drew their breath in agreement. "We should be ready and have some men hiding and ready to kill them if something goes wrong," Ocelot said.

As the men took defensive positions, they heard Withered Hand calling again. This time Snake answered: "Come to our camp and visit us but unstring your bows so we know you are friendly."

When the two men arrived in camp, their bows were unstrung, and they were both carrying large cloth bags. They wore shirts and shorts, things rarely seen on Aché, except when they stole them from the Apa.

"I am Monkey," said the one called Withered Hand. His right hand was clenched and stiff, the result of a snakebite long before. "This is my brother, Piranha."

"We heard you were captured by the Apa," Ocelot said.

"We were," said Withered Hand. "We still live with the Apa."

"*Taa*," exclaimed Ocelot. "They did not kill you? Did they eat your children?"

"No," said Piranha. "They do not eat children; they are like us—the Apa love children. Our children are happy. They are learning to speak the Apa language. We work in the fields, and they give us food—manioc, corn, and even meat from strangehorns and horses."

"We have presents for you," Withered Hand said, reaching into the bag he carried. He handed a brand new machete to Ocelot and an axe to Snake. He gave a shiny cooking pot to Deer and handed brand-new, wooden-handled knives to the rest of the men. Piranha pulled shirts, shorts, hats, and cloth from his bag. Everyone—even the smallest child—got a tool or a piece of Apa clothing.

The band members looked with great astonishment at the gifts. They had never seen a brand-new machete or axe. They turned them round and round in their hands. Everyone gathered around to look at the amazing things.

"Why are you giving us these things?" asked Ocelot. "You hardly know us."

"We want you to come with us and live with the Apa," Withered Hand said. "There are more things like this at the farm. You can live without fear of jaguars. You will not have to clubfight. Your children will not be hungry. You will not have to run from the Apa—they will be your friends."

The band members were stunned. They had never heard such things. The thought of living with the Apa was something so foreign to them that they could not imagine it, yet here were two Aché men telling them that it was possible and it would be good.

They would need some time to think and talk.

≡ EPILOGUE

The band followed Withered Hand and Piranha through the forest. They traveled along the Little River to its junction with the Big River, then continued heading downstream toward the Apa farm where they would live. Some were excited, some frightened, but all were apprehensive. They had decided to leave the only life they knew for the promise of a better one. They wondered what staying in one place all the time would be like. They were uncertain what the Apa would be like. They dreamed of eating well, of not being afraid. They hoped their children would have better lives.

To live in the jungle is to be part of the jungle. The living, breathing jungle that cloaks the continent with a diversity of trees and vines and flowers and butterflies is trees and vines and flowers and butterflies, harpy eagles and capybara, monkeys and toucans, palms and bees, and snakes and jaguars. And it is Aché.

The jungle represents a multitude of life, organisms, and individuals that are both a part of and in opposition to it. The jungle is their medium, their home, their fragile niche created by competition, and each niche is unique and ephemeral. The ever-changing jungle gives life, harbors life, takes life, is life. Each ant born in the jungle dies there, and the jungle hardly notices. It goes on. And the Aché, the children of the jungle, also go on.

As life continues for the mate of the giant anteater killed in the meadow, the boy orphaned by a jaguar attack, and the woman who loses her child, so it will go on for Armadillo and Snake and the rest of their band. They hope for a richer future for themselves and their children, a promise of security described by Withered Hand. They walked away from Turtle with confidence and trepidation. Now they walk toward a new way of life with great hope and heads full of dreams for themselves and their children.

The jungle slowly shrank away behind them as they strode purposefully toward their future.

☰ ABOUT THE AUTHOR

Kevin T. Jones is the former state archaeologist of Utah, an adjunct assistant professor of anthropology at the University of Utah, and a research curator at the Natural History Museum of Utah. He is also the owner and principal investigator of the archaeological and environmental consulting firm Ancient Places Consulting. He sings and plays mandolin in the bluegrass band The Lab Dogs. Kevin has been married to Barbara Evert for thirty-four years, and they have an adult son, Nicholas Evert Jones.